Murder
of the
Obeah Man

Judy Fishel

Flying Heron Books
2020

Flying Heron Books
516 SW North River Point Drive
Stuart, Florida 34994
For permissions and discount information contact jjfishel@gmail.com

Book interior design by Vickie Swisher, Studio 2020
Library of Congress Control Number 2020900268
ISBN 978-0-9906112-4-0
Publisher's Cataloging-in-Publication Data provided by Five Rainbows Cataloging Services

Names: Fishel, Judy, author.
Title: Murder of the Obeah man / Judy Fishel.
Description: Stuart, FL: Flying Heron Books, 2020.
Identifiers: ISBN 978-0-9906112-4-0 (paperback) |
    ISBN 978-0-9906112-5-7 (ebook)
Subjects: LCSH: Murder—Fiction. | Obeah (Cult)—Fiction. | Jamaicans—
    Florida—Fiction. | Florida—Fiction. | Detective and mystery stories. |
    BISAC: FICTION / Mystery & Detective / Amateur Sleuth. | FICTION
    / Mystery & Detective / African American. | FICTION / Mystery &
    Detective / Traditional. | FICTION / Mystery & Detective / Women
    Sleuths. | GSAFD: Mystery fiction.
Classification: LCC PS3606.I84 M87 2020 (print) | LCC PS3606.I84 (ebook) |
    DDC 813/.6—dc23.

This book is dedicated to

All the Virginias in my life,
all of them strong, independent women:

Virginia Marcella Ruhnke,
my mother

Frances Virginia Fishel,
my mother-in-law

Thamora Virginia Fishel,
my daughter

Virginia Rose Fishel,
my granddaughter

And to Virginia (Jeenya) Birdsong who,
while she exists only in my imagination,
has haunted my dreams for at least a dozen years
demanding that I tell her story.

I want to thank

Eula Clarke, who said to me,
"You cannot write a book about Jamaica
until you GO to Jamaica."

And our three Jamaican bird guides,
Veda Tate, Deceita Turner, and Wolde Kristos,
who drove us around Jamaica, from one end to the other.
They helped us see many of their lovely birds
while answering my questions and telling us what they knew
about Obeah Men and duppies, as well as for sharing
their experiences growing up in Jamaica.

The Characters

There are many characters in this book but only a few you'll want to remember. These you will get to know only a few at a time. This might help you understand how they are all related.

The Overmon Family
Josiah Overmon – the Obeah Man
his wife Dolly
his sister Sharona
his brother Elijah – the chef
his step-brother Seth – the manager of the Garage

The Birdsong Family
Jeenya: herbalist, healer, and spiritual advisor
her husband Zeke
their grandson Homer

The Armstrong Family
George – works at the Garage
his wife Angela – friend of Jeenya

The Hackett Family
Victor works at the Garage
his wife Elaenia died ten years ago

The Detectives
Ricardo (Rick) Montoya
Hazel Fontaine

The Location

Jamaica Lakes: A Jamaican neighborhood in Palm City, Florida.

A Few Important Words

Obeah: Pronounced different ways (O-bya) (O-be-uh) (O-BE-uh)

It is often described as a mixture of witchcraft, magic, and sorcery often using fetishes or charms. They cast spells for good or evil purposes.

Jamaican Patois: A patois is a dialect created from multiple languages. The Jamaican Patois is a mixture of English, Portuguese, Hindi, Spanish, and several West African languages. It's NOT broken English. Below are some common examples.

Duppy: The ghost or spirit of a person who died, often looking for revenge.

Dis – This	De – The	Patoo – Owl
Dere – There	Ting – Thing	Tink – Think
Mi – my	Someting – Something	

John Crows – Turkey Vultures
Black-black – Very black
(Note: that repeating words make them stronger.)

Table of Contents

PROLOGUE

Josiah Overmon had it all—at least, he thought he did. He was tall, perhaps six foot four and, at the age of seventy-four, he was still handsome. While not overly wealthy, he was definitely the richest man in Jamaica Lakes. In fact, he *owned* Jamaica Lakes. Everyone here loved and respected him, at least he thought they did.

And why shouldn't they love him? When people needed money for gas, he gave them a little. When they asked him to build a park, he created a large, beautiful park around the large lake. They wanted a Jamaican restaurant and grocery so he built these and other shops. They wanted an Obeah man and, even though he never wanted to do this, he did have the training, so he agreed to be the Obeah Man—his way.

If you asked the people in Jamaica Lakes what they thought of Mr. Overmon, every single person would say the same thing. Mr. Overmon was a wonderful man. He built Jamaica Lakes. He cared about everyone here. Everyone loved Mr. Overmon.

But, if you got to know some of them a little better, perhaps had dinner together and maybe shared a few drinks, they might tell you a different story.

One might say, "Sure, we're grateful to Mr. Overmon for all he's done, but we'd be happier if he'd let us work in some of the shops he built. But no, he just lets his relatives work there. We'd like to build our own businesses, but no, Mr. Overmon won't allow that. He has to be the one to control everything."

Another would perhaps say, "Mr. Overmon? Sure, he be one fine gentleman you know, but he not perfect like some people 'round here be tinking. He be way too full of hisself. We say, 'Yes sir, Mr. Overmon. Thank you, Mr. Overmon. You be right Mr. Overmon.' That man tinks because he built Jamaica Lakes—because he be so rich— that he be better than anyone else."

Yet another might venture his opinion, "It is true that everyone here will tell you we respect the old man. Some even say we love him and I expect a few of them do but not all of us. That man is certainly not perfect. Like he thinks he can have any woman he wants, old women, young women, married women, single women, and the old man thinks he is doing them a favor you know, like he's making them so happy. Maybe some of those women are happy but I can tell you—their husbands are not so happy."

Perhaps, if Josiah had a few years more, he might have understood. He might even have changed. But Josiah didn't have a few years more.

1

The Black-Black Night

Jeenya

An old woman shouted into the dark for all to hear and went unheard that night as usual. Her granddaughter heard the shouting but she just shook her head at such nonsense and went about her work.

"Hey dere, Miz Jeenya. You heah me? Don't know 'bout you but dis dark tonight be so black-black it hurt mi eyeballs. I speck you be sitting dere in de black-black, tinking dere be someting bad, maybe someting evil. You tinking 'bout de duppies out dere, Miz Jeenya? You tink dey be walking around, looking to do some mischief? You 'fraid, Miz Jeenya? You scared? Dose who don't believe in de duppies and all, we not afraid. You hear dat, Miz Jeenya? We NOT afraid."

Jeenya Birdsong shivered. It wasn't the cool air making Jeenya's skin prickle, and it wasn't the drums beating back in the woods. Deep in her bones, she sensed something terrible out there in the darkness, perhaps something truly evil.

Jeenya and her husband, Zeke, huddled together on the old porch swing. Zeke held one arm protectively around her shoulder as if to keep the chill away.

"You cold, honey?"

"I'm not cold, Zeke. Just one of those strange feelings I get. I sure wouldn't want to be alone on a night like this."

Elsewhere in Jamaica Lakes, others also felt uneasy. Later, some claimed to have had a premonition of evil, of something demonic lurking unseen, perhaps unseeable.

In most of Palm City and nearby towns along Florida's Treasure Coast, bright streetlights and a constant flow of cars provided illumination. Here, there were no streetlights. By dinner time, most cars were parked in their driveways and most sensible people stayed home. It wasn't the kind of night where people wanted to be out walking around.

Beyond the church, beyond the parsonage, beyond the small cemetery, there was a patch of woods and, coming from those woods, was the hypnotic rhythm of drums and the vigorous singing and shouting of the Revivalists. Rev. Wolff was out there preaching and shouting about fighting evil while his followers tramped 'round counterclockwise in a circle, jerking their bodies back and forth, shouting and waiting for spirits to possess their bodies. Those sounds, though familiar, seemed louder that night.

In another part of the community, a tall man stood watching something in the distance. The pounding of the drums didn't bother him. He sometimes said those drumbeats were a sign of life, like the beating of his heart.

He smiled a little. Tonight, those drumbeats could be a sign of something else.

He cocked his head a little, as if alert to any sort of movement. His lips twitched, forming a momentary smile. When the door in a small building opened wide, he took a deep breath, held it, and slowly released the warm moist air.

Slowly, quietly, he walked through the darkness, pausing occasionally to listen. Finally, he slipped around the back of the small building. He heard voices and stopped, then stepped back, deeper in the shadows. He would have to wait a little longer.

Jeenya shivered again, this time violently. "You can't feel it, can you?" she asked. "I'm not scared of the dark, Zeke. Never have been. But there's something monstrously wicked out there tonight. Feels to me like the old devil hisself crawled up from hell and is walking down the streets, peering in windows, looking to do some sort of dreadful mischief."

Zeke shook his head. "Jeenya, honey, I'll never understand where you get these weird notions."

Sounds of the Revivalists and their unending fight against evil continued as Zeke and Jeenya stood and felt their way through the darkness to the front door. The meeting in the woods would continue until at least one, maybe one-thirty in the morning.

When Jeenya turned out the small bedroom light, the darkness seemed to grow thicker. She tried to relax, thinking about the herbs in her garden. Tomorrow, she needed to cut lavender, rosemary, fever grass, and cerasse.

"Hoooo. Hoo hoo hooooo. Hooooooooo."

Jeenya cringed. "Zeke, you hear that?"

"That's just the old owl, honey. He's up there in the mango tree right outside our window, just where he sits most every night."

"He sounds different tonight, Zeke. Louder. Maybe more wavering, and something else I can't explain. You couldn't hear it, could you? The Patoo only cries like that when something awful is happening—like when someone is dying."

"Now, Jeenya, we hear that old bird plenty of times. You don't usually get all upset and nobody we know ever turns up dead. It's the darkness making you nervous. Maybe that poor old owl is scared of the darkness too."

"No need making light of it, Zeke. Granny taught me to listen to the Patoo. I can feel it in my bones. Growing up in Kingston, you never learned the old ways. You might not believe me, Zeke, but I'm thinking someone died tonight."

"Last month," Zeke said, "when Sissy Tomlinson died, you didn't hear the owl, did you? Do owls only talk to you some of the time?"

"Sissy was ninety-four, God bless her soul. She'd been sick and was in a heap of pain. Death came as a blessing for her. This is different."

Jeenya didn't want to tell Zeke what she really thought. She had a dreadful feeling that this time it might be a person not expecting to die, not wanting to die—maybe it was even murder. But, if she said that, Zeke would think she really was crazy.

"Even if someone is dying," Zeke said, "that owl didn't tell you who is dying or where to find the body, did he now? You can't call the police and tell them an owl told you someone was dead. The fact is, you can't do a blessed thing. Go to sleep, Jeenya, my love. If somebody really is dead, I expect we'll hear all about it in the morning."

Jeenya sighed and pulled the blanket up to her chin. Zeke was right. There wasn't a thing she could do. She closed her eyes and tried regular breathing, hoping it would help her relax, but it was a long time before she slept.

The great horned owl left the mango tree and flew powerfully, silently, his yellow eyes searching for prey. Near the few windows that still showed light, perhaps waiting for Revivalists to return home, it was a little easier for the owl to see what he was looking for.

Suddenly he dove toward the earth, grabbing an unwary mouse. The owl's sharp talons and powerful beak grasped the tiny squealing rodent, killing it quickly. Back in his perch high in one of the ancient live oaks, the owl gulped it down. Later, the owl would regurgitate the indigestible portions of his meal.

He paid no attention to humans going about their business below.

2
Rumors Begin to Spread

Residents of Jamaica Lakes

As dawn broke, Eula May Carter and her little dog, Princess, were out for their morning walk. Princess was first to realize something was wrong. She barked and kept barking. When Eula May saw the police car, she scooped up the small dog and rushed down the street to share the news with her friend, Elsie. The first quiet ripples of rumor began to spread.

"Dolly Overmon is imagining things again," Elsie told Eula May. "I heard she reported burglars trying to get into that house of hers four or five times just in the last month."

Eula May nodded. "Everyone knows about Mrs. Overmon. She's the nervous type, I guess."

Elsie told Betty and Seymour. "The police are checking like they always do," Seymour said. "It's their job but they won't find a thing wrong. They never do."

Jeenya and Zeke Birdsong sat quietly on an old wooden bench on their patio, drinking coffee and waiting. If something really had happened, someone would tell them soon enough.

The sky was still strawberry pink when Seymour's wife, Sarah, noticed the Fire-Rescue truck pulling up. "Don't look like no imaginary burglars this time," she told Patty and Angela. "Looks to me like somebody got hurt." Maybe Mrs. Overmon hadn't been imagining those intruders after all.

The ripples now spread further and faster.

Angela hurried to share the news with the Birdsongs.

"Late last night," Jeenya said softly, "I heard the Patoo and I knew something bad was happening."

Angela stared at Jeenya. "Miz Birdsong, what do you think it was?" Angela had also grown up in rural Jamaica. She respected Jeenya's abilities to interpret such omens.

"Deep down inside my bones," Jeenya said, "I had a feeling that something awful happened. This morning, right here sitting in the garden, I looked up in the sky and saw them, the John Crows. They're still up there circling and you know what that means."

The two women, one old and one young, looked into the brightening sky and saw the terrible omen. Soaring in circles high above were dozens of vultures, the bald-headed turkey vultures. Everyone back home in Jamaica knew the carrion-eaters were omens of death.

Residents of Jamaica Lakes

After she called 911, Dolly Overmon called her sister, Emily. Then she called her husband's sister, Sharona, who passed the word along to her brother, Elijah. They shared the information with their children. Finally, realizing no one else was likely to give him the news, Dolly called Seth.

On her way down the street, Emily told her sister-in-law, Jayne, who told Tina. People began to gather across the street. "The Fire-Rescue truck was here a while," a tall man with a white beard said. "Now, they gone. Didn't see them take nobody with them."

"That," an older woman said quietly, "might mean someone died."

"A heart attack?" her friend asked. "Could have been his heart."

"Could have been a false alarm, don't you think?" a teenaged girl suggested.

A young man pointed across the street. "Look over there. See those policemen? They're stringing up that black and yellow tape. That's to keep people out. They don't put that tape up for heart attacks. They don't put it up when someone gets sick or has an accident. They put that tape up when there's some sort of crime."

"True," an older woman said. "You don't think somebody killed Josiah, do you?"

"Josiah Overmon? You got to be kidding. No one 'round here would dare kill the Obeah man."

Neighbors stood quietly and watched the Overmon's house as, one by one, Josiah's sister and a little later, his brother, Elijah, appeared speaking quietly to one of the policemen, then stepping inside the house. Somewhat later, Seth appeared and joined the others. After a brief time inside, they came back out, spoke to the policeman again, and returned to their homes. Nobody saw Josiah.

A woman in a blue sweater spoke up. "If Josiah was okay, he'd be outside talking to the police himself. I'm starting to think he really is very sick or injured—maybe even dead."

Another woman joined the crowd. "I overheard Sharona talking to one of Elijah's boys. She told the boy his uncle was dead. She said he was murdered."

No longer gentle ripples of rumor, news of Josiah's murder created huge waves that washed through the small Jamaican community, destroying their feeling of security.

Jeenya

Jeenya and her young friend, Angela, still sat on the patio and Zeke was still watering herbs when Seymour and Sarah came with the latest news. "You heard, earlier," Sarah said, "about the police going to the Overmon's house?"

Jeenya and Angela nodded. Zeke pulled up a chair. "What happened?" Angela asked hesitantly. "Was there really a burglar this time?"

"Not a burglar," Seymour said, taking a deep breath. "Josiah Overmon is dead. He was murdered."

There was a shocked silence.

"Murdered?" Zeke finally said. "But why? Everyone liked or at least respected Josiah. It doesn't make sense."

"It had to be a stranger," Sarah said quietly. "That's what everyone is saying. Nobody in this neighborhood would be crazy enough to kill the Obeah Man."

Seymour nodded solemnly. "Josiah's duppy would track him down. It will find the one who did this and kill him for sure. At least that's what people are saying."

Zeke frowned. "But why would a stranger come to Jamaica Lakes and kill Josiah Why would anyone want to kill him?"

"I don't know," Sarah said. "But as soon as I tell my neighbors, I'm going back down by Josiah's house. I have to see what the police are doing. I know it's dumb but I cannot just sit at home thinking about it, wondering what's happening. I need to be there." She and Seymour said their goodbyes and hurried down the street.

"I don't know how you do it, honey," Zeke said to his wife, shaking his head in disbelief. "When you said all that stuff last night about the owl telling you someone was dead, it seemed ridiculous. It still sounds ridiculous but now I am starting to wonder."

"This is awful," Angela said. She wiped off a few tears. "It doesn't seem real." Her eyes suddenly opened wide. "I was there. Late last night, I was at Josiah's work shed." She began to shake.

"Calm down," Jeenya said. "Let's fix a pot of tea. What do you think about rosemary and black mint with a touch of pimento? It will help both of us relax."

Seated at the kitchen table, Angela took a swallow. "George doesn't like me going to see Josiah, you know, but I needed more of that special tea, the tea that's supposed to help me get pregnant. Last night, I even had one of Josiah's special herbal baths."

"What time were you there?" Jeenya asked.

"I had to wait until George went out. He was going to the Revivalist meeting as usual, but it was cold out and he came back for his jacket. I was running late but Josiah and Sharona were waiting for me, same as always. It was nearly ten when I got there, so it must have been ten-thirty or a little later when I left."

"Did you notice anyone hanging around? Did you hear anything?"

"I couldn't see a thing. It was way too dark. Maybe the killer was there, waiting for me to leave. What if he saw me? He might think I could see him."

"Take another swallow. You'll feel better. With you being one of the last people to see Josiah alive, you really should talk to the detectives."

Angela shook her head. "I can't do that. You know I can't. George would find out. He'd know about me going to see the Obeah man when he told me not to."

"Angela," Jeenya said softly, "why don't you leave something here, maybe your sunglasses. When the detectives are here, I'll call you and have you come get your glasses. Then you can talk to the detectives here. It would just take a few minutes."

Jeenya watched Angela leave and then she hurried into the bathroom. She couldn't let Zeke see her crying. She had told Zeke about knowing the Overmons when they were children, but he didn't realize how much she had admired and then loved Josiah. Finally, she wiped her tears, washed her face, and went back into the garden.

"Something wrong?" Zeke asked.

"Must be the pollen," she said. "Just took an allergy pill." Jeenya headed toward the flower garden. But instead of helping her relax, the garden reminded her of Josiah. He had invited her and Zeke to join him at Jamaica Lakes. He had allowed them to live in a nice house, rent-free. He had encouraged her to grow her herbs and vegetables, and he bought them to sell in the grocery and to use in his Obeah shed.

But where could Jeenya go that wouldn't remind her of Josiah? She'd have to leave Jamaica Lakes to forget him. Now she realized she didn't really want to forget Josiah. She wanted to remember all that she had loved about him, about the good things he'd done, about how he'd changed the lives of everyone in Jamaica Lakes.

He wasn't perfect. She knew that, but she knew her life would have been different without Josiah, without his family and, especially, without his mother. She still missed Mrs. Overmon but now she was glad Josiah's mother hadn't lived to learn that her son had been murdered.

She wondered about the detectives. Who would be assigned to this case? Would they send Rick? That would be logical. Ricardo Montoya was the only person in the Palm City Police Department who knew anything about the people in Jamaica Lakes.

She remembered Rick as a teenager, coming on his bicycle to spend time with their grandson, Homer. Certainly, the police would know enough to send him. If it was Rick, she might be able to help him a little. She and Zeke could, at least, share what they knew about the people in the neighborhood.

Residents of Jamaica Lake

Meanwhile at the parsonage, nearly a dozen people had gathered, all shocked and horrified, all nervous. Herman Wolff tried to comfort his people, to calm their fears, to assure them it wasn't their fault. It couldn't have been.

3

The Detectives Arrive

Jeenya

Jeenya walked out back where Zeke had a basket of freshly cut callaloo and some hot peppers. Chester called to say they were running low. With or without Josiah, they had to fill the shelves. People still had to eat.

"Zeke, I have a hunch the police will be sending Rick to find out who killed Josiah."

Zeke looked up from his work. "A hunch? Not the sort of feeling you had last night? Just a simple hunch?"

She smiled. "If they send Rick, I'll call and ask him and his new partner to lunch. It would be interesting to see what they can tell us and I'm sure we can help them. We know people here. We can tell them about Josiah's family."

"Uh-huh," Zeke responded. "I guess we could."

"I'm planning to wander down by Josiah's place and talk to Sarah. She doesn't know Rick but, when she sees the detectives, she can call me and tell me what they look like. It will be pretty clear if she sees Rick."

"With that scar of his," Zeke said, "he'd be hard to miss."

Rick Montoya

As Jeenya and Zeke spoke, Palm City Police Detective, Ricardo Montoya, was crossing the bridge that rose high above the south fork of the St. Lucie River.

The sky was an icy blue with a few thin cirrus clouds near the horizon. He glanced with a smile at a line of seven large brown pelicans flying so close to the water's surface that he wondered if they didn't sometimes get their bellies wet. Pelicans, he thought, with their six-foot wingspan and oversized bills, had to be some of the strangest-looking birds anywhere.

The bridge over the wide, slow-flowing river took him from where he lived in Stuart to Palm City where he worked. As soon as he'd heard from the lieutenant, he had called his partner and then called the Cocky Rooster to order bagels, coffee, and a few snacks.

At the café, Ramona greeted him with her usual happy smile. "So, Detective Ricardo, another big case, huh? You're like those detectives on TV, I bet." She filled his large thermos with hot coffee and handed him a box with bagels and cream cheese, pears, and a bag of her famous homemade cookies: chocolate chip with walnuts.

Rick packed the food in the back seat of his unmarked police car, a four-year-old silver Ford Focus. He could tell you the history of each dent and scratch including the three bullet holes in his trunk, a parting gift from Marty Zander nearly a year ago.

Marty had been depressed. He'd lost his job more than two years earlier and had no luck finding another. His family's savings were gone and their debt had grown larger every day. No longer able to pay the mortgage, they were about to lose the house. That's when Marty decided to end it all.

Marty planned to kill his wife and five children first, then himself. He spent a long time explaining to his wife how he didn't want her to go through the pain of losing him and living homeless with the kids. Mrs. Zander comforted him and tried to convince him to change his mind.

Their oldest girl who was not quite ten heard the conversation and called 911. Rick and his old partner, Andy Sutton, were in the area and arrived four minutes later.

Marty took off running and hid, possibly in a closet or under a bed. Rick and Andy decided not to take the time to look for him. With Mrs. Zander and the five children in the car, he and Andy left, wanting to get the family to safety before returning to deal with Marty.

As they drove away, Rick looked in the rear-view mirror. He saw Marty appear in the driveway with his gun. He warned the others to duck and watched as Marty shot the car three times. Then Rick watched in horror as Marty held the gun to his head and blew his brains out.

Sometimes Rick wondered if they should have stayed that day to look for Marty. Maybe they could have gotten help for him. Other times, Rick knew they'd done the right thing. Police work was like that. Decisions were rarely clear-cut. It wasn't always a choice between right and wrong. You had to think fast and do what seemed best.

He hoped he wouldn't need to make that sort of choice on this case. He slowly ran his fingers along the scar that ran down the left side of his face, remembering a war where right and wrong were never clearly defined.

He parked in front of the police station. Where was Hazel? She lived closer to the station than he did. He poured himself a cup of coffee but was too tense to drink.

Finally, after four or five long minutes of waiting, he saw her arrive with her husband.

Rick watched as Hazel kissed Tim and got out of the car. With her red hair done as usual in a single braid down her back and, with her cool green eyes, she was extremely attractive. Zeke and Jeenya would be impressed.

Some people, he thought, make the mistake of assuming that a pretty woman is a pushover. Jeenya and Zeke weren't like that. He felt certain they'd understand that Hazel was tough—tougher than many of the men in the department.

"Have a good day, dear," Hazel's husband called cheerfully.

Rick frowned. Was the man even thinking? Did he really think they could have a good day investigating a murder? Or was he being too critical of Tim? Perhaps, for Hazel, a good day would be one where they could quickly and easily find the killer or at least find enough information to narrow the list of suspects to a manageable number.

Less than fifteen minutes after the lieutenant had called, Rick and Hazel were heading down the road, chewing bagels and sipping coffee.

"So, what did Nate tell you?" Hazel asked. "He just told me some guy was dead and to get my ass over here ASAP. I don't even know where we're going."

Nate Holiday, the lieutenant in charge of the detectives, wasn't known for polite language but it annoyed Rick that Nate would talk like that to a woman. Nate never talked to him that way.

"We're going to Jamaica Lakes," Rick said. "I suspect Nate chose us because I have friends there. The people in Jamaica Lakes, as you might guess, are all from Jamaica and, like with a lot of minority groups, they don't like talking to outsiders—especially the police. But some of the people there know me a little. Hopefully, that will help."

"Nate tells you more than he tells me. Don't know if it's because I'm a woman or because I'm new."

"Hard to tell with Nate. He might just have been in a hurry, expecting me to pass the information along."

"So how do you feel about women in the Police Department?" she asked. "I'm good with a gun, really good, but if I'm attacked, there's no way I could defend myself the way you could. Does that bother you?"

"I thought about it," he said. "Sometimes being able to fight is helpful but, since I joined the department, I haven't needed to fight more than three or four times. You could defend yourself a lot better than some of the older men on the force, especially those who put on too much weight. I'd say you're better at some things; I'm better at others. That's why we're partners. We make a good team."

"What would you say I'm good at?" Hazel asked.

"Why are you so down on yourself?" Rick asked. "Somebody say you weren't good enough?"

"Answer my question. What would you say I'm good at?"

"First thing, you're definitely better than I am at understanding what women are talking about. You're great at asking questions that make people feel comfortable before getting to the painful stuff, especially with women.

"I know some men don't respect a woman asking them questions, so there'll be times when I take charge. Most of the time, I'd rather watch and listen. I like observing their expressions, listening to their tone of voice and watching their eyes. That's one reason I requested you as my partner."

"You requested me? Honestly? I heard some of the guys talking about how you got stuck with me, thinking you must have done something pretty bad to irritate Nate enough to get stuck with me."

"One of the first things a good detective learns, Hazel, is never to believe everything you hear. You need evidence. Maybe those idiots didn't know I requested you. Maybe they were irritated that I chose you rather than them. Maybe they knew the truth but wanted to watch you squirm, wanted to see how well you'd take it. Don't let them get to you."

"I know not to believe everything a witness says, but I thought I could believe the guys in the department. Anyway, did Nate the Nasty have anything else to say?"

"You talking about our fearless leader, Nate the Great?" Rick smiled, noting that she was more cheerful now. "I'm looking forward to the day that man retires. I asked him about the cause of death and got his usual helpful response. 'Look at the evidence, Montoya. Come to your own conclusions.' But this time, believe it or not, Nate actually broke down and gave us two helpful clues. 'First,' he says, 'I understand your victim could be someone important.' And his last comment? 'And Montoya, it wasn't a heart attack.'"

"Right. Like he would send us out for a heart attack. I guess he was telling us not to waste any time getting there. You talked to your friends yet?"

Rick shook his head. Although he and Hazel had worked as partners for only three weeks, she knew he frequently visited an older couple in Jamaica Lakes and, although he occasionally tried to explain, nobody else in the department understood why Ricardo Montoya, who wasn't Jamaican, would spend time visiting some old people from Jamaica.

The first day they'd worked together, Hazel had asked, "I don't want to pry, Rick, but I don't understand how you happened to meet these Jamaican people."

"Their grandson, Homer, and I were friends." It wasn't easy to talk about Homer, but Rick was glad she'd asked. "I met Homer Birdsong in high school. We were both into sports. Homer lived in Jamaica Lakes. He lived with his grandparents. His mom, down in Miami, had a drug problem. When she was arrested for selling drugs and was looking at years in prison, his grandparents got permission to raise Homer. They didn't want him in foster care."

Rick hadn't wanted to say anything more that day and changed the subject.

On their way to Jamaica Lakes, Hazel brought up the subject again. "You were telling me how you and Homer were friends in high school. Are you still close?"

That was the question Rick had been dreading. "Homer and I both went to the University of Florida. We were roommates. On September 11th, Homer and I were watching TV. We saw those planes hit the towers again and again. Homer…"

He took a couple sips of coffee. "Homer wanted to join the army. I convinced him to wait until we finished the semester. It was the first semester of our sophomore year. Then we signed up together, we went to boot camp together, and we both ended up in Iraq. We were together in one of those crummy armored vehicles that day. A roadside bomb went off, and Homer was hurt, hurt really bad. There was blood everywhere.

"Homer asked me to tell Jeenya and Zeke he loved

them, that he was sorry he'd let them down. I knew what he meant. They were hoping he'd be a doctor or lawyer or something. I told Homer he didn't let them down, that they'd be proud of him. I promised to go see them as soon as I got home. Homer died in my arms that day. I held him and couldn't do a thing to help. All I could do was cry.

"I was in military hospitals for five months before they let me go home. The first thing I did was to visit them, Jeenya and Zeke, and you know what they did? They comforted me."

He knew Hazel had noticed how he limped when he was tired. She didn't say anything but he could see her frown. She didn't know how many scars were hidden under his clothing, but Rick couldn't hide the dark scar that went from his left eyebrow down to his jaw. Now, as he ran his fingers slowly along the scar, she asked about it.

"That scar?" she asked. "That's from Iraq? From that roadside bomb?"

He nodded.

"And when you rub it like that? Does that mean it's still sore?"

"Just remembering."

"Remembering Iraq?"

"Remembering Iraq and Homer and our reasons for being there." Then he changed the subject. "Hand me one of those cookies, will you?"

4

The Crime Scene

Rick

Rick was glad Hazel asked all those questions. It would be difficult to explain about Homer and Zeke and Jeenya in the middle of a murder investigation.

"I haven't called the Birdsongs yet," he said. "I don't think they'll have any information about this man's death. After we get the basic facts on the case, we'll drop by and see them. I expect they'll insist on feeding us lunch. If they don't, I know a nice little café."

He turned and smiled at Hazel. "You'll love Zeke and Jeenya. But you need to understand that, like a lot of grandmothers, Jeenya is trying to marry me off. I'll need to explain right off that you're married or she'll be ordering our wedding invitations tonight.

"They worry about me living alone and feeling lonely. They worry about me getting hurt on the job. Nobody else worries about me like that. It's like they're the only real family I have.

"The Birdsongs should be able to tell us about the victim. They'll share things with us that other people might not mention. And, if this victim is who I think he is, I've seen him a time or two and things will definitely be interesting."

Rick turned left on Orange Grove Road. "We're just about there." He turned right on Tangerine Street and stopped. Larry Tipper, one of the older policemen on the force, was directing traffic.

"Hey there Rick, Hazel. The best place to park," Larry said, pointing, "is down here along Montego Bay." In the paved area behind the grocery store, a police cruiser and the medical examiner's car were already there.

"Back at the corner," Larry said, "you hang a right. The first house on the right is where the victim lived. Not far past the house, there's a shed or small cottage. That's where the body is. He seems to have been an important man around here. The victim owned the little grocery store. His name was Josiah Overmon."

Rick parked and the two of them walked back to Ocho Rios. Across the street, a man sprinkled white powder around his yard. "Looks like salt," Rick said. "Maybe it's fertilizer."

"Or maybe ant killer," Hazel suggested.

"Neighbors know something's wrong." Rick pointed to half a dozen small groups across the street, all watching with solemn faces.

As Rick and Hazel passed Mr. Overmon's house, an older uniformed policeman walked toward them. His face was red, his hair gray and thinning, and his uniform a little too tight. "Harvey Markwell," Rick said. "How long now until retirement?" He knew Harvey was counting the days.

"Sixty-three and a half days." Harvey's shy smile showed a couple teeth missing.

"You and Larry first on the scene?"

Harvey nodded.

"Then show us the scene and tell us what you know so far."

Harvey led the way to a small cottage in front and to the left of the house. "Larry and I were called out to this same house five times in the past six weeks. The victim's wife, Mrs. Overmon, kept calling us, telling us someone was trying to break in, but we never saw any evidence and nothing was ever missing. This time when she called 911, she said her husband was hurt, but she didn't say how bad. They sent out the Fire-Rescue people just in case it was something serious, but Larry and I were guessing he'd tripped and sprained an ankle or something.

"We sure never expected to walk in and find ourselves a murder. Maybe Mrs. Overmon was right all along. Maybe someone has been sneaking around. One of the men with Fire-Rescue checked the body and pronounced him dead. That's when we called the station and told them we needed detectives, the crime scene people, and the medical examiner."

Rick looked at the small building. The homes in this area were all concrete block structures, probably built strong enough to protect people from the all-too-common hurricanes in south Florida. This small structure, however, was a wooden building set on a concrete slab. The outside was painted pale blue with navy blue trim, matching the colors on the main house. He saw only the one window. It looked out on the road but, with the lacy white curtains, you couldn't see inside. Possibly, at night with a light on inside, you'd see shadows.

"Did you talk to his wife?" Hazel asked.

"Yeah. Couldn't get much out of her. Her name is Dolly. Nice lady, but she's terribly upset. Says there isn't anybody who'd want to kill her husband. I told her she'd need to talk to you guys."

Harvey led them around the side of the small structure to the open door. "The door was open like this when we got here. The wife isn't sure if she opened it when she came looking for him. She thinks it was already open."

The body lay face-up on the shiny blue linoleum, his head toward the open door. The dark-skinned man appeared to be in his sixties or older with black hair and a neatly trimmed gray beard. Blood covered his neck, beard, and white dress shirt and puddled on the floor around his head.

Rick raised his left hand to the scar on his face and slowly traced it down to his chin. Seeing a body, seeing blood, always reminded him of Iraq. He'd seen too many bodies there and he would never forget watching Homer die. The scar reminded him that, for some reason, he was still alive.

Homer had talked about fighting to protect American freedom. Rick could never see how killing people in Iraq had any effect on American freedom. He had decided, if he lived long enough to come home, he'd fight for justice. He understood justice. Now, with this man lying dead on the floor, it was Rick's job to get justice for him, his family and his friends.

"Nate was right," Rick said. "It wasn't a heart attack."

"Cause of death looks pretty obvious," Harvey said. "We looked around for a knife but didn't want to contaminate the scene. No sign of the weapon. I imagine the killer took his knife with him.

"No evidence of a robbery either," Harvey continued. "He's got a money box, open there on his desk, with four twenties, six tens, three fives and seven one-dollar bills. Looks to me like somebody had a personal grudge. They sliced his throat and left him to bleed out. The medical examiner is here and has seen him already. According to Dr. Parker, based on the state of rigor, he's guessing the time of death was between ten last night and three this morning. We'll have a better idea after the autopsy."

Rick nodded. He liked working with Frank Parker. "Doc still here? I'd like to talk to him."

"A couple minutes ago he stepped inside the house to see the wife," Harvey said. "He wanted to ask her if the victim had any health problems. And then he'll make sure the wife is doing all right. When he comes out, I'll let him know you want to see him."

Harvey stepped back so Rick and Hazel could get a better look inside. The two of them stood at the open door. They didn't want to step inside until the forensic team was done.

From what Rick could see, there were two rooms, a larger front room and a much smaller back room. A blue and white striped curtain hanging between the rooms could be pulled across for privacy. A blue plastic chair and a small white table were visible in the back room. A metal basin on the table held what appeared to be a yellow-brown sea-sponge. Behind the basin there was a stack of white towels, all neatly folded.

The single window didn't let in much sunlight. Two metal fixtures on the ceiling, each with a pair of fluorescent bulbs, provided the necessary light. A big wooden desk and a well-worn, brown leather office-chair filled the left side of the room.

Behind the desk, the wall was layered with solid

wooden shelves painted white. Large clear plastic storage tubs, filled with paper and plastic bags, were on the lower shelves. On the higher shelves were Mason jars with dried plants and other mysterious substances. A plastic bin on the desk was half full of small plastic bags of herbs.

"What is that disgusting smell?" Hazel asked, wrinkling her nose and hunching her shoulders.

It was a strong smell, more intense than Rick remembered, probably due to the large quantity of herbs stored in the small building. What smelled so disgusting was the overpowering smell of that awful tea Homer once talked him into tasting. "It's the herbs we smell."

"Herbs? You sure? It doesn't smell like any herbs I know."

"A few are special Jamaican herbs. Zeke and Jeenya grow them in their garden. They probably grew most of the herbs you find here in this room. But I agree with you on the smell. It really is disgusting.

"Jeenya told me once that the worse the herbs smell and the worse they taste, the more people will believe the stuff will help them. That's probably true for us too. If a doctor gave you medicine that looked and smelled like ground up peppermint candy, you'd have a hard time believing it could do much good."

Three simple but comfortable-looking chairs were pulled up to the desk across from the office chair. Two mugs sat on the desk, a dark blue mug in front of the office chair, a pale green one on the other side. Off to the left was a blue and green teapot, a matching sugar bowl and a plate with what appeared to be cookie crumbs.

Toward the back of the room stood a small table with a hotplate and battered tea kettle. On white wooden shelves above the table were at least a dozen mugs in a variety of solid colors. An orange mug was filled with spoons. Further down on the shelf were a dozen or so boxes of cookies and a kitchen canister labeled "Sugar." A blue plastic dishpan held additional mugs, probably ready to take into the house for washing.

A few minutes later, the crime scene officers arrived. They would take pictures of every detail, look for weapons, and check for prints, fibers, hairs, and other evidence.

"Call me when you're done," Rick said. "We'd like to get a close look before they carry him away."

Rick and Hazel were turning toward the house when they saw Dr. Parker heading their way.

"I was hoping to see you before I left," the medical examiner said quietly. "The transport van should be here soon. Everyone so far takes one look at all that blood and concludes the man was killed with a knife. There's no doubt someone used a knife to slit his throat, but I don't think that was the cause of death. There wasn't enough blood. I suspect the cutting was done postmortem."

Jeenya

Jeenya was going through the refrigerator to see what she could fix for lunch when the phone rang. It was Sarah.

"Hi Jeenya. I just saw the detectives, a man and a woman. At first, I couldn't see his face. When he turned to look inside the Obeah shed, I could see one side of his face, but it was the wrong side. Finally, he turned to talk to someone and I could see his whole face.

"That scar on his face really is awful. I know you said the scar would be hard to miss but I had no idea it would be this bad. And, Jeenya, I know you said his partner was a woman but I wasn't expecting someone so beautiful. Just wait until you see her."

Jeenya, told Zeke about the phone call and then hurried to the grocery story. As she passed Ocho Rios, she noticed that the crowd milling around to see what was happening had grown much larger.

At the store, there was also a crowd, many there to buy salt. Others were just standing around talking about who might have been crazy enough to kill the Obeah Man. A few of the men were talking about how ugly the scar was on the detective and about the woman with the detective, how beautiful she was, and whether she was his girlfriend or his wife, or something else. As far as Jeenya could tell, none of them suggested that she might also be a detective.

After looking at what was available, Jeenya decided to make fish soup for lunch. She didn't know about Hazel, but she remembered that this was one of Rick's favorites. She had no problem finding the ingredients she needed and hurried home to get the soup started.

5

The Victim's Wife

Rick

Harvey led the way to the Overmon's front door and knocked.

"This house used to be smaller, like the others in the neighborhood," Rick told Hazel. "They built additions several times, a good sign the Overmons were earning a little more than most of the folks in the neighborhood."

A girl, perhaps ten or twelve years old, came to the door. She looked like she'd been crying. "These are the detectives," Harvey told her. "They need to talk to your mother."

"You are detectives? Both of you?" The girl stared at Hazel, her eyes wide. "I didn't know they had lady detectives. Come on in. Mama is 'specting you. She told me to bring you some coffee."

The girl led the detectives into a small but neat living room. Three framed Jamaican travel posters were on one wall. Family pictures covered the other walls. It reminded Rick of other homes he'd visited in the area.

"The detectives are here, Mama. And one is a lady detective, a lady detective with real pretty red hair. I'll go get the coffee."

Dolly Overmon sat on a flowered sofa blowing her nose. She took several deep breaths. "That's my Julie. She is such a great help. So are the other kids. If I didn't have my kids needing me to be strong, I don't know what I'd do."

"I'm Detective Hazel Fontaine, and this is Detective Rick Montoya. We're terribly sorry for your loss, Mrs. Overmon. Finding your husband like that must have been a terrible shock and we really hate to disturb you. But, if we're going to find the person who did this, we need all the help we can get."

Julie returned and served coffee and gingersnaps. "I hope you like 'em," she said. "These are my favorites."

"Thank you, sweetheart. They're perfect," her mother said. "Now, if you'll go help Jerry and Aunt Emily with the little ones, that would be a big help. Why don't you take them some gingersnaps and milk?"

Dolly seemed to force a slight smile as her daughter left the room. "Being useful helps Julie deal with the situation. I wish it could be that easy. So, what can I tell you, detectives? The officers I talked to earlier asked who'd want to hurt Josiah, who his enemies were. Josiah never had any enemies. Everyone loved Josiah. Nobody would want to hurt him."

Rick studied Mrs. Overmon. He couldn't remember ever meeting her. He guessed she was at least twenty years younger than Josiah. She was a pretty woman even with an extra twenty or thirty pounds that she'd probably put on having children. Her hair was cut short and curled in toward her round face and she had dimples when she smiled.

"Why don't you start by telling us about your family?" Hazel suggested.

Dolly nodded. "Josiah and me, we've got five children. Julie is thirteen. She's the oldest. The others are ten, four, two and the baby is four months old. Josiah had three other children with his first wife, Marie. When she died of cancer, close to fifteen years ago, Josiah took the children back to Jamaica to live with their grandparents. I never met any of them. Now I guess I'll need to call and let them know about their father. I hope I can find their number or address or something.

"Their grandparents didn't have much and it would be hard for them to feed and clothe three children and put them through school. They say schools in Jamaica are free but buying school uniforms and books can be expensive. Josiah sent money every month to pay the bills. We'll have to keep doing that."

She glanced at the travel posters on the wall. "Josiah was born in a little town southeast of Montego Bay but then he grew up in Kingston."

Rick watched Mrs. Overmon wipe fresh tears away. He watched Hazel who was doing her best to start the conversation with easy questions. He could see how each time Hazel mentioned Mrs. Overmon's husband, it obviously caused Dolly a great deal of pain and, while less obviously, Hazel was also feeling the pain.

"Josiah didn't know his father very well," Dolly continued. "His father was an Obeah Man and traveled a lot. Josiah hardly ever talked about him. All I know is that Josiah loved his mother. Sometimes, you know, I got the feeling he didn't much like his father. When Josiah was eighteen, he heard about jobs here, working in the citrus groves. All this area was citrus back then. Josiah came to Palm City and worked picking oranges for several years.

"His mother got cancer, maybe ten years ago, and died a couple months after it was discovered. His father died less than a year later. I never knew Josiah's parents you understand, but I wish I had."

"What about your family?" Hazel asked.

Rick nodded. They both understood that Dolly needed more time before focusing on the death of her husband.

"Well, we lived in Bull Bay, just east of Kingston, but we moved to Miami when I was only seven. Dad was a history teacher in Jamaica; he was a garbage man here. It wasn't anything I liked to tell people but, unlike construction workers, Dad had a steady job and the pay was good.

"Mother worked in an office for a small moving company. My older brother had worked in the groves with Josiah and he suggested we live here in Jamaica Lakes. That's how I met Josiah.

"Mom and Dad planned from the beginning that all us kids would go to college. I studied education and got a job teaching second grade here in Palm City. Josiah was a lot older than me but that didn't matter." She dabbed her eyes with a tissue.

"After I got pregnant, I quit teaching. Maybe, when the children are older, I'll return to teaching again. Josiah and me, we were married thirteen years, almost fourteen years ago."

Dolly took a deep breath, sighed, and tried to smile. "I'm getting off track, aren't I? Let's see. Josiah has two younger brothers, Elijah and Seth. He has an older sister,

Sharona. All of them live here in Jamaica Lakes. My sister, Emily, lives here and my brother, Chester, lives here. Another brother lives in Boston. What else do you want to know?"

"How old was your husband?"

"He was only seventy-four. His brothers were planning a big party in April for his seventy-fifth birthday." Tears that had been threatening now poured down her face. She reached for another tissue.

"I know this isn't easy," Hazel said. "Let's take it one step at a time. Why don't you tell us about yesterday? Start with when you woke up. Tell us everything you remember."

Dolly twisted a little clump of hair behind her ear and frowned. "Josiah was up before me. He almost always was. I fixed breakfast and started getting the two older kids ready for school. While they were eating, I stepped outside and called Josiah. He was in his work shed out front.

"He came inside a few minutes later. Josiah liked eating breakfast with the older children, asking them about school and about their friends. While he was eating with them, I got the three younger kids up, the two in preschool and the baby."

She continued with every detail of the day. "Josiah owns all the little stores around the corner. There is a Caribbean grocery, mostly Jamaican, selling a little of everything, but mostly what we can't find in the big stores. Nearly all the people here in Jamaica Lakes are from Jamaica you know."

Dolly leaned forward and peered at Rick. "I feel like I've seen you before. Aren't you the young man who was friends with the Birdsong boy?"

"Yes, ma'am. Homer and I went to school together. He and I were best friends." He fingered his scar briefly.

"I remember. The two of you boys used to go to the store with Jeenya's shopping list. You'd get everything on her list and pick up a couple sodas and candy bars for yourselves.

"I also remember hearing about the two of you getting jerk pork in the café one day. I guess you didn't grow up eating spicy food. They said you downed the whole pitcher of ice water before Homer convinced you to eat rice. I always wondered if Homer ordered a dish that was too spicy on purpose or if you told him you were fine with spicy food."

Rick smiled. "I remember that like it was yesterday. I had never tasted anything that hot. But Homer didn't do it on purpose. I always put hot sauce on what I ate at the Taco Shop. Their hot sauce didn't bother me. But that jerk pork was an entirely different level of hot."

"I hear you still visit the Birdsongs now and then. That's real nice of you. They're good people. They took it awful hard when Homer got killed over there. They expected him to finish college and go on to be a doctor or lawyer or maybe an artist. They love telling people what a great artist that boy was.

"I guess you know Jeenya and Zeke grow most of the Jamaican herbs and vegetables for Josiah's store." She managed a half-smile. "I do feel better knowing you're the one trying to find his killer. You'll understand our community better than most of the police."

"I know a little," Rick said. "But I have a lot more to learn. I hope you'll trust us and tell us what you know."

"Yesterday," Hazel said, "what did your husband do

after breakfast?"

Dolly looked out the window. "Josiah went over to the store first thing like he always did. He had to be sure they weren't running low on inventory. They don't have much storage space, you understand. He came home for a quick lunch at around twelve-thirty and then went right back.

"During the afternoon he left Chester, his assistant, in charge of the store while he drove down to the farm stand. Josiah got some vegetables from Zeke and Jeenya, especially Jamaican vegetables. The rest he got at Fred Buckles' farm stand. Josiah enjoyed picking out the best quality, you know. 'Can't do that if they deliver,' he always said. He did that three or four days a week. He's gone an hour and a half, maybe two hours, each time. I guess he was running other errands too, getting things for the store."

Rick listened and took notes. He underlined two names. Chester was the assistant at the grocery. The farm stand belonged to Fred Buckles.

"He was always home for dinner at six." Dolly continued. "When he was done eating, Josiah went out to his work shed. He and his sister, Sharona, worked together every night. They mixed herbs to sell in his store. He also had regular customers that came by to talk to him and buy herbs for making tea."

Rick added Sharona's name to his list.

"How late did he usually work in his shed?"

"Sometimes pretty late. I couldn't say exactly what time. People came by to talk or to ask his advice. It never surprised me if he was out there late. I try to go to bed at ten most nights. Josiah came in when he was done."

"What about last night?"

"He hadn't come in when I went to bed. I was expecting him to be there when I woke up, you know, but he wasn't. I thought he'd gotten up early, but it didn't look like his side of the bed was slept in. I wondered if he slept down here on the sofa. Sometimes he did that when he'd been working real late. He didn't like to disturb me. Josiah was thoughtful that way.

"When I couldn't find him downstairs, I wasn't worried. I figured he was already out in his shed. Once the older kids started eating breakfast, I stepped outside and called him. When he didn't come, I assumed he was mixing herbs, or that someone stopped by to talk to him."

Dolly was twisting her hair again, twisting it so tightly it must have hurt. "So, I went out there. I was going to ask if he wanted me to take his breakfast out to him. That's when I saw him, lying there on the floor. First, it looked like he was sleeping, but then I saw the blood. It looked like somebody cut his neck.

"I was terrified, you know. Too scared to move. Too scared to scream or anything. I just stood there like a statue, like Lot's wife, turned into a pillar of salt."

Rick watched as she told the story. Dolly was starting to shake. She seemed to have trouble catching her breath. Rick knew she was picturing her husband's body in her mind. She finally managed to take several deep breaths and turned back to Hazel.

"I knew I shouldn't scream," Dolly continued, back in control. "The children would hear me. They'd all have started screaming too without knowing why. I pulled myself together, came inside and called 911.

"I was pretty sure he was dead, you know, but I kept hoping. I couldn't tell them that on the phone. I wanted them to send a doctor just in case. I told them he was hurt. The policeman and the Fire-Rescue man both checked him. They said there was no reason to take him to the hospital. Josiah was dead."

"After you called 911," Hazel said, "what did you do next?"

"I called my sister, Emily. I didn't know what to else to do. Emily told me to call Sharona, so I did. She's an incredibly strong woman. She didn't scream or cry or get hysterical. She was real quiet for a minute or two. Then she said she'd be right over.

"Emily and Sharona got here about the same time. They both took a quick look at Josiah. They didn't go inside, you know, just looked through the open door. They knew right off he was dead.

"Then Sharona took charge. She asked Emily to help with the children. She told me to fix a pot of coffee. She called Josiah's brothers. When the police arrived, Sharona was outside ready to show them where Josiah was and she tried to answer their questions. After all, she was out there with him last night until pretty late. She knew who came in to see Josiah. I wouldn't have had any idea.

"She talked to family members when they stopped by, told them they could come in to see me for a few minutes but then to go on home or go to work. She knew you'd want to talk to me alone, not with a roomful of relatives. It really helps having a strong woman take charge."

Dolly blew her nose and glanced toward the back room. We could hear the sounds of cartoons playing. "Julie and Jerry, the two big kids have been such a help. They got the little kids up and dressed and helped me feed them. Since then, they've been helping Emily in the back room. Julie and Jerry are old enough to understand what's happened. They asked me if it was all right to turn on cartoons and I said sure. Cartoons might not seem appropriate when your daddy is dead but the little ones don't understand."

She looked at Rick. "Those policemen out there tell you somebody's been messing around in our yard the past month or so? I'd always call 911, but the policemen never found anything wrong. They seemed to think it wasn't anything serious, maybe just an animal.

"So, when they got this call, they expected it was like before—until they saw Josiah lying on the floor. I still hoped that he was just hurt not dead, but somehow, I guess from looking at all that blood, I knew he was probably gone."

Hazel tried moving the conversation away from the terrible image of Josiah dead on the floor. "Did your husband do or say anything out of the ordinary in the past week or two?"

"The other policemen asked me that too. There isn't anything I can think of."

"Has anyone argued with your husband or made any threats?"

"No. He would have told me if there had been any problems."

Hazel gave her a card. "If you think of anything at all, Josiah saying something a little odd, talking to someone he didn't normally talk to, any little changes in his schedule, anything at all, please give us a call."

"Thanks for your help," Rick said. "I can promise you we're going to do everything we possibly can to find the person who did this."

6

Pouring Salt Around the Houses

Rick

Rick found Harvey and Larry outside Josiah's shed. "Why don't the two of you start checking out the neighborhood? Start at one end of Montego Bay and work your way down to the other end. Then come back along the opposite side. That's only two blocks. Do the same thing along Ocho Rios. Find out who lives in each house and ask three questions:

1. Get the names of everyone in the house over twelve years old.

2. Ask where they were last night between ten p.m. and three a.m.

3. Ask who and what they remember. If they remember anything, get the approximate time and place."

He waited while the men got out paper and pens and then he repeated the questions. "If you need a notebook," Rick added, "they sell them over there in the store."

Rick and Hazel walked over to the Caribbean Grocery.

A thin man wearing neat-looking jeans with a white dress shirt and dark blue tie was deep in conversation with four younger men. He looked their way. "You the detectives?"

Rick nodded.

"Dolly called to say you were coming. Be with you in a minute." He returned to his conversation.

Rick and Hazel looked around. Along the right side of the store they saw fruit and vegetables, including some Rick couldn't identify. In the back, fresh and dried herbs were in plastic bags. There were candles and incense and, in one corner, some cheap cooking pots. A large freezer had a sign listing the frozen meat that was available.

"Goat?" Hazel asked. "These people eat goats?"

"Why not? We eat lamb. It's not much different. Goat curry is a popular Jamaican dish, one of my favorites. Maybe Jeenya will cook some while we're here.

"What is all this stuff labeled 'jerk'?" Hazel wanted to know. "There's jerk seasoning, jerk dry rub, and jerk sauce. And what about Pickapeppa? That sounds super spicy."

Rick laughed. "Jerk is the one that's super-hot. It's the spicy sauce they put on meat. You heard Mrs. Overmon. After I got used to the burning in my mouth, it really tasted good. It's like barbecue sauce but a hundred times hotter.

"Now Pickapeppa is something else. That stuff is delicious. I keep a bottle at home. It's like Worcestershire sauce but with a lot of what they call pimento in it. To us that's allspice. It's great on steak or chicken or whatever you're cooking. I use it in scrambled eggs."

Hazel watched the customers as she listened. "Rick," she said very quietly. "Something strange is going on. Seven customers came in while we were talking. All seven went straight to the baking goods area. Each one picked up two or three boxes of salt and checked out. Here's another one."

Rick watched the older man approach the shelves. He picked up five boxes of salt and headed to the cash register. "I have no idea. I don't remember any really salty dishes."

"Thanks for waiting. I'm Chester Gunn, the manager here. Come on back to the office." Chester was the only man in the store wearing a tie. He led the way but hesitated at the door. "That is Josiah's chair. I reckon I can sit there, at least for now."

Rick and Hazel introduced themselves. "What can you tell us about Mr. Overmon?" Rick asked. "What was he like as a boss?"

"Mr. Overmon was a good man and a good boss. We got along real fine. I can't understand why anyone would kill him. Everyone in Jamaica Lakes had a lot of respect for Mr. Overmon. Some say he was like the mayor of Jamaica Lakes. Anybody with problems could go talk to him. He always did his best to help. He was a fine man."

"Tell me what you can about Josiah's last day."

"Josiah was working here in the office, the same as he did every day. He was writing up orders and working on the record books. At noon, he went home for lunch like he always did and he came right back. It was around two when he left to run errands. He came back close to five with half a dozen boxes of fruit and vegetables from the farm stand. Don't know where else he went."

Hazel asked Chester, "I watched your customers this morning. They were all buying salt, nothing but salt. Do Jamaicans use that much salt in cooking?"

Chester shook his head. "That salt they're buying, none of it is for cooking." He leaned forward and spoke in a hush, "Some people around here, well, you might say they're a little superstitious. They think that when a person dies, his duppy, what you'd call a ghost, wanders around. Duppies, supposedly, do bad things to people, getting revenge for whatever was done to them."

As Chester spoke about duppies, his voice shook a little. Rick wondered if Chester was scared of Josiah's duppy too. Maybe he had a reason to be worried.

"Salt is supposed to keep duppies away," Chester added. "People around here, especially those who are more educated, say they don't believe in duppies. But nearly everybody, including Josiah's friends and relatives are getting salt to pour around their houses.

"I just sent three of our staff out to supermarkets to buy up all the salt they can find. I expect we'll be able to sell all the salt we can get hold of."

Chester laughed nervously. "I have no idea if salt really keeps those duppies away but I guess it can't hurt none, sprinkling a little salt around your house.

"So, what have you been hearing," Rick asked, "about who might have killed him? Looks to me like everyone in the neighborhood knows he's dead. They must have some suspicions."

Chester chewed on his lip. "Well, the people I talked to this morning are pretty sure Josiah's killer is not Jamaican. If the killer was one of us, he'd be terrified, knowing for sure that Josiah's duppy would find him and do awful things. When a duppy comes after you, they say you die a slow, very painful death."

Rick was contemplating this idea of being tortured by a ghost when his cell phone rang. "Thanks. We'll be there in a few minutes."

7

A Look Inside the Obeah Shed

Rick

Rick and Hazel thanked Chester for his help and returned to Josiah's work shed as the crime scene officers were packing up. The transport van was parked in front of the house.

"I'd guess we've got close to a hundred prints," a tall thin woman said. "But none with blood on them. People could have been in and out of here for weeks, months, or longer. I can't see how finding their prints will help much."

"Same for fibers," said one of the men. "As we understand it, this was kind of like a public place. Anyone around here could come in to pay their rent, get a little tea, or just sit and talk. Matching up prints or fibers isn't likely to help us find the killer."

Rick and Hazel stepped inside. "I remember Mr. Overmon with a black beard," Rick said to Hazel. "Not gray, but it's the same man. He sometimes talked to Homer and me in the store. He was an impressive-looking man: very tall, really good-looking, and always extremely well-dressed. I was never quite sure why, but Mr. Overmon always seemed to stand out in a crowd; he just looked like he was important. Now, stretched out on the floor like this, he doesn't look quite so impressive."

Rick studied the body carefully. Mr. Overmon's hands were covered with paper bags. They would be checked for skin that might be under his nails if he had been able to fight back. "I can't see any evidence of a fight," Rick said. "I would guess that either he was surprised and didn't have a chance to fight back or it was someone he knew and trusted."

"What was in his pockets?" Hazel asked as they brought in the body bag."

"The usual things," a short woman said. "It didn't look to me like the killer touched anything. The victim's wallet still had cash, driver's license, credit cards, family pictures, and things like that. It wasn't a robbery. He had close to two hundred in cash in his wallet along with a handkerchief, two pens, his set of keys and what looked like a shopping list for the store: two cases of apples, a case of pears, a case of plantains, ten large sacks of yellow onions and three sacks of Vidalias. Way too much food for one family, even a big family. There were check marks by each item except the Vidalias."

"What about all that stuff on the shelves?" Hazel asked.

"Don't worry," the woman said. "It took us close to an hour, but we collected small samples of each of them. It doesn't look like poison was used so we won't start testing them right off. If there is any evidence of poison, we'll have samples ready to go. And, when you're checking things out, take a look at what's in the cookie tin on the top shelf."

"All right," Rick said to the forensic officers. "We've seen enough. You can take him now."

Rick and Hazel watched in silence as the crime scene team carefully lifted Josiah, placed him in the large black body bag, zipped it up, and carried it out to the transport van for the trip to the morgue. As the van headed down the road, Rick and Hazel turned back, went inside the shed and took a good look at the smaller room in back.

On the floor, near the plastic chair, was a drain like you'd find in a shower. Along the back, the area they couldn't see from the door, there were more wooden shelves and tubs filled with plastic bags, each neatly labeled: anxiety relief, pain relief, stomach ailments, fertility, vitality, cancer, stop smoking, stop drinking, happy marriage, good health and resist sin.

"That's amazing," Hazel said. "It looks like he could treat almost anything. With the drain, the basin and, and the towels, I would guess they mix these herbs with water, and either rub people down or pour water over them."

Rick nodded. "I remember Jeenya saying something about herbal baths."

Back in the main room, they studied the large plastic tubs. Most were labeled with the names of herbs. The container on the desk held different kinds of tea. Hazel read aloud the labels she could see. "He has tea for diabetes, constipation, diarrhea, babies, joint ache, headache, stomach ache, cough, cold and flu." Moving to another shelf she continued. Here he has tea for female problems, healthy prostate, high blood pressure, morning sickness, and fertility. He had more herbs for tea than bath herbs."

Higher on the shelves, various containers seemed to include unmixed herbs, stored alphabetically from Anise to Thistle, Thyme, and Tobacco. At least a dozen quart jars contained a substance that looked like Vaseline. They were labeled "Sinkle Bible."

Near the corner of the top shelf was the cookie tin. Hazel took it down and opened it on the desk. "It's full of little toys," she said. "Look at this cute little wooden baby. It's smaller than my thumbnail. What do you think these are for?"

"If I had to guess," Rick said, "I'd say they're good luck charms, maybe magic. That baby might be intended to help a woman get pregnant. The dollar bill might help you get rich. The little car might help you get a car, or keep you safe while riding in a car, or maybe both. Who knows?"

Hazel quickly put the baby back in the tin. "I wish I hadn't touched it," she said. "I hope that wasn't long enough to make it work for me. I'd rather not get pregnant right now."

Rick laughed. "Right. If you show up pregnant next month, I'll tell Tim to blame it on a lucky charm you had the misfortune of touching. I'm sure he'd believe that."

Rick checked the desk drawers. Among the usual mixture of paper, pens, pencils, stapler, and paper clips, Rick found what might have been a schedule with initials marked by the dates. He copied the schedule for the past week.

A yellow pad showed what looked like sources for various herbs. They were divided into two columns. Under the heading, JB, was a long list. Under JSCo Miami was a shorter list. JB had to be Jeenya Birdsong. JSCo was probably a supplier in Miami who either imported herbs from Jamaica or got them from someone who grew things further south that wouldn't grow locally.

"We're done here," Rick said, "unless there's anything else you want to look at. Let's go talk to Mr. Buckles."

Ten minutes away, down a dusty dirt road, Rick and Hazel found Fred Buckles at his small farm stand. "I can't believe it," Fred said over and over. "Mr. Overmon was here yesterday. I can't believe he's dead. I can't imagine that anybody'd want to kill him. He seemed like such a fine gentleman."

He called out to his wife. "Laurie. When you get done over there, come meet these people."

"Yesterday," Rick asked, When Mr. Overmon came by, did you notice anything different?"

"Not really. He came in a little later than usual. He picked up apples, pears, plantains, and some onions."

"Let me guess," Rick said. "He was looking for Vidalia onions too, but you didn't have any."

"That's true," Fred said. "You found his shopping list?"

Rick nodded. "It was in his pocket. I just wanted to be sure that's what it was. So what time was Mr. Overmon here?"

"Yesterday he came in about half-past four and seemed to be in a real hurry. Sometimes that happens. He wrote me a check and drove off in his truck. I don't think he was here more than ten or fifteen minutes. What's going to happen with the store now? His assistant going to run the place or do you think they'll end up selling the store or closing it down?"

"For the time being," Rick said, "his assistant is running things. Later, Mrs. Overmon or someone in the family will have to make the decision about what to do with it."

Laurie Buckles finished ringing up the customer's purchases and joined her husband. She was about forty or forty-five, slender, with pale blue eyes and long blond hair pulled back in a ponytail. Her face was plain until she smiled. She had a lovely smile.

"Laurie, sweetheart, these folks are detectives. They came to ask us some questions and they brought bad news. Mr. Overmon is dead. He was murdered last night. They're checking out everywhere he went yesterday.

"Dead? Mr. Overmon?" It took Laurie a few minutes to accept the fact that Josiah really was dead. Rick noticed tears in her eyes and wondered why.

"Mr. Buckles," Hazel asked. "You said Josiah came in at half-past four. We know he left the store at about two. Any idea where else he went?"

"I have no way of knowing. Mr. Overmon never told me anything about where he went. Sometimes his assistant would call and ask to talk to him, and Mr. Overmon didn't come until an hour or two later. It seemed like he'd gone somewhere else before he came here and he was keeping it private.

"Laurie's been wondering the same thing. You tell the detectives what you think he might have been up to."

"I hate to say anything bad about Josiah," Laurie said, "especially now that he's dead. He seemed like such a nice man. But even nice men aren't perfect. I do have a suspicious mind and I could easily be wrong. But my suspicions might help you find the killer. If it doesn't, I'd rather you don't tell people about it, especially his wife."

Rick and Hazel nodded.

"Sometimes Mr. Overmon would come in late in the afternoon smelling of perfume. Once, he had his shirt buttoned up wrong. I mentioned it and he seemed embarrassed but grateful. I suspect he was seeing another woman. I couldn't tell you who she might be so I don't know how much help it is."

"That could be the most helpful information we've gotten all day," Hazel said. "Everyone else tells us what a good man he was, how he didn't have any enemies, and how nobody would have hurt him. If you're right, if he was seeing another woman, a boyfriend or husband might have caught them together and gotten mad. Possibly mad enough to kill him."

"It could also have been the woman who killed him," Rick said. "Maybe he tried breaking it off, and she got upset."

"That's possible," Hazel agreed. "But a woman would have been more likely to kill him immediately, not late at night, not the way Josiah was killed."

"Good point." Rick turned back to Fred and Laurie. "Anything else you remember?"

"I do remember one thing," Fred said hesitantly. "One day, maybe a couple months back, Mr. Overmon came in smelling of alcohol. I thought he might have stopped to see a friend and had a few beers. But I suppose he could have had the beers with a woman. He might have been meeting her in a bar."

"That would give us something to check out," Rick said. "We could see if anyone remembers seeing him in a bar, but there are a lot of bars or other places to get a beer. I don't know what the chances are that a bartender would remember an older black man. But it's possible."

"Even if they do recognize him," Hazel said, "they aren't likely to remember who he was with unless she was very special."

They might have, Rick thought, if she was young or if she was white. People remember things like that. He was thinking what else to ask when his cell phone rang.

"Montoya. Hi Jeenya. We were thinking about coming to see you. We'll be there in about twenty minutes. Fish soup sounds wonderful. Anything you cook is delicious."

8

—

Lunch with Jeenya and Zeke

Rick

Rick and Hazel stopped to see what Harvey and Larry had learned. They were pleased to see that they had a nicely done map with names and information about the residents, but there wasn't a single person who admitted they had heard or seen anything last night.

"As long as you aren't needed anywhere else," Rick said. "Check with Mrs. Overmon. See if she has a picture of Josiah we can borrow. If she gives you one, get a dozen copies made and return the original. Next, I'd like you to start visiting bars in Palm City and Stuart first, then Jensen Beach and Salerno, showing people the picture.

"We think Josiah might have been spending time in a bar when he's supposedly out running errands. He might have been meeting a woman, or perhaps several women, in the bars. He might even have spent a couple hours in a bar yesterday afternoon. See what the bartenders can tell you."

As they drove the last few blocks to the Birdsong's home, Rick wondered what Hazel would think of his friends. Zeke didn't look all that impressive. He was maybe a little under six feet tall, a thin man with frizzy graying hair and wire-rimmed glasses that sometimes slid down his nose. He was the quiet one of the pair and, with his erect posture and the way he spoke, Rick always thought he seemed like a professor.

Rick remembered seeing Zeke looking pretty sharp in his Post Office uniform, but, since he retired, he'd been wearing denim overalls and aging T-shirts, looking more like a farmer. Well, Zeke should look like a farmer. He spent much of the day working in the garden. Rick hoped Hazel would also notice Zeke's warm smile and, when she listened to him, that she'd realize what an intelligent man he was.

Jeenya was about the same height as her husband but more full-bodied and always full of energy. She was the one who made friends quickly. She had that warm, bubbling laugh that made people want to laugh with her. Rick still stood in awe of Jeenya. She would look into his eyes and sometimes seemed to know what he was thinking.

Would Hazel feel that way, he wondered, or would she simply see a friendly old black woman?

Jeenya

Jeenya thought carefully about what she'd wear for lunch. She knew Zeke had no intention of dressing up. He looked like a field hand in his stained overalls, a long-sleeved plaid shirt and a faded blue and orange Florida Gators baseball cap.

She changed from her usual faded cotton house dress and selected a sky-blue dress with bright yellow daisies. She belted it with a bright red sash and wore a matching bright-red-and-blue bandana over her hair. She laughed when Zeke whistled his approval.

Jeenya watched out the window as Rick parked the car. She watched him study the new sign Zeke had made for her. It was three feet high and five feet long, painted a soft pastel green with black letters. She thought it looked quite professional.

Jeenya Birdsong
Herbalist
Healer
Spiritual Advisor

As the detectives got out of the car, Jeenya got a good look at the young woman, a very good-looking young woman. Sarah was right. This woman was lovely. As the two detectives came up the walk, Jeenya opened the door.

"Rick Montoya," Jeenya said, grabbing hold of him and giving him a long, warm hug. "It is so good to see you. When we heard about Josiah, we were hoping the police department would have the good sense to send you.

"Later, when I heard you really were here, I started fixing lunch. There's a big pot of soup on the stove. And, as long as you two are working on this case, Zeke and I are expecting to see the two of you here for breakfast and lunch every single day. Dinners too, if you're working late. But we shouldn't stand out here like this. Come on inside. Now Rick, introduce us to this lovely young woman."

"Jeenya, Zeke, this is my new partner, Detective Hazel Fontaine and, before you even ask, Hazel is married. So, Jeenya, that means no matchmaking."

Jeenya hugged Hazel. "Rick is family, you know, more

like family than my own daughter and, while you're working with him, honey, you're family too. You can feel free to show up here anytime. You can eat here, use the bathroom, or just sit in the garden and take a break. It's also the best place in town to simply stop and talk."

"We really appreciate that," Hazel said. "Rick talks a lot about the two of you. I'm glad I've finally met you."

Zeke shook Hazel's hand. "You gotta watch out for my wife, Detective. She isn't just offering you and Rick something good to eat. She's planning on getting you to share what you know about the case. She likes to keep up with what's going on around here."

Rick laughed and gave Zeke a quick hug.

Zeke leaned back and looked up at Rick. "Tell me again how tall you are. I keep forgetting."

"Six foot five. I grew that last inch in college."

"Our Rick," Jeenya said to Hazel, wrapping one arm around his waist, "he is very tall and very handsome. There's got to be a good woman looking for a man like Rick."

Jeenya knew Hazel was studying them. It must be difficult, Jeenya thought, for this pretty red-haired woman to understand why Rick loved them so much, and why she and Zeke would consider Rick part of their family.

"You're looking beautiful, today," Rick told Jeenya. "I love your dress." He smiled at Hazel. "Jeenya, being a gardener, always seems to wear lovely flowered dresses."

Jeenya laughed. "And what else should I wear? Maybe something with puppies and kittens and baby ducks? I don't think so."

They all laughed at the idea. Rick needed to laugh more often, Jeenya thought.

As Hazel studied the Birdsongs, Jeenya thought about Rick. He had been such a gift to them, never taking the place of the grandson they lost, but reminding them of the wonderful years they had spent with Homer.

Jeenya had loved Rick and worried about him when he was a teenager, knowing that Homer wasn't just Rick's best friend; he was Rick's only friend. Back then, Rick was tall and skinny; now he had filled out and was solid muscle. Then he was cute; now he was handsome, even sexy. That terrible scar only made him a little mysterious.

She wondered about Hazel. With her cool green eyes and with hair the color of burning embers, Hazel was stunning. Rick said she was married but the way Hazel sometimes looked at Rick already made Jeenya uncomfortable. She hoped it was her imagination. Rick didn't need a married woman flirting with him.

It might not be easy finding Josiah's killer, Jeenya thought. It could be another of those terrible cases that went on for years, maybe forever, without discovering the killer. She hoped she and Zeke could find ways of helping Rick without being too obvious.

The four of them sat around the kitchen table and began the meal with plates of salad. She had picked greens and tomatoes straight from the garden. Then she added walnuts, chunks of cheese, and slices of pear. She wanted it to be special.

"Mrs. Birdsong," Hazel began.

"Jeenya. Please, call me Jeenya."

Hazel smiled. "Jeenya. I keep wondering about your name. Is Jeenya a Jamaican name or a family name? I never heard it before."

Jeenya chuckled. "Actually, Hazel, most Jamaicans

have names you're already familiar with. My given name is Virginia but, when my little brother was learning to talk, Virginia was too hard for him to say. He called me Jeenya, and it stuck. I know half a dozen other Virginias. It was good to have a name that was different. Now, I can't remember the last time anyone called me Virginia. I'd think they were talking to someone else. That's true for Zeke too. People almost never call him Ezekiel."

"I have another question," Hazel said. "On your sign, it says you're a spiritual advisor. I've been trying to guess what this means."

"That's a really good question," Jeenya said. "I'll bet Rick would have trouble answering it."

"Answering what?" Rick asked.

"Explain to Hazel what a spiritual advisor does."

"Well, you know what advisors do," he said. "When you have a problem and don't know what to do, they give you good advice. A spiritual advisor gives good advice in a spiritual way."

Jeenya laughed. "Such a logical explanation, Rick, but logical isn't always true. I don't actually give much advice and, when I do, it isn't really spiritual unless the person I'm talking wants that.

"Most people don't want me giving them what I think is good advice. The problem is they aren't sure what they do want. I'd say a spiritual advisor begins by listening. People don't want to talk to their friends or relatives about their problems but they do want to talk to someone so they come talk to me. I am a good listener. I ask questions to help them tell me what they're really worrying about. I ask them how they feel about it and sometimes I just let them cry. Eventually, most of them decide for themselves.

They don't need me telling them what to do."

"Thanks," Hazel said. "Sounds like you are a lot like a psychiatrist, but I'd rather talk to you than to one of those. It sounds like you really care. Most psychiatrists don't."

As they ate, Rick shared what they'd learned that morning, at least what he considered acceptable to share, mainly that everyone they talked to seemed to think Josiah Overmon was a good man, highly respected, and a man with no enemies. He went on to describe what they'd heard about duppies, why so many people were buying salt, and why so many people insisted the killer must be from outside the neighborhood, that it had to be someone who wasn't afraid of duppies.

"Sounds like you learned a good bit," Jeenya said. "I'll bet by tonight, everyone in Jamaica Lakes will know how you were so puzzled about people buying salt." She set a steaming bowl of fish soup with sweet potatoes and peas in front of each person. Then she added a plate of freshly baked bread.

"Ummm," Hazel said appreciatively. "Whatever that is, it sure smells good."

"This is a special Jamaican fish soup," Jeenya said. "My grandmother used to make it this way." For a few minutes, all conversation stopped and the group enjoyed their food.

Zeke put down his soup spoon and frowned. "Rick, you didn't say anything about Josiah being the Obeah Man. Did anybody mention that?"

Hazel looked at Rick. He shook his head. "No, I don't think so. What's an Obeah Man?"

"Rick Montoya," Zeke said, "Are you telling me, with all that time you spent hanging out with Homer, he never told you anything about the Obeah Man?"

"If he did, I've forgotten. It doesn't sound familiar."

"You've heard about Voodoo in Haiti and Santeria in Cuba, haven't you?"

Rick nodded. "I remember my Cuban grandparents, my father's parents, talking about Santeria. They never talked to me about it but, when they thought I wasn't listening, they'd talk about one or another of their neighbors using dead chickens to do some sort of magic. I've also heard about Voodoo but never knew any details."

"In Jamaica," Zeke said, "we have a variety of traditions involving different kinds of rituals or magic. If you want to understand the people here, you have a lot to learn."

"Okay, Professor Birdsong, let me get my notebook." Rick pulled a well-worn leather notebook and a pen from his pocket and opened it to a new page. "Ready," he said with a grin.

"African slaves from many different tribes brought their traditions with them when they were brought to Jamaica. Some cast spells to cure people, to make their enemies sick or even to kill them. Later, some of these people mixed herbal cures along with the magic.

"Secrets were passed along, usually from parents to their children through the years. These practices were called Obeah. Josiah Overmon's father was a well-known Obeah Man back in Jamaica. Josiah and his sister, Sharona, were trained in the tradition. So, you could call her an Obeah Woman.

"Another set of practices, probably from different tribes, was Myal. Just over a hundred years ago, much like the Great Revival that spread Christianity across the United States, there was a huge revival movement in Jamaica. Part of this movement was led by people with little Christian background including many of those from the Myal tradition. They heard a few sermons and were converted. Then they began preaching what they knew, combining African ideas with the little they knew about Christianity. They're often called Revivalists. We have a group of these people here in Jamaica Lakes."

"Last night," Jeenya added, "Rev. Wolff, the pastor of our little Jamaican Church, and his Revivalist followers were meeting out in the woods behind the church. I wish you and Hazel could have heard them. Sitting here in the darkness, we could hear the drums beating, the voices shouting. And if we listened carefully, sometimes we could even hear the tinkling of the tambourines.

"Zeke and I have never been to one of their services, but we've been told all about it. They say the Revivalists stomp their feet and march around a table, always counter-clockwise for some reason. They sing and shout, shaking their heads up and down, hoping a spirit will come and take possession of their bodies."

"Take possession of their bodies?" Hazel asked, raising her eyebrows. "That sounds gruesome. Exactly what happens when a spirit takes possession of a person?"

"As I understand it," Zeke said, "in some African American churches, people do something surprisingly similar. They say people 'get happy.' They shake all over. They shout and sometimes fall down, usually with someone there to catch them and lower them gently to the floor. African-Americans didn't get this from Jamaica. Slaves in both places brought it from Africa."

Jeenya took up the story, knowing Zeke was eager to get a second serving of soup. "The tradition I learned from my grandparents is something different. They were balmists or what we usually called herb-yard people. Here, you would call us herbalists.

"In Jamaica, many balmists mixed their knowledge of herbal cures with a few of the Revivalist traditions. People often didn't feel they were getting a proper cure if there wasn't a little singing, some Bible verses and always some anointing with oil to go along with the herbs.

"When I came to the States, I went to nursing school and became a registered nurse. I worked in the Palm City Hospital for years. I also tried helping people in the neighborhood who didn't have health insurance. Some of them didn't want American style medicine. They wanted herbal medicine, so they came to me.

"If they had a problem that wasn't serious, I'd give them herbal teas. If they had anything serious, I'd send them to an old doctor I used to work with. He'd treat them for a minimal payment and let me know how I could help. But I stick strictly to herbalist practices. I don't mix in the singing, the Bible verses or the anointing with oil. I understand that, back in Jamaica, most herbalists have also abandoned that sort of thing.

"Now," Jeenya continued, "we really should get back to Josiah. When he was fairly young, his father trained him in Obeah but Josiah didn't like it. He didn't want to have anything to do with Obeah. There was too much emphasis on casting evil curses. Josiah came to the States mainly to get away from his father. He got work here in Palm City picking citrus fruit.

"Then, after one of those terrible freezes that killed off the nearly all the citrus, Josiah bought up this land and created Jamaica Lakes. Some of the people remembered his father and begged Josiah to use Obeah to help them.

Josiah finally agreed, but he insisted on doing it his way.

"He refused to do evil spells, spells that supposedly would make a person sick or kill them, but he was willing to do what he called 'helpful spells.' If someone felt sick or had strange pains and they were sure an enemy put a spell on them, he'd do spells to get rid of the evil spell. He'd also do spells to protect people from duppies.

"Josiah and I used to talk from time to time. I asked if he really believed his spells worked. He said they seemed to work in Jamaica, maybe because people there believed in them so strongly. Here, he wasn't sure. 'But, as long as they made people feel better,' he said, 'it couldn't hurt.'"

"Is that why so many people keep saying he was a good man?" Hazel asked. "Because he only did good spells?"

"Not exactly," Zeke said. "That might be part of it, but there are plenty of people around here who were angry when Josiah refused to do the spells they asked for. Some of them probably turned to the Revivalist meetings.

"The Revivalists would never believe Josiah was a good man. They believe Obeah is evil, even if it is only the good spells. They consider it their job to fight evil. But they'd never tell you that. They'd be polite and say what everyone else says, 'Josiah Overmon was a good man.' Now that he's dead, I suspect they might think their prayers have been answered."

"Now, Zeke, that is not true," Jeenya objected. "Not here. Everyone in Jamaica Lakes knew Josiah. They all shopped in his store. They all knew he didn't do evil spells. They might have disapproved of his being an Obeah Man, but I don't think they saw him as evil. I certainly don't think they'd be happy about his death."

Zeke smiled at his wife. "I expect you're right, dear.

You know the people here better than I do."

"I'm glad you explained all this," Hazel said. "But it doesn't get us any closer to finding a good suspect. Can you think of anybody at all who hated Josiah enough to kill him?"

"Are you asking if we know anyone who isn't afraid of Josiah's duppy," Jeenya said, "I've been thinking all morning, and nobody comes to mind.

"Oh, I almost forgot. I talked to a young woman this morning. Angela Armstrong was with Josiah last night. She and Sharona may well have been the last two people to see Josiah alive, other than the killer, of course. Would you like to talk to her?"

"Definitely," Rick said. "Where does she live?"

"That's a problem. Angela was seeing Josiah for help getting pregnant, but her husband is a Revivalist and didn't want her seeing the Obeah Man. If you go to their house, George will hear about it and want to know why. He might figure out she was seeing Josiah and get mad.

"Angela said she'd talk to you here, not at her house. I'll give her a call. I'm to tell her she forgot her sunglasses, in case George is home. She intentionally left them here this morning so she'd have a good reason to come back."

9

Josiah Loved Women

Rick

"You're the detectives?" Angela asked. "I need to tell you what I know and get back home soon so George won't know I'm talking to you."

"Jeenya explained," Hazel said. "We'll keep it short. About how often did you visit Josiah Overmon?"

"Every two weeks, always on Friday nights. He was trying to help me get pregnant. He gave me herbal teas and his sister, Sharona, sometimes gave me an herbal bath but nothing seemed to help.

"Mr. Overmon told me to see a doctor, a gynecologist, and I did. They couldn't find anything wrong with me and wanted to check George's sperm, but George refused. He said his first wife, back in Jamaica, had four kids, that nothing was wrong with him. What else could I do?"

"About last night," Hazel said. "Josiah's sister was there with you?"

"Sharona is always there when I come or when any other woman comes alone to see Josiah. They don't want people to talk. And it's good to have a woman to do the herbal bath. It's not like getting in a bathtub, you know. They take a special mixture of herbs, put it in a basin, pour hot water over them, and then they use a sponge and rub you down. It's supposed to get your blood flowing and make you more healthy."

Hazel nodded. "Tell us about last night."

"I was planning to get there at nine-thirty, expecting George to go to the Revivalist meeting at nine. I was about to leave when George came back. He said it was cold out and he'd forgotten his jacket. He might also have been checking on me. I waited a little longer before I left.

"It was nearly ten when I got there. Mr. Overmon was real understanding about my being late. Sharona did the bath and he prepared a special tea for me to drink. Then he gave me a two-week supply of tea to use at home. He was very encouraging. He said the herbs were working. He told me I was glowing with energy."

"What time did you leave?"

"It was about twenty 'til eleven. It was a terribly dark night, so I had my flashlight.

"Did you see anyone?"

"I'm pretty sure there were a few people walking along Montego Bay Road up ahead of me. They were a long way up the road so I didn't recognize any of them. I couldn't say if they were men or women, old or young. All I saw were gray shadows moving."

"Did you hear anything unusual?"

"I could sometimes hear people talking inside their homes but not well enough to understand what they were saying. And, of course, I could hear the drums and the shouting at the Revivalist meeting. I was glad for that. It meant I'd be home before George got back."

"When you were there, did Josiah seem any different? Did he say or do anything out of the ordinary?"

"Not really. He seemed real cheerful, like he'd had a good day. Even Sharona, who's sometimes exhausted, seemed to be in a good mood. It's really scary to think the killer could have been out there in the darkness, waiting until I left."

"You need to be careful the next couple weeks," Rick said, "at least until we catch the person who killed Josiah. You're right, thinking the killer might have been waiting for you to leave, you and Sharona. He might think if he could see you that you could see him, even if he was well hidden. If I were you, I wouldn't go out alone after dark."

After Angela left, the conversation went back to the murder.

"I'm glad we got to talk to Angela," Rick said, even if we didn't learn much. "Now, I still have a few questions. You told us about Josiah Overmon, the Obeah Man. What about his personal life? What can you tell us about that?"

Jeenya looked at Zeke.

Rick continued. "What sort of reputation did Mr. Overmon have here in town?"

Zeke looked at Jeenya with a slight frown.

"We heard a rumor," Rick continued, "that Josiah might have a girlfriend, maybe several of them."

Jeenya frowned at Zeke and turned back to look at Rick. Finally, she answered. "I must say, Mr. Detective Ricardo Montoya, you seem to be doing one fine job. I can't believe you got anyone to tell you about Josiah and his girlfriends. A lot of people know, but we don't talk about it. I won't ask how you found out."

"I think," Zeke said, "Josiah had so much money and

so much power that he felt he could have whatever he wanted. It's like with all those other powerful people: presidents, governors, senators and all. They want it; they take it. None of them ever think they might get found out. They don't worry about consequences."

"With Josiah," Jeenya added, "this was a huge problem ten or fifteen years ago. If a woman came alone to see him, and if she was more or less willing, he'd close the door to his shed and they'd have sex. This was especially true with women who were having trouble getting pregnant. I don't know if he felt safer with them, thinking they wouldn't get pregnant with him either, or if he thought he was actually helping women whose husbands had lazy sperm or something. Some of those women ended up pregnant. But people talk. It wasn't long before everyone knew what he was doing. One couple got divorced. Several others moved away.

"Finally, Sharona forced Josiah to change. I heard she up and told him that, whether he liked it or not, she was going to be right there with him every single time a woman came to see him. She would do the women's herbal baths and then make herself busy with the herbs while he talked to them. As far as I know, Sharona was still doing this every single night."

"Okay," Hazel said. "So, no more sex at work. What about girlfriends away from work?"

Rick nodded to Hazel. From her hint of a smile, he knew she understood that Rick liked her questions.

"Over the years," Jeenya said, "Josiah was still seeing an occasional woman in Jamaica Lakes, but it's hard to keep secrets around here. Apparently, some of the women were paying their rent that way but I haven't heard of anything like that in years. Visiting women outside the area, that seems to be different. Josiah probably thought he could keep that a secret.

"The last that I heard, it was a Stuart woman. I don't know her name, but someone told me her husband is a truck driver. He must have gotten home earlier than expected one day and caught the two of them together. Somehow, the husband found out where Josiah worked. He showed up at the store one day, found Josiah, and started shouting. He said Josiah better not show up at his house again. The man threatened to kill him if Josiah messed around with his wife again."

"That's what we heard," Zeke said. "But Josiah wasn't stupid. I'm pretty sure he would stay away from that man's wife. That's why we never mentioned the story. I guess Josiah might have found another woman though, and her husband or boyfriend could have found out.

"That's a good thing to investigate if you can figure out how to find the woman. Those people are not from Jamaica. They wouldn't know Josiah was an Obeah Man. They'd have no reason to be scared of Josiah's duppy coming to get them."

Jeenya

After Rick and Hazel left, Zeke turned to his wife with a grin. He nodded toward Hazel. "Pretty woman that one."

Jeenya nodded.

"I noticed, my dear, you left out some very important information."

Jeenya looked at her husband with a slight frown. "What information is that?"

"You didn't tell Rick about thinking the old devil was

walking down the street last night. You didn't tell him about the owl telling you someone was dead. You didn't even mention the John Crows circling up in the sky this morning."

Jeenya laughed. "You are so right. You grew up in Jamaica. Even if you don't believe it, you should have an appreciation for that sort of information. But I can just imagine what Rick and Hazel would think."

"So can I," Zeke said with a solemn look. "They would think you were totally out of your mind."

10

The Obeah Woman

Rick

"So, what did you think?" Rick asked when they left the Birdsong's house.

"It took me a while to understand," Hazel said. "At first glance, they seemed to be an ordinary old black couple. But there's definitely something special about them. Jeenya seemed so happy to see us. I could see how proud she was of you. It was like she said. You are family. She loves you like you were her own grandson.

"Zeke was quiet at first. But once he got to explaining about what an Obeah Man was and the history of all these religious traditions coming from Africa, I could tell he knew what he was talking about. I'd say he's smart and well-educated too. I'm glad I had a chance to meet them, and I look forward to seeing more of them.

"I do have a question. Was Jeenya serious when she said she was expecting us for breakfast and lunch every day while we're working here or was she just being polite?"

"She was serious, very serious," Rick said. "She'll want to get to know you better. You can be sure of that.

She didn't have time to do much of that, today. And she'll want to be updated on our investigation since she does like to know everything that's going on. She understands that we won't tell her everything, but she'll be happy knowing what we're willing to share. Then she'll take our little bits of information and connect it with other things she knows and then try to help us out. Jeenya understands people and why they behave like they do much better than anyone else I know. I'm glad you liked them."

"It was more than liking them," Hazel said. "It's hard to describe. With Zeke, I felt something strange. It was a sense that he wasn't just smart. He was fascinating.

"With Jeenya, even though she'd never met me, it was like she'd known me forever and somehow that she cared about me."

"I know what you mean," Rick said. "The way I would describe it is that she always seems to look me straight in my eyes and when she does that, she seems to know what I am thinking. Now, when I'm near Jeenya, I'm careful to think about something she would approve of."

"That's exactly what I mean," Hazel said. "With Jeenya, it's like being in a trance where I can feel what she is feeling about me."

"Hazel," Rick said, "you are amazing. It took me years to recognize this. You felt it the first time you met her."

After several minutes of silence, Hazel brought the discussion back to their task. "Where do we go next?"

"First, we need to stop by Mrs. Overmon's and get her husband's phone numbers: home, work, and cell if he had one.

"Next, we need to call Nate, and tell him what we've learned so far. He can get someone at the phone company to check their records and tell us about phone calls in and out. If Josiah and his girlfriend were trying to set up times when her husband was away, there'd be phone calls."

Back at the Overmon's house, Julie answered the door again.

"Mama's taking a nap," she said softly. She sniffled and her cheeks were wet. "Why don't you talk to Auntie Sharona? She lives next to us and she knows almost everything Daddy knew. She's out working on her porch. I just took her a pitcher of tea and a plate of cookies. Without Daddy...." She paused to blow her nose. "Without Daddy, Auntie Sharona is the only person left in Jamaica Lakes who knows how to do Obeah stuff."

They found Sharona on her porch drinking a glass of iced tea. She found glasses and poured tea for Hazel and Rick. "Please, do help yourself to the gingersnaps. Julie loves them, but they are not my favorites."

"We should tell you," Hazel said with a smile, "that we've just learned that you know everything Mr. Overmon knew and that now you're the only person in Jamaica Lakes who knows how to do Obeah stuff."

Sharona laughed. "It's that phrase, 'doing Obeah stuff,' that gives it away. You've been talking to Julie. She's a very bright kid. So far, among Josiah's children, she's the only one interested in learning about Obeah. I've promised her that, if she's still interested when she's sixteen, I'll take her on as my apprentice. For the first few years, I'll only let her make herbal teas and things like that. Doing real Obeah isn't something for a young person to get mixed up in."

"It looked like Julie had been crying," Hazel said.

Sharona frowned. "Julie tries hard to be strong, strong like her Daddy. She doesn't want her mother worrying about her. But when Dolly goes to take a nap, that's when Julie loses it. The poor girl is probably ashamed that you saw her crying. But she's still a kid. She needs to cry."

Rick nodded. "We had a few questions for Mrs. Overmon, but Julie says she's taking a nap. You should be able to help us, possibly more than she could."

Sharona provided the three phone numbers Josiah used, his home phone, the grocery, and the cell phone he carried.

"What can you tell us about the last week or so?" Hazel asked. "Were there any problems, anything Josiah was worried or upset about? Anything we should know?"

"Wish I could help you, but I can't," Sharona said, shaking her head. "Josiah was in a good mood all week. As far as I could tell, he didn't have any problems bothering him."

"What about that last day?" Hazel asked. "Anything…"

Sharona interrupted. "Let me ask you people a question first. When do you plan to take down all that ugly black and yellow tape? I need to know when I can go in and clean up all that blood and the mess your people made looking for fingerprints that won't do them any damn good since half the people in Jamaica Lakes have been in there one time or other. I need to know when I can get in there to get the herbs I need. I have to know when I can start working in the shed. You answer my questions, I'll answer yours."

"I wish I could give you a clear answer," Rick said. "It will depend on how the investigation goes. If we arrest someone and get a confession, you can probably do all that the next day. It's our lieutenant who makes that decision.

"If we don't arrest anyone, we need to wait for test

results on Josiah. If he was poisoned, they might need to go back and test every substance in there, looking for the poison. Even if the tests show there wasn't any poison involved, it might take as much as a month before they'll release Josiah's workplace."

"You telling me I can't count on using any of those herbs for a month or so," she said. "That is a problem. People still want their herbal teas and baths and all. That means I have to order all new herbs from Jeenya and from our supplier in Miami. I'll need to mix all those herbs and then bag and label them. I can sell tea from my porch, but I can't do herbal baths out here."

She glared at the two detectives as if all this was their fault. "I don't understand why you expect to find anything useful in that little shed. That killer came in with his knife. He cut Josiah's neck, letting him bleed all over. And it's pretty obvious he carried that knife away with him. I know your people were looking for that knife but it wasn't there. Now, you're talking about poisons? That is foolishness. Can't you see that? That man killed Josiah with a knife."

"We understand how you feel," Hazel said. "Having to follow procedures can be terribly frustrating but procedures exist for good reasons. Maybe the killer poisoned your brother so he couldn't fight back and then used the knife.

"But we do understand your situation and we'll do whatever we can to get the lieutenant to release the shed as soon as possible. Now, about that last day," Hazel continued. "Anything any different about yesterday?"

Sharona glared at Hazel but answered her question. "I didn't see Josiah at all until after dinner. You'd have to ask Dolly about his morning and ask Chester if anything happened at the store. Josiah was in the shed when I came in at seven last night. Things were a little slow. Patty Jordan called us to cancel, saying her parents were visiting from Jamaica.

"Sarah and Seymour Olsen came in at about eight-thirty. Sarah has terrible cramps and problems with an upset stomach. We've been trying different herbal teas, looking for what works best for her. She said the last mixture was the best one yet. Seymour has high blood pressure and doesn't like taking his pills. After three months on Josiah's herbal mixture for blood pressure, Seymour's doctor said the herbs were actually more helpful than the pills.

"Then Eula May Carter came in with her little dog. Both Eula May and Princess are getting old and they both take herbal teas to give them a bit more energy. We even gave that poor dog an herbal bath. Eula May has been going around telling everyone how well it worked. She says Princess is getting as frisky as a pup.

"Josiah and I worked on herbal tea mixtures for a while, waiting for Angela Armstrong. She has to wait until her husband leaves the house. He doesn't want her coming to see us. We expected her between nine-thirty and nine forty-five since George usually goes out Friday nights at between nine and nine-thirty. Angela came in a little late. I'd guess it was almost ten. I gave her an herbal bath using a different mixture Josiah recommended. It helps the blood flow and makes a person feel much better. When women want to get pregnant, it's supposed to help the ovaries function and make her more passionate, you know, during sex."

She was watching the detectives' response to that, but they simply nodded.

"When Angela left," Sharona continued, "I finished sealing and labeling the last packages of tea for the grocery. Then I left. Josiah said he'd be done in fifteen or twenty minutes. He was packaging the herbal bath mixtures. He has seven different mixtures he normally uses. As far as I can tell, there wasn't anything at all unusual last night."

"I understand," Hazel said, "that you are always there the whole time. Were you there with your brother the entire time last night?"

"The whole night," Sharona said. "I needed to use the bathroom, but I waited until Angela was gone. When I tell the people I will be there every minute with the women, then that's what I do."

"One question we were going to ask Mrs. Overmon," Rick said. "Do you know if Josiah made a will?"

Sharona frowned and looked into Rick's eyes, squinting a little. "Now, you tell me," she said in a deep, tightly controlled voice, "just why you need to be asking 'bout that will. You thinking somebody in the family is in too big a hurry to get what they had coming and they murdered Josiah to get they inheritance? That's what you all be thinking, isn't it? Why else you ask a question like that? Nobody in this family would do that. I can swear to the Almighty God in heaven, nobody in this family would kill Josiah."

Sharona took a deep breath and seemed to calm herself. "Yes sir, Josiah had himself a will. I have a copy, Dolly has a copy, and so do our brothers. Josiah left each one of us what he should have given us years back. We all knew he was going to do it and we weren't in any rush. He left each of us the houses we've been living in for years, living rent-free, you understand, so it's like we owned them all along except Josiah paid the property tax. We couldn't complain about that.

"The Café, Beauty Shop, Boutique, and Grocery all go to Elijah. He and his family already run the café and the other shops. Seth gets the Garage of course."

She turned to face Rick and looked him in the eye. "He left me the use of his shed and I'm in charge of his real estate deals. I go on collecting rent and mortgage payments. I decide when and where to build more houses and who I rent or sell them to. We don't want troublemakers coming to live here, no drug dealers, no gang members, no thieves, you understand, only good, hard-working family people.

"For doing this, I keep one quarter of the income and Dolly gets one quarter. Plus, he left his bank account to Dolly and there's a good bit in there. I'm to invest the rest to send his children to college. I can also use this money to help out in any kind of emergency. If there's any left, it all goes to Dolly."

"That's very helpful," Rick said. "Knowing this, I can see that no one in the family had any motive to kill your brother. I didn't think they would, but it's our job to check every possibility. Most families aren't as close as yours.

"Now, I have another question, a more personal question, one I hated to ask Mrs. Overmon, but I imagine you'll know more than she does."

Sharona glared with slitted eyes. "So, Mr. Detective, what sort of nasty personal questions you asking this time? You be asking about Josiah's sex life?"

Rick nodded. "Not so much about his sex life at home. I can't see how that would be relevant. Given the number of children they have, I assume they were happy together. But we have heard rumors that Josiah might have had a girlfriend, possibly a girlfriend with an angry husband."

Sharona snorted. "I can't think why people 'round here be talking 'bout things that not their business. I'm guessing it was one of Herman Wolff's people told you that, people who go to those Revivalist meetings, beating they drums and all that nonsense. Those people haven't any love for us and our people. Well, I could tell you things 'bout them too, things they wouldn't like talked about in the open. But I would never do that."

"We sure don't like poking around, looking into your private lives," Hazel said, "but someone murdered your brother. You cannot imagine how many people told us that everyone in Jamaica Lakes respected and liked Mr. Overmon. And they said nobody here would dare kill an Obeah Man, because they'd be so scared of his duppy.

"We tried to think of a situation where someone outside the community, someone not afraid of duppies, might have had a reason to kill him. We have no intention of spreading stories, but we would appreciate your help. Did Josiah have any girlfriends who might have husbands or boyfriends that are angry enough to kill him?"

Sharona scowled. "From the sound of the questions you're asking, I'm thinking you already know something. I'd better tell you the whole story before you start asking questions all over Jamaica Lakes. People out there have wild stories mixed in with a few facts.

"My brother was one of those men who loved women, plenty of women, and he enjoyed having sex with them. But the only women he really loved were his first wife, Marie, who died of cancer, and now Dolly.

"Back ten or fifteen years ago, he sometimes had sex with women who came to his Obeah shed. There were a few angry husbands back then, a couple divorces, and one woman even committed suicide. But those divorces and even the suicide might have been caused by other problems, you know.

"I had myself a long talk with Josiah back then and he agreed not to work with any woman in the shed if he was alone. From that day on, I spent every single evening in that shed of his, working along with him. If a woman wanted an herbal bath, I took her into the backroom, pulled the curtain, and I did the bath. It wasn't right for a man to be doing baths for a woman.

"People in Jamaica Lakes stopped worrying. Josiah still visited a number of women at home, maybe while collecting rent, and he might have accepted less rent if they invited him in. But it wasn't tied to his being the Obeah Man. There were still angry husbands so Josiah and I had another long talk. He agreed to leave the women here completely alone. If he wanted a girlfriend, he'd have to find one away from Jamaica Lakes. That was about five years ago. I can't imagine one of those husbands living here would suddenly decide to kill him."

"That's extremely helpful," Rick said. "Can you give us any information about the women outside Jamaica Lakes that he's been with recently? Were there situations where someone could have been angry enough to kill him?"

"Well, Josiah did get himself into one sticky situation you might hear about," Sharona said, "a real nasty problem six or eight years back. You'll hear about it from others so I might as well tell you. A good-looking girl named Collette lives a couple miles down the road. She went to high school with a couple of our children and they all rode the bus together. She was here off and on visiting her school friends. Miss Collette Cooper looked like she was at least eighteen or nineteen, but she was really only fourteen at the time. Josiah took one look at her and he was desperate to have her.

"One day when it was raining, he offered Collette a ride home. He asked if she'd like to go with him some time, out in the woods to collect herbs. My dear brother didn't have any idea how to collect his own herbs. He bought them from Jeenya or ordered them from Miami or Jamaica. But somehow, he talked this fool girl into having sex with him, out there in the woods.

"Josiah never forced anyone you understand. You might hear he raped this woman or that one, but he never did. Those women were all willing, every last one of them.

"First thing we knew about little Miss Collette was when she came back six months later, asking Josiah for money to go to the doctor. The little tart was six months pregnant. It was too late to send her off for an abortion. Josiah paid all her medical bills and then he paid her two hundred a month for things the baby needed. While Miss Collette Cooper is not written into the will, she and her daddy were told that, if anything happened to Josiah, our family would continue the payments until Collette gets married or until the child is eighteen."

"What you're saying," Hazel said, "is that Collette's father had no reason to kill Josiah."

"Exactly. Now, two other women I know of could be more of a problem. I know their names but don't have any addresses. Suzy Cornblatt is a trashy white woman who lives in a Stuart trailer park. She stopped at the store to see Josiah once. Stringy blond hair, too much makeup, and ugly scarlet lipstick. Suzy's not married or engaged so far as I know, but her current boyfriend is the jealous type and he's stupid. He also has a filthy mouth.

"Clancy Cottonwood is his name. He works at a motorcycle shop out near Walmart. Clancy is as ugly as a wild boar, and he comes rumbling through Jamaica Lakes every week or two on his big black Harley. He parks in front of the grocery and shouts a string of obscenities in the door, telling everyone what he'd like to do to Josiah if Josiah messes with Suzy again. I haven't seen Clancy the past couple weeks but, if Josiah did visit that woman again or call her on the phone, Clancy might have been mad enough to kill him.

"And then there's sweet Juanita Juarez. Her family used to work in the sugarcane fields. She and her husband live out on the Indiantown Road. According to Josiah, she's as black as we are even though she's from Mexico.

"Her husband, Jesus, is a cross-country truck driver, and he's gone sometimes for a week or two at a time. Juanita gets terribly lonely when he's gone and she called Josiah just to talk. Other times she asked him to have dinner with her. Josiah talked about her now and then. I don't think he told his wife about her, you know, but he'd talk to me.

"One day last week, Juanita's husband, Jesus, stopped by the store to see Josiah. I wasn't there but Chester told me about it. He said Jesus was about six foot three or four, maybe half Mexican, half African-American, and he looked like one of those football players, like the tackles with all those muscles.

"Josiah took Jesus back into his office, hoping to keep the conversation private. Chester told me he heard a lot of shouting but he wasn't sure what they were saying. He said when Jesus came storming out, slamming that office door, he wasn't happy. He stomped straight out the front door and back to his truck without saying another word.

"Clancy, the motorcycle-riding boyfriend seems to be all mouth. I have a hard time picturing him actually doing anything. If you asked me who was most likely to be a killer, I'd say Jesus, especially if Josiah visited Juanita again. Is there anything else I can tell you, detectives?"

Rick and Hazel shook their heads.

"Well, I have one more thing to tell you. The man who killed my brother might already be regretting what he did. Josiah's duppy knows who did it and he knows where this man lives. It won't matter that those fools don't believe in duppies. And it's not only his duppy they should be fearing. My brother didn't like using the most powerful Obeah spells but I'm not afraid to use them and I don't need to know who the killer is to use those spells.

"You wait and see. The man who killed my brother will get sicker and sicker. He'll think he's going crazy. He'll think somebody's following him, watching him all the time. Who knows? He might even confess hoping that the duppy won't find him if he's in prison."

Sharona laughed. "And you know what, detectives? I can kill a person that way and you policemen cannot do anything at all. You won't have a single shred of evidence because I don't need to go anywhere near that killer. You and your people don't believe in magic and evil spells and all. You'll just have to believe the poor man got to feeling so guilty it made him sick or made him take too many pills or something. But people here in Jamaica Lakes? Every single one of them, even Herman Wolff's Revivalists, will know for certain it was my spells that were responsible."

11
What the Medical Examiner Found

Jeenya

The two detectives drove to the police station, still stunned by Sharona's words. "I don't know if I should even write up that last part," Hazel said, "about how she can kill people using magic spells and how we can't do anything about it."

"We need to," Rick replied. "She threatened to kill someone. She might go farther than magic spells and somehow get to him, give him food containing poison so people will think her magic worked. We need to know about the threat. I don't believe in duppies or evil spells, but I sure wouldn't want that woman putting a spell on me. Listening to her could make a believer fear for his sanity or," and now he paused, "or for his life."

"Hazel," Rick said as they got out at the station. "I just had a thought. Maybe it's a little crazy, but what if Sharona did it? What if she killed him? We know she was the last one to see him. She's smart and she's tough. He trusted her. Maybe she got tired of waiting for him to die so she could take his place."

"I was thinking the same thing," Hazel said slowly. "But how would you prove it? We can't use finger prints. Hers would be all over. Nobody would have seen her do it. Unless she hands over the knife she used, unless she confesses, there isn't much we can do. Let's hope it was someone else, someone we can take to court."

They reported back to the lieutenant who had interesting news. "Everyone looked at the corpse," Nate said, "and you all figured the victim died from getting his throat slit. Right?"

Rick remembered Dr. Parker saying the cutting looked like it had been done postmortem, but he didn't say anything. He frowned slightly at Hazel and she got the message. Nate liked being first to know things.

"It took the medical examiner about three minutes flat to see past what the rest of you saw," Nate said. "The killer used a garrote and strangled the man first. It wasn't anything like piano wire. Dr. Parker said that when they use that, killers can come close to cutting a man's head off. This was a thicker cord, something smooth with no fibers, something like a phone cord that wouldn't cut the skin. It killed him though, killed him quickly according to the Doc.

"There was no sign the victim fought back. Then, when the man was dead, your killer took his knife and cut the man's throat. That's why there wasn't blood everywhere. Doc said if that man's throat had been slit while his heart was still pumping, his blood would have been all over the walls of that little shed.

"Doc spoke to the crime scene officers, and they went

back over every inch of the scene this afternoon. They never found anything that could have been used to strangle him. The killer took that away with him, along with his knife. So, now we have an interesting question. Why kill the man first and then slit his throat?"

Nate Holiday grinned broadly showing teeth that should have had braces when he was young. "And there's another thing the two of you don't know. That wasn't all our killer cut." He left a dramatic pause.

"Your killer pulled down that man's pants and cut his genitals. Not all the way through, but enough to make his point. Then he pulled the pants back up and refastened his belt. By the time the killer got around to doing this, there was so little bleeding, you couldn't see any blood there until he was undressed. So, what does this tell us?"

Rick nodded to his partner.

"It tells me," Hazel said, "this killer was very angry, and it had something to do with sex. We aren't that surprised, sir. We've already learned that Mr. Overmon has been getting in trouble with husbands, boyfriends, and at least one father because he couldn't keep his pants zipped. There is no evidence of him ever raping anyone but you could probably list at least twenty or thirty women he's had sex with, women other than his wives. We already have a list of names to check out.

"First, there's Juanita Juarez and her husband, Jesus, both thought to be Mexicans. Jesus apparently threatened to kill Josiah about a week back. He's on the top on our list of suspects.

"Then there's Suzy Cornblatt, a white woman, living in a Stuart trailer park. No husband, but she's got a jealous boyfriend, name of Clancy Cottonwood. Clancy works at a motorcycle shop out near Walmart.

"We'd like to get someone in the department to get all the victim's incoming and outgoing phone calls for the past couple of months." Hazel continued.

"We have the three phone numbers Mr. Overmon was using, his home, his office, and his cell phone. I'd guess he used his cell phone to talk to these women. This might help us locate some of the girlfriends."

"Maybe," Rick added, "they can also find the home addresses and phone numbers for these two women. And, while they're at it, we'd like to see priors for the women, the husband, and the boyfriend.

"As soon as we get this information, we're planning to drop by and visit the women and ask what they were doing Friday night, and what the boyfriend and husband were up to. But we have plenty of other people to talk to for now."

"Good work," the lieutenant said. "I knew, if anybody could get those people out there to talk, it would be the two of you. So, what's your plan for tomorrow?"

Rick looked at Hazel and nodded.

"We're thinking about visiting the pastor," she said, "the Rev. Herman Wolff. In addition to the usual church services, he apparently leads these weekly rituals out in the woods. They're called Revivalists. Herman Wolff is the leader of the opposition, the religious group that hates the kind of spellcasting Josiah supposedly could do as the Obeah Man. But I'm not at all sure they'd go so far as to cut the man's throat and genitals.

"Next, we need to go back and talk to Chester Gunn, again. He's the manager at the grocery. He didn't tell us about the angry husband or boyfriend who came in to see

Josiah. The victim's sister, Sharona, said Chester didn't hear any details. He just heard a lot of shouting. That's what he told her. It's possible he heard more than he told Sharona and there might have been other people in the store who heard more."

Nate winked at Rick. "Smart partner you have here. She's got a good head on her shoulders. She looks pretty good too. If I was your age, I wouldn't mind working with her."

Rick cringed, knowing how much Hazel hated comments like this. But they both knew it wasn't just Hazel. Nate talked this way with most of the women on the force. And it would be hard teaching this old dog any new tricks, especially with this old dog being their supervisor. Rick tried to ignore the rude remarks. Nate was due to retire in a year or two anyway.

"That part about cutting his genitals," Rick said. "We're keeping that out of the news, aren't we?"

"Damn right we are," Nate said. "Stuff like that scares people. It makes the family even more upset. And keeping it out of the news helps us know, if someone confesses, whether he's telling the truth or not."

Hazel and Rick sat down at a worktable and, using notes they'd taken, put together a written report of the day. Hazel called her husband. "Hi Sweetheart, we're about done. You want to defrost a tuna casserole or would you rather go out?" She turned to Rick. "We're going out for pizza. Want to come along?"

"No thanks," Rick said. "I'm exhausted. You and Tim have a nice time. See you in the morning."

Rick stopped on his way home and picked up a pizza of his own. Pizza sounded good when Hazel suggested it, but he needed time alone to think. Besides, he'd been out with Hazel and Tim several times and it always felt uncomfortable. Tim said and did little things to put Rick down or to make him appear foolish.

Hazel always apologized afterward. "Don't pay any attention to Tim," she said. "He didn't mind so much when I was working with Benny Jackson. Benny was too old and fat for Tim to worry. But he sees me working with a strong, good-looking man like you, and I guess he gets jealous. He'll just have to get used to it." The tone of Hazel's voice and the way she looked at him, made Rick wonder if, perhaps, Tim had a reason to be jealous.

Rick showered and then stretched out in the old black leather recliner, staring at the wall and eating pepperoni and mushroom pizza. He went back over the day's conversations. Was he missing anything important? He didn't think so. He called Jeenya to find out if the grocery store was open on Sunday.

"Sunday mornings are for church," she said. "But the store is open in the afternoon from one to five. We'd love to have you join us for church."

"All right. What time is church?"

Rick called Hazel. "Want to go with me? Good. I'll pick you up at nine. We'll meet Zeke and Jeenya and go to church together."

He could hear Tim complaining in the background. "That man spends the entire day with you and he has to call while we're eating dinner? I deserve a little time alone with my wife."

As Rick returned to his pizza, he began to wonder how long Hazel's marriage would last. He couldn't picture Hazel putting up with a jealous husband. But, he realized, you never can tell. She might be enjoying the attention. Maybe she went out of her way to make Tim jealous.

I'd better stop doing this, Rick told himself. I'm getting to be suspicious of everyone. First, we suspected Sharona of killing her brother and now I even suspect Tim and then Hazel. Next thing, if I keep doing this, I'll start suspecting Jeenya and Zeke.

Back in Jamaica Lakes that night, Ida Lee was at her window.

"Hey dere, Miz Jeenya. How come you take up so much time with your detective friend and his girlfriend? The detective is 'sposed to be finding the killer, not sitting around talking to you. Or maybe he thinks you did it. That would be a real hoot, wouldn't it? If I get a chance to talk to the detective, I'll tell him my theory. I 'spect you waited till your husband was sleeping, and took one of your kitchen knives. Then, you went down the street in the dark and killed that poor old Obeah Man who never did nobody no harm."

✦

12

The Rock and Roll Church

Rick

Rick looked approvingly at Hazel. She wore a simple blue dress with a dark red jacket.

"Am I dressed all right?" she asked. "I have no idea what these people wear to church, but I wear a dress like this when we manage to go to our church. It's been a long time, you know, since Tim and I were inside a church."

"Jeenya will approve," Rick said. He wore his only suit with his favorite blue and gold tie. "It's been a while since I've been to church too."

"I'm curious about what this church will be like," Hazel said.

"When I visited Homer, we sometimes went to this little church. The service wasn't like anything I'd known before but the people were nice. They acted like they really were glad to see me."

Jeenya

Jeenya and Zeke had breakfast, as usual, on the patio. This morning, they shared johnnycakes, fried plantain, and some good blue mountain coffee with Rick and Hazel. "You should eat a good breakfast," Jeenya said. "Our church services tend to run a little long."

"What Jeenya means," Zeke added, "is that church might go on for hours so you really need to eat plenty for breakfast. It's also a good idea to use the bathroom before church."

Hazel returned through the kitchen and found Jeenya stirring a pot. "Something smells good. Smells like curry."

Jeenya smiled. "Our Rick told me he was hoping we'd have goat curry some time. I started fixing it last night when I knew you were coming. This was Homer's favorite, too."

While they didn't often attend church here, Jeenya loved the small church. It reminded her of pictures she'd seen of the old New England churches. It was a wooden building with a small steeple, white with a gray trim around the windows and doors. Instead of the classic stained-glass windows, this church had windows of solid colors, all the colors of the rainbow. The sign in front read "Jamaica Lakes Independent Church of The Living God."

As they walked up to the door, Zeke and Jeenya were greeted over and over by different churchgoers. "Jeenya. Ezekiel, it is so good to have you and your friends worshiping with us." "It's been a while since we've seen you here." "Glad you came to join us this morning."

Rick and Hazel were also welcomed warmly. An elderly gentleman shook their hands and said, "We are so pleased you are here with us this morning. Come back anytime."

Jeenya spoke softly to Zeke, "Take a look at the woman over there with Mercy Venable. She look familiar to you? I could swear I've met her, or maybe she reminds me of someone."

"I know what you mean," Zeke said. "But I can't place her."

Rev. Wolff greeted people at the front door. "So glad you're here with us today. Praise the Lord for this beautiful day. Praise God for He is very good."

Zeke introduced Rick and Hazel, and Rev. Wolff smiled warmly. "I've heard about the two of you. We're happy you've joined us this morning."

Inside were twelve rows of well-worn wooden pews. "Twelve rows," Jeenya whispered to Rick, "for the twelve apostles."

A large table stood in front, covered with a white cloth. Placed on the table there was a large open Bible, two vases of flowers, probably from a member's garden, and six candlesticks on each side.

"Twelve candles too," Rick whispered.

"And how many windows?" Jeenya smiled as he turned to count windows, six on each side.

Rick

Rick looked around, remembering Homer calling it the "rock-and-roll church." He studied the dark wooden pulpit. Behind the pulpit was a large wooden chair that looked almost like a throne. It appeared to be terribly uncomfortable.

A battered, white piano was off to the left. An older man, short and fairly heavy, walked up to the piano. He sat down, raised his hands high above the keys, and appeared to attack the piano. He wasn't actually playing rock-and-roll, of course, but it was spirited music played with unmistakable enthusiasm.

A group of women, mostly older women, all dressed

in white, walked forward and sat in the front pews. The pastor came in and took his seat in that uncomfortable-looking chair. Two children, a boy and a girl, lit the twelve candles.

In the back of the church the choir in green and white robes was lining up. As the music started, they began moving forward. Rick had forgotten this part, the way the choir seemed to glide: left step, pause, right step, pause, all in unison. They almost seemed to be dancing.

It had been a long time since he'd been sitting here with Homer but the memories were coming back. As women came in with huge colorful hats, he remembered how Homer would poke him in the ribs and grin.

After an opening hymn by the choir, the congregation stood and joined the singing, most clapping hands, many rocking back and forth, and a few raising and waving their arms. One song was familiar and Rick joined in.

He glanced over at Hazel. She was making an effort to clap in time to the music. He tried not to smile. This must be a shock to her after the formality of the Catholic Church.

Rev. Wolff picked up his Bible and held it up. "This morning's lesson from the Old Testament comes from the book of Zephaniah. For those of you who aren't sure where to look for Zephaniah, it is near the end of the Old Testament, followed by three very short books, Haggai, Zechariah, and Malachi." Jeenya nudged Rick, handing him an old Bible open to the book of Zephaniah.

"I am reading today," the pastor said in a slow, solemn tone, "from the first chapter of Zephaniah, verses 14 through 17.

"The great day of the Lord is near, near and hastening

fast; the sound of the day of the Lord is bitter, the mighty man cries aloud there.

"A day of wrath is that day, a day of distress and anguish, a day of ruin and devastation, a day of darkness and gloom, a day of clouds and thick darkness, a day of trumpet blast and battle cry against the fortified cities and against the lofty battlements.

"I will bring distress on men so that they shall walk like the blind, because they have sinned against the Lord; their blood shall be poured out like dust, and their flesh like dung."

The pastor must have searched a long time, Rick thought, to find a scripture describing what sounded very much like Josiah's murder. It seemed to say God had killed Josiah Overmon and let his blood pour out because of his greed and his sins against God.

After a long prayer, Rev. Wolff began preaching. It was nothing like the quiet, thoughtful sermons in the churches he'd attended with his family, but Rick remembered similar sermons when he had come here with Homer.

Rev. Wolff was shouting in a rhythmic, almost singsong fashion, rocking back and forth and waving his arms. Members of the congregation shouted back: "Hallelujah!", "Praise the Lord!", "God is great!" and "Amen, brother, Amen."

Rick tried listening, but the sermon was hard to follow. It seemed to be a dramatic retelling of that horrible scripture. It was about darkness and devastation, death and blood, sin and the wrath of God.

Finally, they sang again. Some of the people were up in front, dancing, shouting and shaking all over. Finally, the singing and shouting and dancing quieted down and the pastor said a long benediction.

After church, Jeenya and Zeke introduced Hazel and Rick to a few more members." We had an excellent turnout today," one woman said. "Rev. Wolff sure is one fine preacher," a man said. "That was a fantastic sermon, wasn't it?" Rick nodded politely. That wasn't exactly how he'd have described it.

Jeenya steered Hazel and Rick toward the road. "I'd like to say hello to Mercy and her friend."

"Good morning, Mercy," Jeenya said. "I want you to meet Hazel Fontaine and Rick Montoya. They're the detectives looking into Josiah's death. You remember Rick, I'm sure. He and our Homer were good friends."

Mercy nodded.

"This is Mercy Venable," Jeenya continued when Mercy made no effort to introduce her friend. "She's lived here in Jamaica Lakes almost as long as we have. I don't believe I know your friend."

"I'm Esther Warren," the younger woman said with a shy smile. "Iris Venable and I are good friends. My mother and Mrs. Venable were friends too. I'm just visiting Jamaica Lakes for a week."

"Esther," Mercy said, "this is Jeenya Birdsong. That's her husband over there. They grow Jamaican vegetables for those of us who miss having callaloo and bitter cerasse. They have the most wonderful herb garden."

"I've seen your garden," Esther said. "Even out on the street, I can smell the herbs. It makes me feel like I'm home in Jamaica. I'm so pleased to meet you."

As Jeenya continued introducing Hazel to some of the members, Rick spoke to the pastor.

13

The Stranger in Jamaica Lakes

Jeenya

"**B**efore we go home," Jeenya said, "we'd like to take a short walk around the park. Zeke and I take this same walk every Sunday after church."

"I saw you speak to Herman," Zeke said to Rick. "Did you have a question for him?

"We have several questions," Rick said. "Hazel and I have been invited to the parsonage this afternoon at three."

"That's good," Jeenya said. "Herman should have a different view of what's going on around here. I haven't talked to him all that much, but I've always found him to be a good and honest man."

She was pleased that Rick thought to do this. The more people the detectives talked to, the better their chances were of learning helpful information.

"This is a lovely park," Hazel said, looking toward the lake. "In nice weather, it would be a great place for a picnic."

"It is," Jeenya agreed. "You remember all those wonderful picnics we had here, don't you Rick?"

"How could I forget? You'd bring a nice tablecloth and put it down on one of the picnic tables. You fixed so much food we all had things to carry. Homer and I usually carried the cooler."

"This place," Hazel said, "must be packed on holidays like the Fourth of July."

"Sure, we come out on the Fourth for a picnic," Zeke said, "but if you really want to see a mob, you ought to see the park on one of the Jamaican holidays. Then it really is packed. Jamaican families and friends from all over the county gather here to celebrate on August 1st, Jamaican Emancipation Day, or on August 6th, our Independence Day. Josiah always found someone to set off fireworks.

Jeenya stopped at a tree with feathery leaflets. "This is what I wanted you to see," she said softly. When Homer died, we wanted a special memorial. This is a jacaranda tree. It has bright blue flowers in the spring, a shade darker than the sky. Josiah agreed this would be a wonderful way to remember Homer."

Jeenya reached out and touched the smooth trunk. "Homer loved those blue flowers. If you check the paintings in our living room, you'll find three pictures Homer painted for an art class. All three are of jacarandas."

"When we planted the jacaranda," Zeke said, "Josiah asked if we'd plant a tree for him when he died. He wanted a royal poinciana. I thought for sure he'd outlive both of us but I told him, as long as one of us was still alive, we'd plant a royal poinciana right in front of the lake. I plan to go out to a nursery tomorrow, looking for one, for a tree that's tall and strong. We'll wait, of course, until they bury Josiah. Then we'll plant his tree."

Hearing a high-pitched yapping, they all turned to see

a short older woman walking a small dog. "Hello Eula May," Jeenya said. "I'd like you to meet our friends. You might remember Rick Montoya. He and our Homer were good friends."

Eula May nodded. "I remember."

"This is Hazel Fontaine. Rick and Hazel are the detectives trying to find who killed Mr. Overmon."

"It's good to meet you, Eula May," Rick said. "And I can guess who this is." He looked down at the little dog. "You must be Princess."

"Goodness," Eula May said. "Even if you are a detective, I don't understand how you'd know my dog's name. Jeenya and Zeke tell you that?"

"We didn't mention you or Princess," Jeenya said.

Rick smiled. "Could I get away with calling it intuition?" He smiled. "Actually, when Sharona told us who saw Josiah the night he was killed, she mentioned a woman named Eula May with a dog named Princess."

"That is amazing," Eula May said. "Absolutely amazing. Since my name is Eula May, you figured out this had to be Princess? I guess you got to be real smart like that to be a detective."

Rick knelt down to pet the small dog. "Hi there, Princess. I understand you've been feeling better after your herbal bath. I was hoping I'd get a chance to meet you." The little dog, in response, bared her teeth and growled.

Eula May laughed. "I must apologize for her behavior. She's not used to white folks, you know."

Once they were out of hearing, Hazel asked. "What kind of strange dog was that? She looked like a cross between a chihuahua and something mean and ugly."

"You sure got that right," Zeke said. "Princess has got

to be the ugliest dog in the neighborhood but Eula May never figured that out. And it isn't just white folks she snarls at. That dog doesn't like anybody except for Eula May. She just adores Eula May."

"Now Zeke," Jeenya said, "to understand why Eula May and Princess get along so well, Hazel and Rick have to know how they met. Eula May's husband, Berny, had been sick for years. One morning he just didn't wake up. He died in his sleep.

"For months, Eula May was grieving. She never left the house. A couple of her neighbors did some shopping for her. Others brought food. Most days she hardly ever got out of bed. She just lay there and cried. Nothing seemed to help. We thought she was going to die.

"Then one day, that ugly little dog showed up at her door. She barked a little and whined. Eula May came to see what was making all the fuss. She looked at the dog and started laughing. It was the first time in months she'd laughed. Eula May said the dog went straight to her blue chair. Eula May sat down and the dog hopped up in her lap. That afternoon, Eula May and the dog took a ride to the pet store.

"Eula May says she let that dog choose her own dog food, her food dish and water dish, her leash, her doggie bed, and even some toys. When they got home, she put on the little dog's leash and the two of them went for a walk.

"Somebody asked what her dog's name was. They say Eula May leaned down and she asked that dog what her name was. The dog barked and Eula May said, 'Princess. She says her name is Princess.'

Since that day, Eula May goes everywhere with that dog. Some people will tell you Eula May saved that dog's life but I believe that ugly little dog saved Eula May's life."

14
Goat Curry for Lunch

Jeenya

They passed the church again on their way back to the house. Only a few people were still standing around talking. "I keep thinking about that woman," Jeenya said, "the woman with Mercy Venable. Her name is Esther Warren. I do wish I could figure out why she looks so familiar.

"From her accent, I'm pretty sure she lives in Jamaica, but I still have a feeling that I know her. I can't remember any Warrens ever living here in Jamaica Lakes."

"She said Mrs. Venable used to be a good friend of Esther's mother," Hazel added. "Does that help?"

"Not really," Jeenya said. "Mercy always had a lot of friends."

"It's possible," Hazel said, "this woman is married, that she has a different last name now."

"I can smell the curry," Rick said as they entered the house. "It smells heavenly."

Jeenya's smiled broadened, remembering similar comments from Rick and Homer when they were teenagers. "I need to get the rice cooking," she said. "You want to set the table for me?"

Hazel joined Rick, carrying dishes and silverware and arranging them on the table. "Can you manage spicy food?" Rick asked Hazel.

"Sure," Hazel said. "No problem."

Jeenya shook her head. Rick had told her about Hazel. He said she'd never admit there was anything she couldn't do. As the only girl in a family with four older brothers, she had to compete with them, showing she was smarter, faster, tougher, and meaner than any of them. Even if Hazel had never eaten spicy food, she was sure to do her best to swallow it with a smile. Jeenya liked that sort of spirit.

Jeenya was stirring the curry pot when Hazel came and took a peek. "It looks great, Jeenya," she said, "but the smell isn't quite like the curry I'm used to eating. Is it the goat that makes the difference?"

"Goat might taste a tiny bit different," Jeenya said, "but it doesn't change how the curry smells. Instead of Indian curry powder, I use Jamaican curry powder. There are many different recipes, but what I use includes cardamom, cinnamon, cloves and allspice. I add fresh-cut thyme, grated ginger and garlic and, of course, a few peppers. I made it much milder than usual today, knowing you were coming, but I'll warn you. It's still a little spicy."

Jeenya put the lid back on the crock pot and turned to Rick. "Last night after dinner, Zeke and I went to Josiah's house for the wake."

"The wake?" Rick asked. "I thought wakes were held in funeral homes."

"That would be true for most of us in Jamaica Lakes," Jeenya said. "but the Overmons always have to do things the traditional way. In the old days, out in the villages, the men worked together to build a wooden coffin while the women washed the body and made new clothes or, for a man, at least a new shirt. All the buttons would be removed and pockets were sewn shut. When they put the body in the coffin, they would nail him in thinking it would be harder for the duppy to get loose. Then, for nine nights, they'd hold a wake."

"It's different now," Zeke said, "and, for Josiah, who knows when they'll get the body back from the medical examiner? Then it will go to a funeral home where they embalm it. In the old days, bodies got pretty smelly after nine days. Flies would be buzzing around."

"Why nine days?" Hazel asked.

"What I heard, growing up," Jeenya said, "was that the duppy needs nine days to wander around, visiting his family, his friends, his house and all. I guess he's saying goodbye. He wanders for nine days while they're having the wake. Then he normally rejoins his body and they're buried together. But, if he's not buried properly or if he still needs to get even with somebody, he might continue wandering a long time."

"That's spooky," Hazel said. "The more I hear you talk about duppies, the more I feel like, if I turned around real fast, I'd catch a duppy sitting in the corner."

"With the coffins we have now," Rick asked, "can they still nail a dead person in?"

"Not usually. I don't think anyone will try nailing Josiah in," Zeke said. "But I suspect they'll pile up heavy rocks on top of him before they close it up. That's another way of keeping a duppy from wandering."

"The Overmons," Jeenya added, "and others who

follow traditional ways still hold the nine-night wake. They'd tell you that family and friends gather each night. To tell the truth, though, most people only come for the first and last nights. "With most families, they'll read the Bible, sing hymns, and then eat together at a wake. But the Overmon's, last night, didn't include the Bible or the hymns. They talked about how wonderful Josiah was, they comforted each other and they had plenty of good food. But not one person said anything about his murder."

"You ever think, honey," Zeke said, "that the reason they weren't talking about the murder could be because we were there? They'd know for sure that, if they said anything interesting, we'd share it with Rick."

When the food was ready, Zeke said the blessing, and they began filling their plates. Hazel took a large serving of white rice and a small serving of curry to start. Jeenya watched as she took a small bite and quickly drank her entire glass of iced tea.

"Rice," Rick whispered, gesturing toward Hazel's plate.

Hazel nodded, ate a large forkful, and relaxed. "It is a little spicier than I expected," she finally said, noticing everyone watching her. "But it is delicious." She tried another bite with even less curry. Before long, she reached for a second helping.

"That sermon this morning," Hazel asked. "Was that the sort of sermon the pastor normally preaches or was he really talking about Josiah being a sinner and God killing him and letting his blood pour out on the ground? I couldn't believe anything like that would be in the Bible."

Zeke laughed. "You're very perceptive, young lady. I'm thinking Rev. Wolff spent hours hunting for a scripture that applied to Josiah's death but half those people sitting there never realized it. That's because it sounded so much like every one of his sermons. Sometimes we call him Herman Hellfire.

"Jeenya and I both went to the Church of England in Jamaica. You'd never hear that sermon in one of our churches. You'd certainly never see people clapping and shouting in the Church of England. It's more formal, more like the Episcopal Church here. Our priest talked more about Jesus, about loving our neighbors, and about forgiveness. Many of the little country churches in Jamaica are like this one. They concentrate on the Old Testament prophets or on the Book of Revelation. They try scaring people into believing."

"If you think this was a wild service," Jeenya added, "you should be here on a typical Sunday. Rev. Wolff was keeping things calm today, probably because the two of you were visiting. Today, the people were simply rocking back and forth a little, with a few people down in front near the altar, jumping up and down and dancing like they're going crazy.

"Most Sundays, you'd see twice as many people dancing in front by the altar and at least half a dozen people get slain by the spirit, as they say. They actually fall out on the floor with someone there to lower them gently. The ladies in the front row have a stack of cloths to cover the ladies' legs. And there are days we have healings and testimonials. Today's service didn't quite last two hours. You're not used to that, either. I sure wasn't. But, when things really get going, church can go on three or even four hours."

While Jeenya went to get the dessert, she suggested that Zeke show Hazel and Rick the paintings of jacaranda flowers. "Homer was quite an artist," Hazel said. "Those blue flowers are lovely."

"And over here," Zeke said, pointing, is another of Homer's paintings. Can you tell who this is?"

"That's Jeenya, isn't it?" Hazel asked. "I can tell by her eyes and her smile. What a beautiful job he did."

"Homer worked really hard on this one," Zeke said softly. He was planning to do my portrait when he got back, but…" He couldn't say any more.

"Now," Rick said, taking over and pointing at the opposite wall. "Take a look at these paintings."

Hazel went from one to another. "Homer's paintings were acrylic; these are watercolors. Those were very bright; these are more delicate. I don't think Homer did these."

"You're right, there," Zeke said. "Those painting aren't nearly as good as Homer's work. Don't you agree?"

"I'm not sure," Hazel said hesitantly. "Homer's pictures are beautiful. I'd look at those and say the artist was a real professional but I like these pictures even if they look less professional. Did Homer do these when he was younger?"

"You are very kind to an old man, my dear. It's a real honor to have you thinking these pictures were Homer's work at any age. Those are mine."

"Yours?" Hazel said studying Zeke, then the pictures. "I had no idea you were an artist. Artistic talent must run in your family. These are lovely. Instead of being painted by a younger artist, they were painted by a more mature artist."

15

A Tour of Jeenya's Garden

Jeenya

Hazel and Rick helped Jeenya clear the table.

"Esther, Esther," Jeenya mumbled. "You know, Zeke, one of Josiah's daughters with his first wife, might have been Esther. Esther Overmon sounds familiar, doesn't it? She does look a little like Marie, doesn't she? That's who she's reminding me of, Marie Overmon."

"You think she's Josiah's daughter?" Hazel asked. "Were her mother and Mrs. Venable good friends?"

"The best of friends. The two of them were closer than sisters. They used to laugh about Marie marrying an Obeah man, though, of course, Josiah wasn't doing that when he married Marie.

"Mercy and Marie had little girls about the same age, Iris and Esther. I remember seeing the girls playing together at the park while their mothers sat watching them. Marie had another child on her lap and the third one in the stroller.

"I'm not positive this is Josiah's daughter, but she could be. Esther and Iris were good friends when they were young. I wouldn't be surprised if they'd kept in touch over the years. Iris got married and lives in California now."

"But," Hazel said slowly, "do you really think, if Esther had a reason to return to Jamaica Lakes after all these years, that she'd write her friend's parents and ask if she could stay with them? Why wouldn't she write her father?"

Rick had been listening quietly while drying the silverware. "That is the question isn't it? If she is Josiah's daughter, why would she be here in Jamaica Lakes? And, even more interesting, why doesn't she want her family to know she's here? And what's most suspicious is that Josiah's daughter would suddenly appear in Jamaica Lakes and then, a day or two later, Josiah is found murdered. We need to learn a little more about Ms. Esther Warren."

"I agree," Jeenya said. "I'll invite her to drop by to see the garden?" She picked up the phone and called.

"That wasn't hard," Jeenya said. "Esther had just finished her lunch. She'll be here in about fifteen minutes. Jeenya fixed a tall pitcher of limeade and set out a plate of cookies. Esther arrived a few minutes later. "Rick, Hazel," Jeenya said, "would you like to join us?"

"I was hoping you'd ask," Hazel said. "I've been looking forward to seeing what you grow back there."

The four of them began with the vegetables. Jeenya took a deep breath as usual, enjoying the mixture of smells, that pungent smell of the tomato leaves, the smell of decomposing compost, the bitter fragrance of the cerasse.

"Isn't that bitter cerasse?" Esther asked.

"It looks a lot like Chinese bitter melon," Hazel said.

"You're both right," Jeenya said. "It's bitter melon or bitter gourd in China. It's cerasse in Jamaica. They cook and eat the fruit; we usually boil the leaves to make tea."

"Yuck. Homer convinced me to taste that tea once," Rick said. "It was the most disgusting thing I'd ever tasted. Homer kept laughing while I spit it out and tried rinsing that taste out of my mouth."

"It's hard getting used to it when you're young," Esther said. "My mother used to sweeten it with brown sugar, a lot of brown sugar, trying to make it taste sweet. We drank it but it was still awful. As we got older, we got used to it. Now I drink a cup a day. It's good for you."

"You're right about that," Jeenya said. "It's full of all sorts of vitamins. I recommend it when there's a virus going around or if someone is sick and the doctors can't do much to help. If I could grow only one thing in my garden, it would be Cerasse."

She pointed to the back of the garden. "Over there we're growing fourteen kinds of tomatoes: the great big ones, the medium-sized Romas, cherry tomatoes, grape tomatoes and even the yellow ones.

"Over there we have okra, eggplant, chayote, and several kinds of squash. Further down we have lettuce, spinach, other greens, and plenty of hot peppers. Off to the right, we grow pumpkins and yams. And look over here."

"Callaloo?" asked Esther. "I had no idea you could grow callaloo here. Mercy served some for dinner last night. I thought for sure she got it sent in from Jamaica."

"Mercy was here the other day, getting all sorts of fresh vegetables. She said she was expecting company."

They passed a long row of large spiky plants. "I know these," Hazel said. "That's Aloe Vera. I use that on cuts and burns and it's sometimes added to skin creams."

"We call it Sinkle Bible," Jeenya said. "We don't just

put it on our skin. Sometimes we eat a little. It's good for constipation, diabetes, and even for the common cold."

Jeenya kept looking at Esther. It wasn't her imagination. She did look like Marie. It had to be Marie's daughter.

"Over here," she said, "we have the familiar cooking herbs as well as fever grass. Other people call it lemongrass. It's used in Asian cooking, but we mainly use it for tea. We have a dozen kinds of mint and we grow a little ginger."

"I can't remember ever seeing an herb garden like this at home," Esther said. "In Jamaica, most of these plants grow wild. I remember wandering through the fields picking what we needed. Now I understand," she added, "why Mercy keeps going on and on about how much she loves it in Jamaica Lakes. It really does feel like home."

"Next," Jeenya continued, "up along the road where people can see it when they walk by is my flower garden. I have a lot of lavender because so many people use lavender scented oil for healing or relaxation.

"I put in a little row of flowers a couple years back. Then the ladies at the café wanted flowers to put on the tables for Mother's Day. Now, I do their flowers three times a week. Other people stop by and ask for flowers, especially for birthdays and anniversaries. They tell me their favorite colors and I fix something nice.

Now, Rick took over, "And here, ladies, you see Jeenya's famous flock of flamingos." He pointed at a row of strange pink birds made of wood, plastic, metal, and PVC pipe. "Zeke gave Jeenya her first flamingo years ago. She made such a fuss over the silly thing, that he's been giving them to her ever since. And, I'm proud to say, Homer and I presented her with several more."

16

The Visitor from Jamaica

Jeenya

"Esther, you look so familiar. You used to live here, didn't you? That's how you knew Iris?"

I remember seeing you and Iris playing at the park while Mercy and Marie were watching you. You look a lot like your mother."

Esther didn't deny it.

"You seemed familiar to me because you look so much like your mother."

"But why Esther Warren?" Jeenya asked. "Did you make that up or are you married?"

"I married Paul Warren three years ago."

"Why, after all these years, are you back here in Jamaica Lakes?" Jeenya asked. "And why in the world are you keeping it a secret? Did you tell your family you're here?"

"I came," Esther said slowly, "because I needed to talk to my father. I didn't want Aunt Sharona and my uncles asking why I was here and I didn't want them making a fuss over me. I just wanted to talk to my father and leave."

"And did you get a chance to talk to Josiah?"

"Yes. We had a good talk. Now I don't know what difference it made. I stopped by the store Thursday morning.

"Daddy didn't recognize me at first. I asked if we could talk privately in his office. He didn't have an office when I was little. Now the store's twice as big and so much nicer. Mrs. Venable told me about the office and said we should go there to talk. That's when he figured out who I was. He said the same thing you did, that I looked like my mother."

Esther looked at the detectives. "I guess you need to know what we talked about."

Rick nodded. "It would be helpful. If it's not related to our investigation, it doesn't need to be made public."

Esther sighed, looking off into the distance. "We talked about my brother, Daniel. After Mama died, Daddy took the three of us kids back to Jamaica to live with Mother's parents. Mother made him promise to do that.

"Every month, Daddy sent a check to cover our needs. It was for food, clothes, school expenses, and anything else we needed. It wasn't a lot, but it really helped. Grandma and Grandpa didn't have much money. With Daddy's help, I finished high school and two years of college. Sarah was just starting to walk when we arrived in Jamaica. Now she's finishing high school this year and will be starting college in the fall."

"And Daniel?" Jeenya said gently.

"Daniel hated school. Right after Grandpa died, Daniel dropped out. He didn't even finish eighth grade. Grandpa wouldn't have let him drop out, but Grandma didn't know how to stop him. She was too ashamed to tell Daddy.

"But that's not why I came. Daniel has been getting into trouble. First, it was drinking. He started stealing to get money for beer. Then he came up with a plan. He wrote Daddy, telling him he was going to high school, and that Grandma wasn't giving him enough to pay his expenses. Daniel convinced him to send an extra fifty dollars a month, not to Grandma but to him at a friend's address. Now, instead of buying beer, Daniel uses it to buy drugs.

"We found out when Daniel was arrested for selling drugs. The police found a letter from Daddy asking how Daniel was doing in school and if he needed more money."

"What about Sarah?" Jeenya asked. "Does she need money for college?"

"Daddy was still sending money to Grandma for Sarah's school expenses. She also has a part-time job. But Grandma's getting older and is sick a lot. I asked Daddy to send the money to me or Sarah. We could pay for Grandma's medicine and doctor bills and the rest for Sarah. He agreed.

"I first tried writing Daddy but I just couldn't do it. I threw away one letter after another. I wanted him to stop sending Daniel money. I finally decided I should come in person and talk to him but I couldn't stand having to explain all this to the whole family I just couldn't do it."

"You did just the right thing, dear," Jeenya said. "I'm sure Josiah appreciated your coming to him in private. Now, you'll need to talk to Sharona. I expect she will continue to handle the family finances."

"I'll do that, maybe the day before I leave, and hope she can keep the story from getting around. And I have to tell you, Mrs. Birdsong, I'm glad we're talking about this.

"I was halfway hoping you'd recognize me, that we'd be able to talk. I remember you and Mr. Birdsong from when I was a kid. I always wished I had a beautiful name like Birdsong. Then, of all the grownups I knew, I liked you and the Venables the best. You were always so nice.

"The other thing was…" and Esther smiled. "I remember Homer. He was older than I was, but he was so good-looking. I had a crush on him. So did all the girls I knew. Daddy wrote and told us when Homer got killed in Iraq and, even after all those years, I still cried. I always thought how lucky Homer was that he got to come and live with you. When Mom died and they said we were going to live with our grandparents, I hoped they'd be as nice as you."

Jeenya smiled. "And were they that nice?"

"Not like my image of you, but they definitely loved us. And that made it much harder to see Daniel behaving like this.

Then Esther turned to Rick. "I guess you're thinking it's suspicious, me coming here in secret and my father getting killed a day later. Do you have questions for me?"

"I believe your story," Rick said, "but I hope you have a good alibi. One question: where were you Friday night?"

"I knew you'd ask that. Friday night, I went with the Venables to the Revivalist meeting. Mercy got a headache, so she and I left at about eleven. I fixed her a cup of tea and then she went to bed.

"I stayed up reading until Mr. Venable got home at about one-thirty. But, from eleven-thirty and one-thirty, no one saw me. After Mr. Venable came home, I went to bed, but I'd can't prove I stayed in bed. I could have gotten up and left, but I didn't.

"But why in the world would I want to kill my father? He sent us money all those years. He was going to continue sending money for Sarah to go to college. I wasn't mad at him for taking us to Jamaica. We all knew Mom wanted him to do that and our grandparents took good care of us. What possible reason would I have for killing my father?"

"If people knew who you were," Rick asked, "would any of them think you had a motive to kill your father?"

"When we lived here," Esther said quietly, "My mother took care of us. My father was always busy. When we started school, he made sure we did our homework. But he wasn't like other fathers, helping us with homework or playing with us. He seemed to have three jobs: working in his grocery store, supervising the building of more and more houses and, at night, working in his Obeah shed.

"He told me he'd been sorry he didn't make more time to get to know us. With the children he has now, he always eats breakfast with the older ones and has dinner with the whole family. I suggested he take even more time with his children. Children should feel close to both parents.

"But, to answer your question, none of us hated him. We just didn't know him very well. And I can't think of any reason why an eight-year-old girl would hate her father enough to return years later and kill him."

"One reason that comes to mind," Hazel said. "It would definitely make an eight-year-old girl angry enough to kill her father. If her father had been sexually abusing her, or if his brothers or friends had been abusing her, she'd have a very good reason to kill him."

Esther looked shocked—too shocked to respond.

"Nothing like that ever happened," she finally said. "I swear. But it's hard to prove a thing didn't happen. Talk to Daddy's new wife. If he was doing horrible things like that, I think he'd keep on doing it. If he isn't abusing his children now, there'd be no reason to think he did it before."

"You're right about that," Hazel said. "Child molesters rarely stop unless they're locked up. But I believe you. I don't think there will be any problem."

"I wouldn't worry if I were you," Rick said. "If you killed your father, you'd be on your way home, not talking to us. We appreciate you telling us what you talked about. It took a good deal of courage and we respect that. How long will you be here? Are you staying for the funeral?"

"I planned to leave tomorrow. Now, since the airlines let you change your ticket for the death of a parent, I plan to stay for the funeral. I haven't made a new reservation but hope I'll be here long enough for you to find the killer."

"Good. We know how to contact you here. Why don't you give us your address, phone numbers and, if you have one, an email address, back in Jamaica? After you go home, if anything comes up and we have a question, we'll know how to contact you. And you need to take my card so you can call me any time, night or day if you need to talk to us."

Esther dug in her purse. "Here's my husband's card." "The home phone number is the same. You can email him at work or send mail to his office."

"Thanks," Rick said, tucking the card into his wallet. "I hope we have the case wrapped up before you leave, but it could be one of those cases that goes on for years."

"Esther, it was so good seeing you," Jeenya said, giving her a hug. "We won't talk to anyone about who you are and why you're here. Enjoy your visit with the Venables."

17

The Boyfriend and the Husband

Rick

"You believe her, don't you?" Jeenya asked.

"I'd really like to," Hazel said, "but I don't think we can rule her out."

"She makes a great suspect," Rick said with a smile, "and we don't have too many good suspects, but I'm inclined to believe her too. She impresses me as a good woman. We need to get going. We have a busy afternoon."

Rick and Hazel walked over to the store. Chester led them back to the office and got coffee and doughnuts to go around. Rick tried to picture Josiah there at the computer, working on inventory lists, doing bookkeeping, or whatever it was he did in his office. Three gray metal file cabinets stood along one wall. Josiah apparently kept good records.

After one bite of the doughnut and a swallow of coffee, Rick began the conversation. "Most people we've talked to so far seem to think people here in Jamaica Lakes wouldn't dare kill the Obeah Man, being scared of his duppy and all."

Chester nodded seriously. "That's true. You wouldn't believe how much salt we sold yesterday. I thought they were through buying salt but, even those who bought salt yesterday, they're coming back for more today. People who never put salt around their house before, they're buying salt now. I had to send a man back to Publix to buy all the salt off their shelves and we're already running low again."

He leaned forward and said very quietly, "Let me tell you why they're so worried. I've heard stories of at least a dozen people who have seen or heard Josiah's duppy. One woman said Josiah actually touched her. She was lying in bed, not quite asleep, and Josiah touched her hair. She said he ran his hand through her hair.

"Then, there were two men who saw him looking through their windows and several people heard him banging on their door, trying to get in. People hear this, they get real scared you know and they're out buying more salt. It's a shame salt is so cheap. If it was expensive, we'd be making some serious money."

"We've also heard," Rick said, "that Josiah had a number of lady friends, a few with angry husbands or boyfriends. You were aware of this, I assume."

Chester nodded slowly.

Rick, observing Chester's face, thought he was surprised for a moment, then nervous. He obviously wanted to know who'd talked but he didn't ask.

"We need you to tell us what you know."

"I, uh, I don't know," Chester said. "I mean I really don't know very much. Mr. Overmon didn't talk to me about things like that."

"Just tell us what you do know."

Slowly and painfully, Chester went through Josiah's history with women in Jamaica Lakes and Sharona's efforts to put a stop to it. "First, I remember was Philip and Rosie Statler. When news got around that Mr. Overmon had been getting it on with Rosie, Philip threw her out of the house. They finally got a divorce. Rosie moved back to Jamaica to live with her mother who was getting older and was happy to have her daughter around. At least that's what people said. Philip died a couple years ago.

"I also heard how Josiah was sleeping with some of the other women here. A couple of those families moved out of the area. Maybe it was because of Josiah, maybe not. It was a long time ago. I don't even remember their names.

"Then, maybe ten years back, there was Elaenia, the pretty young woman who committed suicide. One night, while her husband was sleeping, she walked down by the lake and took who knows how many sleeping pills. Some people blamed Mr. Overmon but Elaenia hadn't seen him in three or four months.

"There are stories like this about maybe a dozen women but, so far as I know, nothing happened the last eight or ten years, not with women in Jamaica Lakes, anyway. I heard that Sharona convinced Mr. Overmon to stick to women from outside our community. Getting Josiah to stop chasing women completely just wasn't going to happen."

"And recently?"

"Right now, I only know of two women he might have been seeing. I haven't seen either of them but I've seen one woman's boyfriend and the other woman's husband. I'm not good with names but I'd recognize the two men.

"The boyfriend is a white guy, probably close to thirty, with greasy, long black hair. I've seen him three or four times, always wearing black jeans, a black T-shirt, a dirty black leather jacket and a shiny black helmet. He has one tooth missing in front, and the others are crooked and kind of yellow. He comes roaring into Jamaica Lakes on his big old Harley, making plenty of noise. I expect he's making sure we know he's here. He parks right out in front of the store. The idiot never gets off that motorcycle of his. Maybe he's scared of us, scared of people with black skin. Maybe he's scared of Mr. Overmon.

"There's no way of knowing. He sits out there on that Harley and screams all the obscenities he knows. He reminds me of an eighth-grade bully I used to know. He says stuff like 'You better leave my f-ing girlfriend alone.'

"The other one, the husband, is tall, built strong and looks like he lifts weights. He's got dark skin but not as dark as mine. His hair is cut so close it almost looks shaved.

"He speaks English all right but with a kind of accent. He could be one of those Hispanics. I understand he drives a truck and he's sometimes gone a week or more at a time. His wife has one of those Spanish sounding names. They might be illegals up from Mexico."

"Do you remember their names?" Rick asked.

"Let me think. I'm pretty sure I heard it. Let me think a minute. Okay, I got it. The husband's name is Hay-sooce or something like that, a crazy name if you ask me. Someone told me it was Spanish for Jesus. Now you tell me. Why would anybody name their kid Jesus? I sure enough wouldn't. I don't remember hearing his wife's name.

"Anyway, this man, Hay-sooce, was here last week, looking for Mr. Overmon. He came in heading straight through the store to the office. Mr. Overmon was standing by the door like he was expecting him. He let the man in the office and shut the door. I heard a lot of shouting and then this Jesus fellow comes out stomping like an angry bull. He didn't look at nobody. He didn't say nothing. He stormed out, jumped in his pickup and left in a big hurry."

"Tell us," Rick said, "what you do remember hearing."

"I stayed out front. I don't like to listen to other people's business, especially Mr. Overmon's business."

"That's good but you still heard part of it, didn't you?"

Chester nodded slowly. "They started out kind of quiet. I didn't hear any of that. When the shouting started, it was hard not to hear. There was a lot of f-ing this and f-ing that. Both of them were talking like that. Then, I'm pretty sure this Jesus said, 'You mess with my wife again and I'll kill you. I'll slit your f-ing throat.' That's all I remember."

"Mr. Gunn," Hazel said. "You had other customers here at the time, didn't you? Can you remember who they were, and where they were standing?"

"I certainly do. I remember them clearly. If I'd been here alone, the story would never have gotten around Jamaica Lakes. I guarantee you nobody would have known a thing about it. I don't talk about things that are not my business.

"But a few of those men working over at the garage, they don't know how to keep their big mouths shut. They never stop talking and, what they don't know for sure, they go ahead and invent, wanting to make the stories more exciting. You can't trust half of what they say.

"Three of them were in here that day, taking their mid-morning break, getting their sodas and doughnuts.

"Elijah's oldest son, Abe, was here when it happened. He saw the man come in, got his soda and a doughnut and left right away. He wouldn't have heard much of anything."

Chester stood and beckoned for them to follow. At the office door, he pointed to the soda machine. "With the other two, though, that's another story.

"George Armstrong was over by the soda machine. He stopped moving to pay close attention, stood with a can of Dr Pepper, holding it up like he was ready to take a swallow. He looked like he was frozen in place.

"His buddy, Victor Hackett, was getting a doughnut. He watched that man go into the office and saw Mr. Overmon shut the door. Then he stepped closer to the door so he wouldn't miss a word.

"It made me furious, seeing them eavesdropping on Mr. Overmon, but what could I do? It's not like eavesdropping is against the law. It's just not polite. There's no telling how many people they told or how much the story changed as it got passed along."

Rick thanked Chester for his help. Once he and Hazel were back in their car, they discussed what they'd heard.

"You heard what I heard, didn't you?" Rick asked.

"Couldn't miss it. This Jesus threatened to slit Josiah's throat. That cannot be a coincidence."

"The problem," Rick said, "is that those men apparently passed the story all over town. Anyone in Jamaica Lakes could have heard the story and they could have slit Josiah's throat, intending to throw suspicion on Jesus."

18

The Revivalists

Rick

The last visit for the day was with Rev. Wolff and his wife. Rick and Hazel walked past the park, turned down Port Royal Street behind the church, and past the Sunday School building to the parsonage. Rick pointed across the street.

"Right across from the parsonage is the cemetery," he said. "Behind the cemetery are some of the fields where Zeke and Jeenya grow vegetables. You can see their house from here.

"Homer once explained how Zeke and Jeenya got more land than anyone else in town. This whole piece of land was set aside for the cemetery. Josiah knew they wouldn't need it for a long time, maybe fifty years or so. He also knew Zeke and Jeenya were growing vegetables and herbs for their own use. So, he told them they could move to the house where they are now if they'd grow the vegetables and herbs he wanted for the store. He always paid them well, of course, but where else would you find callaloo or cerasse?

"By the time the cemetery needs more land, Zeke and Jeenya will be getting pretty old and they won't want so much land."

The parsonage was a pale peach color with dark green trim. Bright purple and red bougainvillea grew along the sides of the house. Rev. Wolff had the door open before they had time to knock. "Please, come in. I just made a pot of fresh coffee. It's Blue Mountain coffee from Jamaica. People around here say it's the best in the world. This is my wife, Gladys, and please call me Herman. I'm only Rev. Wolff on Sunday mornings."

Gladys brought them coffee and generous slices of cake as they settled into the modern-looking living room. Rick studied the pair. Herman was a short man, perhaps five foot five, with a stocky build; Gladys was maybe an inch or two taller and thin. Both wore neat-looking jeans and identical bright green shirts showing a map of Jamaica.

Herman noticed Rick looking at the shirts. "Our son went to Jamaica a few weeks back and brought these back for us. He's coming for dinner tonight so we thought we'd better wear them."

"You have a lovely home," Hazel said. "How long have you and your wife lived in Jamaica Lakes?"

"Nearly ten years now," Herman said. "My brother, Samuel, was the pastor before that. When he passed away, the people called and asked me to take his place. We were serving a small church forty miles outside of Montego Bay. We'd never been to the States, but now we love it here."

Gladys sat down to join them. "We're hoping our son and his family and maybe even one of my sisters will join us here in Jamaica Lakes. They've been talking about it for years."

"So, how can I help?" Herman asked. "I assume this is related to Josiah's murder but I can't think how anything I know would be helpful."

"Why don't you tell us a little about Josiah," Hazel said. "You weren't as close to him as the people we've talked to. You might be a little more objective."

"Well now," Herman began, as if taking a few moments to collect his thoughts. "Josiah was here in Jamaica Lakes many years before we came. He was responsible for building every house in the community and all the stores too. He donated this land for the church and all, and he even helped people in the community build the church.

"Actually, it was Seymour Olson who started the ball rolling, talking to people about needing their own church. People held bake sales, raffles, a street dance, and all sorts of fund raisers. They tell me Josiah gave a very generous donation. He hired a construction company who agreed to take local people on as unskilled workers.

"They built the church first, then the parsonage. Five years later, they added the new building with space for fellowship dinners and Sunday School classes. During the week, the preschool uses the space and the little they pay helps cover most of the expenses, things like water and electricity.

"I'm not a full-time pastor, you know. A little church like this can't afford to pay a full salary. During the week, I drive a school bus and work as custodian for the middle school in Palm City. My wife teaches seventh grade social studies in Stuart.

"I was introduced to Josiah when I came, of course, but he never once came to church. I hear things now and then about people he's helped in various ways. If anyone needed money to buy medicine or to get gas for their car so they could get to work, they always went to see Josiah.

"I've also heard a little about his personal problems,

but my information was at the tail end of the grapevine, as they'd say. I imagine you've already heard most of the same stories."

"I understand," Hazel said with a warm smile. "There is one thing you can help us understand. We know Josiah was an Obeah Man. Zeke and Jeenya gave us a little background on that. They also told us that, in addition to being pastor of the church, you lead Revivalist meetings. This is all new to us. We were hoping you could tell us what that's about and how it's different from what an Obeah Man does. We understand that both come from Jamaica and both have roots in African traditions."

Herman smiled. "You can check with a dozen experts who've studied our history and get a dozen different explanations. Originally, it was the Myal and Obeah traditions. Each group thought they were good and the other group was evil. They put a whole lot of effort into setting spells on the other group and trying to get protection from the other group's spells.

"Back in the 1860s, we had a Great Revival in Jamaica, a lot like the one in the States. All kinds of people were converted and started preaching, doing the best they knew how. A good number worked within established churches. Others started new churches, often mixing African traditions they knew with what they understood of the Christian Revival Movement. So, we're referred to as Revivalists.

"We have a clearing in the woods that's a sacred place to us. We have little colored flags to mark the area. Some would tell you our little flags and our altar table help bring the spirits.

"Our group meets Friday nights from nine to midnight

or sometimes later. We have a rough wooden table and a couple chairs out there. When we meet, we cover the table with a white cloth and I place a Bible in the center. Around the Bible is a circle of candles. People bring all sorts of food and drink and sometimes flowers to add to the table.

"They also bring drums and tambourines. When the drummers begin, the others march around the table singing, and shouting, inviting spirits to enter their bodies. These spirits might be angels or the spirits of those who have died.

"Some of our people can tell you about their spirit and believe they receive the same one each time. Others know only that they were possessed but have no other memories. For all of us, it's a powerful experience tied to our beliefs. It makes our religion real for us."

"That's very helpful," Hazel said. "And the people here in Jamaica Lakes, how do they divide up between people who believe in Obeah, people who believe in your tradition, and people who don't believe in either one?"

"You do ask difficult questions," Herman said. "But you're right to ask. At church on Sunday mornings, we usually have about thirty adults and plenty of children. We often have three or four times that number on Christmas and Easter. We have three services on holidays to fit in all the people who come. Many of these people might not approve of the Revivalist meetings. A few might even be more inclined to side with Josiah's traditions.

"At a normal Revivalist meeting, I'd say I've got about a dozen regulars and another ten or twenty who come once or twice a month. We sometimes even have people we don't see on a Sunday morning.

"It would be harder to count Josiah's people. They don't

hold any kind of service or meeting. Let's start with the Overmon family–there are twenty or twenty-five of them if you count all the brothers, sisters, nieces and nephews plus Dolly's relatives. Then he has people who stop by regularly for teas or herbal baths or good luck charms. Josiah claimed he never did evil spells, but who knows? I'd guess that, beside his family, he has another forty or fifty people that look to him for help from time to time, maybe more.

"About those that wouldn't look to either of us for help, that's a good question. I'd estimate we have about three hundred adults here in Jamaica Lakes. At least half of them would probably claim not to be part of either group. They might come to church occasionally, they might attend church elsewhere here in Palm City, in Stuart, or in one of the nearby towns or they might not go to church at all.

"I suspect that, no matter what group they're part of, that when Josiah was killed, most of the people in Jamaica Lakes sprinkled salt to keep Josiah's duppy away."

Hazel had another question. "You make these groups seem friendly. I had the impression your followers and an Obeah Man's followers hated each other."

Herman nodded. "That was certainly true back in Jamaica, especially in our parents' and grandparents' time. People went to the Obeah Man and paid him well to cast spells, evil spells, on their enemies. They believed these spells could even kill. Others went to the Obeah Man for protection against such spells.

"When the Christian Revivalists began, they promised protection against evil. I remember hearing my grandfather preaching that we should kill Obeah. He wasn't talking about killing the Obeah Man or Obeah Woman or their followers. He meant we should kill their evil practices.

"But, if you're talking about people here in Jamaica Lakes, we often have one brother coming to me, and the other going to Josiah. You have a husband coming here and his wife going to Josiah. Most of us have friends with people of varying beliefs. While I wouldn't say Josiah was a close friend, I had many conversations with him. I'd consider him a good man, a man who did what he could to help the people of Jamaica Lakes. I certainly don't know anyone who'd have a reason to want him dead."

"You said you had about a dozen regulars," Hazel said. "Would you be willing to give us their names?"

"Certainly. We really have no secrets. First, there's Ben and Leona Fletcher. They have three grown sons and one daughter all living here, but only the parents are regular. Then there's Eugene and Vivian Duckworth. Eugene walks with a limp. He always plays the bass drum so he can sit. Next, there's Walter and Vera Cathcart. They've only been here for two or three years, but they're friends of the Duckworths and they joined us the week they moved in. There's also Matthew and Mercy Venable. I'd say this group could be called the leadership team."

Rick was surprised that Rev. Wolff was so open, listing all these names. He watched as Hazel wrote the names in her notebook.

"Then we have Kitty and Bunny. Actually, their names are Kathryn and Benjamina Ferguson, but everyone calls them Kitty and Bunny. Harry and Arlene Butler are usually there. Add these and you have our list of regulars.

"Others don't come often but still see themselves as part of the group. This includes Luke and Tina Bordon, Albert and Linda Walkover. Paul Green comes often but his wife never comes. George Armstrong came all the time when he was single but his wife, Angela, frowns on what we do so George doesn't come as often now. I understand that Victor Hackett used to come regularly, but, since his wife passed away, he comes very rarely. With the Scotts, Rachel comes often. Carl sometimes comes to church with her but never to the Revivalist meetings."

"That's extremely helpful," Hazel said. "Can you tell us who was at your meeting on Friday night?"

"That's a little harder," he said, "but I'll try. Gladys, see if I make any mistakes."

Gladys nodded.

"Let's start with the regulars. The Fletchers, the Duckworths, and the Cathcarts were there with us. Kitty was there, but I don't think Bunny was." He turned to look at his wife."

"Bunny had a tooth pulled that afternoon and decided to go to bed early."

"Oh yes, now I remember. The Butlers and Venables were there, but I can't remember seeing the Bordons."

"Luke came late," Gladys said, "and left early. Tina's mother was visiting."

"I don't think any of the others were there. Can you remember?"

"The only other person I remember was that friend of Mercy Venable who was visiting. I don't remember her name."

"Oh yes, a very nice young woman. She had a good Bible name, a name from the Old Testament."

"You're right," Gladys said, "Esther. Made me think of old Esther Jamison back home. Anyway, Mercy had a headache. She and her friend went home early. Matt stayed 'til the end. That should be everyone."

"We heard that George Armstrong might have been with you," Hazel said. "You're sure he wasn't there?"

"Absolutely sure," Rev. Wolff said. "If George had come, I'd remember. I've been talking to George for weeks inviting him to join us again. He keeps saying he thinks he'll come. I was looking for him Friday night, hoping to see him, but he wasn't there. I spoke to him yesterday. He said Angela hadn't been feeling good so he stayed home with her."

"You've been extremely helpful," Rick said. "We really appreciate your taking all this time to talk to us." He gave Herman a card. "If you hear anything or think of anything else, that might help us in our investigations, please give me a call."

As they walked down the street, Hazel smiled. "I was a bit nervous about meeting him. Maybe it was that sermon, or maybe it was the name. Herman Wolff and his wife weren't anything like I'd expected. They were very nice."

"That's true," Rick agreed. "They seemed to be totally open and honest and actually quite helpful. When we stop by the garage in the morning, we need to have a serious talk with George. He told Angela that he was going to the Revivalist meeting, but he didn't. He told the pastor he was home with Angela, but that wasn't true either. It will be interesting to see what he tells us."

Back at the Birdsong's, Rick got Seth's phone number from Jeenya and gave him a call. "We're going to need to talk to your men again. It shouldn't take long. Sure, we can be there when you open."

As they were heading back to the police station, Rick's cell phone rang. "Yes," he said. "I'm through work for today. I should be able to get there in about thirty minutes. Thanks for calling me."

"It was one of the staff at the nursing home," he told Hazel. My grandmother had a fall. They aren't sure if she broke anything, but she's in an ambulance on her way to the hospital to get checked out."

"Do you want me to come with you?" Hazel asked.

"Thanks, but I'd rather do this alone. No telling how long I'll be there."

That night, as usual, Ida Lee had her say:

"Hey Miz Jeenya. What's taking you so long? I'd tink with you and dose detectives helping, you'd find de killer by now. You spent all morning in church. Then you cooked some of your goat curry. I could smell it. But dose detectives wouldn't appreciate it like I would. You also went showing off your garden. What you need to do is work harder on finding de killer. Maybe dat old owl could give you some help."

19

Asking Questions at the Garage

Rick

Rick and Hazel arrived at the Jamaica Lakes Garage at nine. "How's your grandmother?" Hazel asked.

"Not too bad. I was at the hospital until nearly midnight. They thought she might have broken a hip but the X-rays didn't show any problem there. She broke her arm though, broke it in two places. She'll be in the hospital for a few days at least. They want to make sure she's all right before sending her back to the nursing home."

"Did you talk to her?"

"They let me see her but she was on painkillers and didn't know what was going on. I'll drop by and see her again tonight."

Rick knew it was more than just the pain killers. He had visited his grandmother occasionally and most of the time she had no idea who he was. He'd tell her his name, but five or ten minutes later, she'd have forgotten.

He sometimes asked himself if he was wasting his time but it didn't seem right to stop visiting. With his mother in California, he was the only family his grandmother had left in the area.

At the garage, Seth was waiting for them. "I told the men you were coming so they are all ready to go."

"We learned yesterday," Rick told Seth, "that a few of your men were at the store a week or so ago. They might have overheard a man threatening Josiah. We'd like to ask them about the incident. It shouldn't take long."

Seth nodded. "I wasn't there, but I heard about it. Sounded like that man was extremely angry."

"And, so we don't need to bother you again," Rick said, "we're also trying to find out where everybody was Friday night, let's say between nine and three. We certainly have no reason to suspect any of you, but we do want to know where everyone was."

Seth frowned a little. "That makes sense. You might as well start with me. George and Victor, two of the boys who work here, stayed at the garage late. George is related to Elijah, his wife's nephew, I think. Victor is Dolly's cousin. Everyone here is related to the Overmons in some way.

"Anyway, the boys had some good ideas. They talked about expanding the garage, maybe adding a gas station or a used car lot. George thought it would be nice to have a bike shop to sell new and used bikes and do minor repairs.

"I ate dinner over at the Café. Then I went home and watched television and went to sleep."

"Can you think of anyone in Jamaica Lakes who'd want to see Josiah dead? Anyone with a motive to murder him?"

Seth shook his head. "Maybe the man in the store that day. From what I heard he was furious. People who live here have no reason to hurt Josiah. They might not all have loved him, but they respected him. If not for Josiah, Jamaica Lakes wouldn't even exist. If someone didn't like him, they'd have moved out years ago."

"I understand," Rick said. "Now, if you'd send the men in one at a time in whatever order is convenient."

Art Logan came first. In answer to Rick's question about Jesus, he shook his head. "That day I stopped by the café to see my wife. She works there. I heard the guys talking about it later."

When asked about Friday night, Art had to think. "Emily works late Friday nights. The café stays open until eleven. I had dinner there, watching her work. Emily's a beautiful woman and I enjoy watching her anytime.

"After dinner, I walked over to Seymour's house to play cards with Johnny and Pete Sampson. We left at about ten or ten-thirty. I got to the restaurant in time to have a beer while Emily finished cleaning up. We walked home together. I remember thinking we needed to get street lights. That was one dreadfully black night."

Elijah's three sons came next, starting with Abe. "Yeah. I was in the store when that man came in. I wondered why he was there. He was obviously upset, so I took my soda and a doughnut and left as fast as I could. I don't like being around any kind of trouble. Wish I could be more help."

"Friday night?" Abe continued. "We all had dinner at my parents' place. Mom made fried chicken. I'm not sure what time we left. I'd guess between nine-thirty and ten. The three of us, Josh, Noah and me, we all live on the same street, one next to the other, so we walked home together.

"That was the blackest night I have ever seen. We were feeling our way down the road, wishing we had flashlights. We were joking about how, on that sort of night, duppies would be everywhere. You know about duppies?"

Rick nodded. "They're sort of like ghosts. We might not believe in ghosts, but we still tell ghost stories on a dark night."

"Yeah. It was just like that. Josh started saying a duppy was following us. Don't none of us believe in stuff like that so we were laughing, but we did start walking a little faster. Then Noah asked if anyone brought salt. You know about people using salt to keep duppies away?"

Rick and Hazel nodded.

"We stopped for a few minutes at Josh's house. Our wives and kids were there having their own dinner. Noah and I got our wives and kids and headed home. I don't know about the others," Abe said, "but I was sure happy to get home. I don't like leaving my wife and the kids alone on a night like that."

Josh was next. "Noah and I stayed late at the garage finishing a job so we were late to take our morning break. We got to the store just as that stranger was leaving.

"Looked to me like he was African-American. He seemed strong like a wrestler. I learned later about him threatening Josiah because Josiah, supposedly, had been visiting that man's wife. I sure wouldn't be visiting that man's wife. After Josiah took a good look at that guy, he probably didn't need to hear any threats. Josiah was not stupid. He certainly wouldn't hang out with that man's wife again. He's the only person I can think of who might have wanted to kill Josiah."

Josh agreed with Abe's story of their walk home. "My wife tried getting us to stop talking about duppies. She didn't want us scaring the kids. I suspect she's the one who was scared. The children, seven of them when you put mine and Noah's kids together, were making a lot of noise. They were chasing each other pretending to be duppies, making the younger ones scream and hang onto our legs. It's not easy walking with kids hanging off your legs."

Noah came next. He vaguely remembered seeing the man coming out of the store and hearing the stories later but he couldn't describe him. "I didn't pay much attention."

He described having dinner at their parents' home. "It's nice to have time to sit and talk, time when we aren't working." He retold the story of the walk home with all the children screaming about duppies coming to get them. "Once we got home, we sure 'nough did not want to go back out in the dark. I didn't even want to look out a window."

Victor Hackett was next. "Yes," he said quietly. "I was there. The way he was shouting at Josiah, I was hoping he wasn't carrying a gun or a knife or anything. He sounded mad enough to kill Josiah right there in the office."

"Can you remember anything he said?" Rick asked.

"I certainly can. I was getting a doughnut not far from the office door. I didn't notice when he came in. I was looking for a cinnamon doughnut. But, when the shouting started, I stepped closer to the office door. I was worried about Josiah, you know, hoping he wasn't going to get hurt. I was ready to open the door and barge in if real trouble started. I'm big enough to take care of myself in a fight."

Rick looked at Victor and agreed.

"I'm thinking that man was probably in his late thirties, maybe six foot two or three, and in good shape. He didn't look like the sort of man to lose a fight. I was concerned when I couldn't hear Josiah's voice at first. I don't know if he wasn't saying anything, or if he was speaking softly.

"Anyway, this stranger kept shouting about a woman named Wendy, Wanda or Wanita, something like that. He kept saying 'You stay away from my wife.' We all knew how Josiah had plenty of lady friends over the years so it was easy enough to figure it out. Josiah had visited this man's wife while the man was working.

"What I remember most clearly was right at the end. The stranger said, 'Mr. Overmon, if you dare go near my wife again, I will kill you. I killed plenty of people in Iraq. I'm not afraid to kill one more bastard. I'll slit your throat from ear to ear and let you bleed to death. You understand me?'

"I could finally hear Josiah's voice. 'I understand,' he said. He said it quiet-like and real calm. 'Now, you get out of my store and go back to your wife. The poor woman gets lonely when you're out of town. If she's not entertaining me, I'm sure she has other men she can call.'

"That made the man really lose it. He started screaming, calling Josiah all sorts of filthy names. He walked out of Josiah's office, slammed the door and stormed through the store. I followed him out to see what he was driving. He had an older black Toyota pickup, one of the smaller ones."

Victor stared at Rick. "You thinking what I'm thinking? You thinking that man killed Josiah? I can't believe Josiah would be calling on that man's wife again but you never can tell. Maybe she was with another man and her husband didn't believe her. That's my guess. Nobody here in Jamaica Lakes had any reason to kill Josiah."

Rick asked about Friday night.

Victor frowned. "You thinking one of us killed him?"

"No, not at all. It helps to know where people were so, if

one person remembers seeing or hearing something, we'll know who else might have been nearby. Just like when we knew Chester heard a man threaten Josiah, we learned a few of you were also there and that really helped. You remembered more than anyone else. You've been a real help."

"Yeah. I get it. Friday night, I went to the café. Since my wife passed on, I usually stop after work to get my dinner. I don't like sitting at a table alone, so I get it packed up to take home. I got jerk pork, red beans and rice, and a slice of strawberry pie. I had beer at home. I got home at about six.

"You can ask Miranda and Belinda, the two ladies who live a little way down the street. They were sitting on their front steps when I came by. They're sitting on those steps nearly every time I go by. I swear, if you ever want to know who went down that street, those two ladies would know. They don't even have a TV. All they ever do is sit out on their front steps or sit inside, looking out windows. It's like Jamaica Lakes is their own private soap opera.

"I ate my dinner, watched TV and went to bed."

George Armstrong was last. "Yes, sir. I was in the store along with Victor. I was trying to decide which soda to buy, thinking about a diet soda. My wife is always telling me how I should eat healthy food. I'd just changed my mind and got a Dr Pepper."

"So, if you were in back," Rick said, "you could hear what they were saying, at least part of it."

"Yeah. I missed the first part. I only know it was loud. This man started screaming at Josiah. If Josiah said anything, I couldn't hear him. At first, I was shocked. Then I got to feeling worried, hoping this lunatic didn't have a gun, hoping he wasn't going to shoot Josiah first and then come out shooting everyone else in the store.

"I backed off a little, moving closer to the men's room, so I'd have somewhere to hide. The only thing I remember was that man telling Josiah to stay away from his wife and how, if Josiah saw her again, this man would kill him. He said he had a knife and would cut Josiah's throat and leave him bleeding, something like that. I backed off when I heard that. You know, that man coulda come back Friday night when it was so dark and all. He coulda killed Josiah, but I didn't like to say anything in case I was wrong.

"Friday night? I think I got home a little before six-thirty. I was with my wife, Angela, the whole night. I couldn't see any reason to go out on a night like that."

"Really?" Rick asked. "You and Angela were home together all that night?"

George nodded his head vigorously.

"That's not what we heard, George. We heard you went out," Rick said in his most serious tone. "We need you to be honest, George. Where did you really go Friday night?"

"Oh, you're talking about Friday night," George said, sounding a little shaky. "I must have been thinking about Thursday night. We were home together on Thursday night."

"And on Friday night?"

"Friday night? There's this church group I'm part of, what we call Revivalists. We get together Friday nights."

"Are you telling us you were back in the woods with Rev. Wolff and the Revivalists on Friday night?"

"Yes, sir. That's where I was. Angela can tell you that's where I went."

"What about Rev. Wolff? Would he tell us you were there, George? Be careful now. We don't appreciate having people lie to us, especially not twice in a row."

George was shaking harder. "Yes, sir, I mean no, sir. You already talked to Rev. Wolff? He told you I wasn't there?"

Rick didn't respond.

"Okay. I'll try not to lie to you. I'll tell you the honest truth. That's where I was planning to go, you see. Out to that Revivalist meeting in the woods. That's what I told Angela. Have you been talking to Angela? But what really happened was this. I walked past the house of this other woman I know. She was on her porch and asked me to come in for a few minutes. Her boyfriend dumped her and she needed a friend to talk to.

"Please don't say anything to Angela or anybody else. Angela will think I intended to go see this woman, that we had something going on, and that's not true."

"I can see the problem," Rick said. "But you lied to us twice, how are we to know this story is true? Can you give us this woman's name? Would she tell the same story?"

"No," George said firmly. "I cannot give you her name. You'd go see her and stories would get started." He looked at Rick. "Well, maybe. I need to ask her first if she's willing to talk to you. You could meet her somewhere else."

"Now George, what are we going to think? I can picture you talking to her. You might tell this woman what to say. If you talk to her first, it isn't much of an alibi."

"I'm sorry," George said, "but this is God's truth. I can't say anymore."

Rick handed George a card. "When you're ready to tell us the truth, the whole truth, give me a call."

Rick and Hazel got back into the car before saying anything. "What do you think?" Hazel asked. "George lied to his wife about Friday night, he lied about Herman

Wolff, and he lied to us. He was nervous about something."

"That's true," Rick said. "But the fact that he's lying doesn't mean he killed Josiah. Maybe this wasn't a woman needing to talk to someone. If they're having an affair, I'd understand him not wanting to give us her name.

"George is a wimp. I can't picture him killing someone and cutting his throat and all. I can't imagine George killing Josiah because his wife was sneaking out to get herbal tea. We need a suspect with a serious motive for murder."

20

The Wife and the Girlfriend

Rick

Rick got a phone call asking them to stop by the police station. It took less ten minutes to get there. "We got that information you wanted," Nate said. "We found addresses and phone numbers for both women. Then we checked Josiah's cell phone record. He sure enough had something going on with both of them. Nearly every day, Josiah called one or the other of those women or they called him."

"What about priors?"

"Nothing on Juanita Juarez. With Suzy Cornblatt, we've got a couple drunk driving reports, both barely over the limit and once, about five years ago, she was picked up for prostitution. After talking to her, the arresting officer decided it was a mistake and let her go. Never happened again.

"Now, about the men," Nate continued, "that's something different. Clancy Cottonwood has been arrested for drunk and disorderly seven times in the last two years but never anything violent.

"The other man, Jesus Juarez, he's got twenty-three arrests for drunk and disorderly over the past two years. Four of those times he beat up another man, putting him in the hospital with broken bones and you might guess why. Each time Jesus claimed these men were messing with his wife. The last time he did six months in jail."

Hazel wrote down the information. "So far," she said, "Juanita's husband, Jesus, is the best suspect and Suzy's loud-mouthed boyfriend looks like the next best. We'll visit both of them today."

Juanita Juarez lived out on the Indiantown Road. She looked suspiciously at Rick and Hazel when she answered her door. "Police?" she asked. "Nothing wrong with Jesus, is there?"

"No," Hazel said gently. "Not that we know about. We're here to ask about Josiah Overmon."

Juanita frowned. "What about Mr. Overmon?"

"Can we come in?" Hazel asked. "It's important."

Juanita Juarez was about thirty-five or forty with shiny black hair pulled back into a ponytail. Her jeans were well worn, but her rose-colored cotton blouse was neatly ironed.

"You don't know what happened to Mr. Overmon?" Hazel asked.

Juanita shook her head and frowned. "What happen you talking about?"

"Josiah Overmon is dead, Juanita. He died Friday night."

"Dead?" Juanita's eyes were wide. "No. Not Josiah. How? An accident? His heart?"

"He was murdered."

Juanita began to cry. "Is my fault? Did Jesus kill Mr.

Overmon? Jesus say he will kill him, but I don't believe him."

"We aren't sure who killed him. That's why we're talking to everyone who might know something."

"How he was killed? Somebody cut his throat?"

"Yes. His throat was cut. We know about the threats that Jesus made that day, but other people heard him too. The story is all over the neighborhood. It's possible someone else killed him that way to put the blame on your husband."

Juanita began to cry harder. She shook her head. "No. Not Jesus. Jesus gets in fights but Jesus not a killer."

"Could you tell us about how you met Mr. Overmon?"

Juanita wiped her eyes and tried to smile. "Last summer, Jesus and me, we had bad fights. He hit me hard. Then he goes away on his truck. I feel lonely and sad. I go to a little restaurant. I order a drink, rum and Coke.

"Mr. Overmon comes in. He sits next to me. He very nice-looking man. He tells me, 'Is never good for a lady to drink alone.' He is polite, very nice. He buys me one more drink. Then he buys me dinner. I tell him about Jesus. He is good listener. We have dinner again next night. He gives me his phone number. Tells me call if I need to talk.

"I don't call for three weeks. Then Jesus hurts me more. I called Mr. Overmon. After we eat, I tell him he come to my house. I say Josiah sounds like a name in the Bible. He tells me I'm right. Then he tells me about Josiah in Bible. "His father was king I never knew about. When that Josiah was a little boy, his father is murdered.

"Then, young Josiah is king. He is only seven or eight years old. He was good man. But men came. They had a big fight, and killed King Josiah. They murdered him."

Juanita was quiet for a time. "Is strange, I think. Mr. Overmon wanted to be a good man like the king. Now, just like King Josiah in the Bible, Mr. Overmon is murdered. I am very sad. Mr. Overmon was very nice man."

"When was the last time you saw or spoke to Mr. Overmon?" Hazel asked.

"Maybe two weeks? Mr. Overmon and me, we fall in love, you know. He really liked making love with me.

"Jesus, he tells me he's going in his truck for a week. But it takes a long time in West Palm Beach to put all the boxes on the truck. Jesus listens to the radio. The radio says it will be cold up north where Jesus will go. Jesus comes back to get coat and warm clothes.

"Most times, Jesus calls when he's coming back. He tells me this time he wanted to surprise me. I don't believe it. I think he wants to see who is here with me.

"We hear the truck, Josiah and me. Josiah gets his clothes on very fast. He says he can't hide. His car is in the driveway. He tells Jesus he writes stories for the newspaper. He talks to me for a story about people who worked in tomato fields before and now they don't.

"Jesus laughs. Not a nice laugh. He asks what newspaper. He says, 'Show me the card with your picture.'"

"Josiah doesn't say anything. He just goes out to his car. Jesus talks very loud. Very angry. He tells Mr. Overmon he never come back. Then Jesus goes back in the house. He tells me to get him a beer.

"Jesus says if I talk to Mr. Overmon again, he will kill him. He makes me tell him Josiah's name and where he works and where he lives. I don't know where Josiah lives. Next day, when Jesus goes away in his truck, I call Josiah. I warn him. He says to me 'don't worry. It will be all right.'

"Jesus goes to Josiah's store, tells Josiah not talk to me. says he has sharp knife and will cut Josiah on the neck.

"The next day, I call Josiah again and we talk. He says it is good if we do not get together for a long time, maybe a month."

"Mrs. Juarez," Rick said. "Can you tell me where you and your husband were Friday night?"

"Friday afternoon, I go to the library. I check out books for children so I practice how to read in English. Then I go to my mother's house. We eat dinner together. I don't think Jesus come home that day. He comes Saturday, he said.

"But he came home Friday night. He tells me later he was back at nine. He looked for me and I wasn't here.

"I come home at ten-thirty. I don't know about Jesus coming home because he goes away again in his truck looking for me. He comes home real late, after two in the morning. He is mad at me for not being home. He says bad things about Josiah. Jesus is very drunk.

"He says he looked everywhere for my car. He drives his truck to the place where Josiah worked. He tells me he drove up and down every street there, looking for my car. He looks at my friend's house. He looks at my sister's house. Then he checked all the bars where I sometimes go. Then he stops in one bar, he says it was the one down the road toward Stuart, and he gets drunk. He says they made him go home because it was time to close the bar."

"I tell him I don't leave note because I think he's not coming home that day. I think he's here to see if Mr. Overmon is here."

"Jesus may be a lucky man," Rick said. "If the bartender can remember when Jesus came in and when he left, he might have an alibi. Where is Jesus now?"

"Driving his truck again. In Kentucky first, then maybe Tennessee. He says he be back in five or six days."

Their next stop was Suzy Cornblatt's trailer. After Sharona's description, Rick was expecting one of the trashy trailer parks, but this was one of the nicer ones in the area. He guessed Suzy was close to forty, maybe forty-five. She did have long blond hair, but it was clean and curled above her shoulders. She wore a touch of pink lipstick and green eye shadow but it wasn't overdone as Sharona had described it. Her eyes were red.

Hazel introduced herself and Rick. Suzy invited them to come inside. "You're here about Josiah?" she asked.

"Yes, you knew he was dead?" Hazel asked.

"I heard about it this morning from one of my neighbors. I don't get the newspaper, myself. I only watch news on television. But I do enjoy those Sudoku puzzles, so my neighbor passes her paper along to me.

"I saw the article yesterday about a man out in Jamaica Lakes being murdered but it didn't give his name. I went back this morning to my neighbor's house and got today's paper. Today, they gave his name. It said he was murdered Friday night. I've been crying off and on all day. You don't think Clancy did it, do you?"

"Tell us about Clancy," Hazel said. "Is there any reason to think he might have done it?"

"Clancy has a big mouth. Everyone says that. He likes to ride around on his motorcycle, giving people a hard time. He's been out there where Josiah lives, shouting at Josiah. I hate it when he does stuff like that.

"Most of the time Clancy's nice enough. He takes me out to dinner a couple times a week. He buys me nice presents. He gives me money for groceries and, once in a while, he helps with the rent. Clancy likes to brag about me being his girlfriend, but it's not like we'd ever get married. I don't think he'd ever dream of asking but, if he did, I'd tell him no thanks.

"I work part-time at a nursing home, taking over when one of the regulars is out sick or away on vacation. I keep hoping they'll take me on full-time. Then I won't need Clancy's help paying my bills. There aren't many jobs you can get without a high school diploma. I'm trying to get my GED but it's awful hard work. I dropped out when I was sixteen and never did learn how to read too well.

"What can you tell us about Friday night?" Hazel asked.

"Friday night?" Suzy frowned. "Friday night? Thursday night Clancy and me went to the movies. We saw one of those vampire movies. He didn't like it but I did.

"But Friday? Oh, I know. One of Clancy's friends, a man who works at the motorcycle shop was celebrating his birthday. He had a big party in his backyard, a nice house out in Jensen Beach. He cooked hot dogs and hamburgers on his grill and his wife fixed potato salad.

"Clancy and me, we stopped at the grocery store and got him one of those fancy Happy Birthday cakes. A couple of the other men got together and bought a whole cooler full of beer and a couple Cokes for me. I hate beer. I like a nice glass of white wine with dinner but I can't stand beer."

"What time did you leave the party?"

"I don't think we left until after two a.m. It's a good thing I wasn't drinking. Clancy and two of his buddies were way too drunk to be driving. We got them all in my car. It took a while to drop them off at their houses. It was after three, maybe closer to three-thirty, when Clancy and

I got home. And let me tell you, it wasn't easy getting him into bed. He sure enough didn't go anywhere else that night. I have only the one bed. I'd know if he left."

Suzy hunted around and found the name and phone number for the man who had the birthday party in case they wanted to check it out.

Rick dropped Hazel off at home and then stopped at the hospital again. His grandmother was still on painkillers. "Grandma? You remember me, don't you? I'm your grandson. I'm Ricardo Montoya. You always called me Ricky."

She looked at him but didn't seem to recognize him. Then she rolled over and faced the wall. Rick gave his card to the nurse and asked that they call him if there was any change.

He called Jeenya and drove back out to Jamaica Lakes. The Birdsongs had asked him to come back for dinner.

21
Playing Detective

Jeenya

That evening Rick, Zeke and Jeenya watched the sun go down. "How are you doing?" Jeenya asked. "Are you any closer to finding the person who killed Josiah?"

"We had two good suspects," Rick said. "The boyfriend on the motorcycle and the husband, but both have alibis."

Jeenya frowned and sipped her lemonade. "I was hoping you could find the killer somewhere else," she said quietly. "Hoping you could prove one of those men killed Josiah. But now I have a feeling neither of them did it.

"I'm beginning to think someone here in Jamaica Lakes killed Josiah. I hope I'm wrong but, when we start pushing people here and their secrets start coming to light, it is not going to be pretty."

Zeke stared at his wife. "Exactly what do you mean, my dear, when you say *we*?"

"Now wait a minute, Jeenya," Rick said. "You aren't thinking about playing detective, are you?"

"I'm trying my best to stay out of this," Jeenya said. "I really am. I'm amazed at what a great job you've done so far. As long as it looked like one of those two men was guilty, I felt confident you'd catch him. But, if you need to take a closer look at the fine people of Jamaica Lakes, you might need a little help. That's all I'm saying. People here are going to be hesitant about saying anything at all to you. I might be able to help out a little."

"I'd rather you didn't," Rick said. "If there's a killer in the neighborhood and they hear you're asking questions, especially if you're talking to people who might have seen something, you'd be putting yourself in danger."

"Rick's right, you know," Zeke said. "We should leave this to the police. We don't know who might have killed Josiah but, when a person kills once, he might go on and kill again. Every time you talk to somebody, I'd be worrying that you could be talking to the killer himself and that you wouldn't have any idea it was dangerous."

"Now, Zeke," she said. "I'll be real careful. Most killers, especially those who'd cut somebody's throat like that, they're men. Isn't that true, Rick?"

Rick nodded. "Not always, but most of the time. Women are more likely to use poison, and lately a fair number have started using guns, especially when their husband has a gun around the house. But it is unusual for a woman to use a knife."

"All right, then. If I mainly talk to women, I shouldn't have much trouble. I have no intention of asking police-type questions, you understand, nothing that should make anyone the least bit suspicious.

"I'm going to visit a few friends I've been meaning to talk to. They'll all be eager to share the latest gossip. I shouldn't have to ask any questions at all. They're all talking about it anyway. I can sit quietly and listen. I am a good listener. I might learn something interesting."

"And, when you do," Zeke said, "I trust you won't go

talking to other people about it. You'll tell me and we'll call Rick. Right?"

"That's exactly what I'm planning to do. And you could do a little of the same, Zeke. Why don't you go down and get your hair cut? Those girls in the beauty shop are always talking a mile a minute about the latest scandal. And then, you might take the car to the garage. It's been making that annoying rattle for a couple months now. It's time to get the men to check it out. And you could stop and pick up a few things for me at Josiah's grocery. People are in and out of there all the time."

Zeke smiled. "And where will you be going, my dear?"

Jeenya had to think fast. She hadn't planned this far ahead. "I'll put together a new mixture of herbs for tea, make up a dozen or so samples and deliver them to the women who usually buy my tea. Most will ask me in. They'll be eager to talk about what they've heard. Even if I tried, I couldn't stop them."

Rick smiled. "You two are wonderful. I feel honored that you'd be willing to do this to help us. Jeenya's plan sounds safe enough. Let me suggest one thing. I don't think you'll have any problems or I'd tell you not to do it. To be on the safe side though, I want you to make sure the other person knows exactly where you plan to go. Make a schedule. If you do anything not on the schedule, call your home phone and leave a message.

"Zeke, if Jeenya doesn't get home on schedule and hasn't called to tell you about a change, call the people she was planning to visit and see if they know where she is. If they don't know, call me right away. And Jeenya, you do the same for Zeke. That way you won't worry about each other and I won't have to worry about either of you."

Zeke and Jeenya agreed. As Rick left, Jeenya started putting together her new tea. She used lemongrass, fennel, twice the usual amount of mint and a little rosemary. Then she added a handful of calendula petals and a pinch of freshly grated pimento.

She smiled as she worked. Her plan was really coming together. Rick and Zeke weren't worried about her listening to the latest gossip. She hoped she could learn something helpful this way without getting any further involved in Rick's investigation. But if she needed to…? Well, that question didn't need to be answered right away.

Jeenya gave Zeke a sheet of paper and asked him to write out their schedules. She wondered if Zeke had any idea that she might go a little further than simply listening to gossip. As she mixed the tea, she told him where she was planning to go.

Rick

Rick was almost home when his cell phone rang. "Great," he said. "Thanks for calling. I'm on the road and I'll be there in twenty minutes."

He parked behind the hospital and went up in the elevator to his grandmother's floor. He spoke to one of the nurses and then went to her room. "Hi, Grandma. It's me, Ricky."

The old woman stared at him. "I don't know you. That nurse said my grandson was coming."

"I am your grandson. I'm Ricky, Ricky Montoya."

"You're not my Ricky. My Ricky is a cute little boy. And you can't be his father. Ricky's father is dead. And where's Alice? My daughter, Alice, where is she? You need to tell her I'm in the hospital. I can't remember what happened.

I must have broken my arm. Do you think somebody hit me? Maybe it was that strange man who was in here last night. Or maybe it was the night before. But that was you, wasn't it? Did you hit me? Did you break my arm? And where is Alice?"

"Grandma, I know it's confusing, especially when they give you pain medicine, but listen. When I was a little boy, I used to visit you and Grandpa. I remember one time, for my sixth birthday, the two of you took me to the zoo in West Palm Beach. Do you remember?"

She frowned, then nodded slightly.

"I saw my first flamingos at the zoo that day. Do you remember what I asked you?"

Her frown deepened, like she was trying to remember.

"You asked me…" she said. "I don't remember…"

"I couldn't believe there really were pink birds. So, I asked…"

"I remember," she said. "You wanted to know who painted them, who painted them pink. I do remember. Grandpa was with us. Where is that man? He should be here with me." She started to cry.

"Grandpa would be here if he could," Rick said. "But seven years ago, he had a heart attack. Do you remember that? They took him away in the ambulance."

She nodded. "Ambulance. Flashing lights."

"But it was too late. Grandpa died before they got to the hospital. After that I used to come get you and take you in my car. We'd go to the cemetery, just the two of us. We put flowers on Grandpa's grave. One year, for Valentine's Day, we put red roses on his grave. Do you remember?"

She nodded again. "Red roses. I kept a rose. Took it home with me. But where's Alice? Why isn't she here?"

"Alice is my mother. She was lonely after my father died, so she got married again. She and her new husband moved all the way to California. Would you like to talk to her on the phone?" Rick called his mother's number and explained what happened. He handed the phone to his grandmother and watched as she listened, tears dripping down her face.

Then his grandmother gave him the phone. Rick talked to his mother for a minute and promised to keep her updated.

"If Grandma is likely to die," Rick's mother said, "then I'd come back for at least a day or two. Otherwise, Rick, there isn't much point, is there? Mom might remember me for a few minutes, but five minutes later she'd ask who I was. If she was in her right mind, I'd try to come see her. But now, what's the use?"

His grandmother stared at Rick. "I forget. Who did you say you are?"

"I'm your grandson, Ricky Montoya. I'm not a little boy anymore. I'm all grown up. I'm a policeman now."

Back in Jamaica Lakes, Ida Lee sat by her window.

"Heh there, Miz Jeenya Birdsong. If you so smart, how come you can't tell who killed him, who killed your good friend, the Obeah Man? Why don't you ask your owl? Owls supposed to be so wise. I 'spect he might even have flown by the Obeah shed right when it happened. If you really be some sort of spiritual advisor, why the killer not coming to see you for some of your spiritual advising? Or maybe he did come. Maybe you just aren't telling anybody 'bout it."

22

Why is She NOT Surprised?

Rick

Rick met Hazel at the police station the next morning. They sat down with the lieutenant and reported on what they had learned so far.

"We seem to be at a dead end," Rick said. "The two men who were mad at Josiah because he'd been sleeping with their wife or girlfriend, both of them seem to have decent alibis. Josiah might have been seeing other women but, if so, no one seems to know about it. Josiah's sister was upfront about these two. That leaves us without a way to track down anyone else."

"I have one thing for you," Nate said. "You asked Larry Tipper and Harvey Markwell to check around for you. They took those photos and went from bar to bar. Must have been an interesting assignment. Anyway, they finally found seven bars where a bartender recognized Josiah. I guess he's been making the rounds. And at all of them, they learned that Josiah liked finding a woman to talk to, sometimes leaving with her. But none of them had seen him in over a month.

"Finally, down in Salerno, they got lucky. The bartender there recognized Josiah. He'd seen Josiah a number of times in the past month, usually early in the afternoon, drinking or eating with women.

"He even knew the man's name. The bartender said last Friday, Mr. Overmon was there from about two 'til a little after four. The bartender said Mr. Overmon tried picking up three different women. They each let him buy them a drink. But then the women left—alone. He says Mr. Overmon said, 'Some days are better than others, aren't they? Today just wasn't my day.'"

"That answers the question of where he went before stopping to buy produce at Mr. Buckles' farm stand," Hazel said. What about the forensic people? Did they turn up anything interesting?" Hazel asked.

"They found plenty of fingerprints in your man's work shed," Nate said. "But we didn't find any prints with blood, nothing putting anyone there late that night. And most of the people in town seem to have gone into that shed from time to time.

"The medical examiner says it's hard to tell about the knife. He couldn't find any good distinguishing marks. He says it was sharp enough, but you can find sharp knives in most kitchens. And finding an old phone cord is pretty nearly impossible. And, unless it had blood on it, you'd have trouble proving it was used to kill this man. So, what are you planning to do next?"

"Has the body been released to the family yet?" Hazel asked. "We might go to the funeral, see who's there and how they're behaving."

Nate picked up a phone and made a call. "The medical examiner says he didn't find anything else suspicious.

He kept samples of blood and tissues that he sent to the lab for testing including drug testing, but he released the body this morning. It's going to the Twin Palms Funeral Home. The funeral is scheduled for Monday next week. Apparently, it's a Jamaican custom to hold the funeral nine days after a person dies. I agree. You two should plan to attend. What else can we do?"

"We could go through his bank records," Hazel said. "I've already requested them. We can see if there's any unexplained money coming in or going out."

"Good idea." Nate nodded. "What else? Come on, you two. Think. What would you look at in other murders you've worked?"

"We could run everyone in Jamaica Lakes through the computer and see if they have a record." Rick suggested.

"What else?" Nate prodded. "Come on. Everyone in that whole neighborhood comes from Jamaica. What does that tell you?"

"Drugs? You're talking about drugs, aren't you," Rick said. "Especially marijuana. It could involve other drugs. I don't know why I didn't think of it. This man sold herbs in the evening. Along with his herbal teas, he could have been selling marijuana and who knows what else. Good thinking. We were so focused on the sex angle, especially when we found out about the genital cutting, that we ignored the obvious. We'll get right on it."

Rick and Hazel sat down and planned their day. Dolly wouldn't be likely to know anything. They would talk to Sharona first. She was helpful, telling them about Josiah's womanizing but she might be reluctant to talk about her brother selling or using drugs. They were almost ready to leave when Rick's cell phone rang.

"That was Jeenya," he told Hazel. "She says they're waiting on us for breakfast."

As the four of them ate, they discussed their plans for the morning. "We'll meet you back here for lunch," Rick told Jeenya. "Hazel and I are eager to see what you two gossips can learn today."

As planned, they started with Sharona. They knocked on her door. "You're asking the questions," Rick said to Hazel. "I'm observing."

"Good morning," Hazel said when Sharona appeared. "We were hoping to catch you before you started work. Is this a good time or should we come back later?"

"As good as any," Sharona said. She led the way and took the largest chair in her small living room. Hazel sniffed, recognizing the strong odor of herbs. Half a dozen boxes lay open and a small table was covered with the familiar plastic bags for tea. "I found these herbs in the storeroom at the grocery. I'm putting together what I can. Then I'll write up a list for Jeenya. So, tell me, have you two figured out which of those jerks killed Josiah?"

"Yesterday," Hazel began, "we had a good talk with each of the women. We haven't talked to the men yet, but we have information from the women about where they were. Clarence has a strong alibi. He and Suzy went to a birthday party in a friend's backyard. Clancy got so drunk Suzy had to help him into the house. They have all sorts of witnesses.

"With Jesus, we aren't so sure. Apparently, he was driving around Jamaica Lakes early in the evening looking for his wife. Later, he supposedly was at a bar. The bartender on duty that night is out of town for a while. Jesus, himself, is in Kentucky for the next week or so."

Sharona nodded. "So, what's up today? More of your nasty personal questions?"

"Not too many," Hazel said. "We have one line of questioning we never got around to. What can you tell us about Josiah and drugs? Was he using any drugs? Was he selling anything?"

Sharona glared at Hazel. "Now why am I not surprised? You have a black man who was murdered, a Jamaican man, and you come to the conclusion it's a drug deal gone wrong. If Josiah was an important white man, you wouldn't come asking this sort of question without any evidence, would you?" Her voice was cold.

"But I'll give you your answer. It's simple. Back in Jamaica, Josiah smoked a little ganja, pot, weed… whatever you want to call it. A lot of people did. When we moved to the States, we were warned that it was illegal here, that we could get arrested just for having a little in our pocket.

"Josiah, the ambitious businessman, decided he'd never touch the stuff again, and certainly nothing stronger. He didn't want any sort of criminal record. I really doubt that you'll find anything more than parking tickets and possibly a speeding ticket in his record.

"The answer is no, absolutely not. Josiah was not using any illegal drugs. He rarely used legal drugs like aspirin or Tylenol. He certainly never sold any drugs. This murder, detectives, is definitely NOT about drugs."

"What about drug use in Jamaica Lakes?" Hazel asked. "I imagine, like in most neighborhoods, you have a couple dealers around."

"You strike out again," Sharona said. "I never heard of anybody in the area selling drugs. A couple Rastafarian families live way out back. I expect they smoke a little ganja now and then, but I never heard they were selling it. I've never even seen any of them smoking in public.

"You're on the wrong track, Detectives. I imagine your medical examiner is testing Josiah for drugs. You don't have to believe me. Believe him."

"Thanks. We appreciate your cooperation," Hazel said, getting to her feet.

"Cooperation?" Rick asked once they left the house. "I guess it was cooperation of a sort, but not cheerfully given. We'd better check with Zeke and Jeenya before we upset anyone else with drug questions."

"Where now?" Hazel asked.

"I was expecting we could spend the whole morning tracking down an assortment of people using drugs. Let's see if we can tie up a couple other loose ends. It's probably a waste of time, but let's go meet Collette Cooper and see if we can talk to her father."

Jeenya

Meanwhile, Zeke and Jeenya began their first day of investigating. They had originally planned to start with breakfast at the café, but now decided a midmorning coffee break would do as well.

Jeenya delivered samples of her new tea to Lorraine Feeney, Elsie Clutz and Zelda Dimmick while Zeke went for a haircut. They met at ten, ordered coffee and lemon pie, and quietly observed the people coming in and going out of the café. While investigating this way was easy, they didn't hear anything but the usual gossip.

Loretta Gunn, Chester's wife, came over to chat with them. "Haven't seen the two of you here in ages. What's the occasion?"

"I was thinking about your lemon pie this morning," Jeenya said. "Thinking about it made me hungry for some. That's one thing I never make myself."

"We hear that those detectives have been visiting you. Chester was one of the first people they talked to, after Mrs. Overmon, of course. So, do they have any good suspects? We're all guessing it was that crazy man who went into the grocery store last week, threatening to cut Josiah's throat."

"We actually have no idea," Zeke said. "Rick and his partner don't talk much about their work. They asked us a couple questions, trying to understand what an Obeah Man was. They'd never heard of duppies, of course, and they were wondering why everyone was buying salt. It's hard for them, working in a community with different traditions."

"That's true," Loretta said. "Chester said they were asking him about the salt. He had a good laugh about that. The woman detective thought everyone here was cooking up some pretty salty food."

"Do you know when the funeral will be?" Jeenya asked.

"I assume it will be on the ninth day," Loretta said. "The Overmon family keeps to tradition. Haven't heard anything official."

"Like you were saying," Jeenya said, "most people think the murderer was the man who threatened Josiah in the store, either him or that idiot on his big motorcycle. Have you heard anyone else suggested as a possibility?"

Loretta shook her head. "Everyone I've talked to says it can't be anyone in Jamaica Lakes. People here would be too scared of Josiah's duppy. It's not just because Josiah was the Obeah Man, you know. It's because Sharona is an

Obeah Woman and, from what I've heard…" Loretta now spoke softly, "Sharona's a whole lot more powerful than her brother ever was. I hear she's doing spells every night, making Josiah's duppy stronger and sending it out to kill the person who did this.

"You ought to hear what else people are saying. Only this morning, I've heard people talking about at least three or four people who insist they've seen or heard Josiah's duppy, usually in the middle of the night. I'd love to know who they are, but nobody seems to know."

"If I hear anything, I'll certainly let you know," Jeenya said.

"So how was your morning?" Zeke asked once Loretta left."

"Pretty useless. I had nice conversations with the three women I visited. They're all eager to try my new tea, but none of them had new information about Josiah. Loretta's story was the most interesting of the morning, but it's not especially useful. What about you?"

"You'll love this story," Zeke said. "I don't know what to make of it. I was in the beauty shop with Geraldine trimming my hair. She asked many of the same questions Loretta asked. Everybody wants to know what Rick and Hazel have found out and who's on the suspect list. I'm playing dumb as usual.

"Anyway, I heard Maggie talking while she worked on Kitty Ferguson. Maggie was describing the last time she cut Josiah's hair. Vivian Duckworth was getting her hair cut at the same time. When Josiah left, Vivian jumped up and dropped her keys right where Josiah's hair lay on the floor. When she picked up her keys, Vivian picked up a fistful of Josiah's hair along with the keys and shoved it in her pocket."

"Josiah's hair?" Jeenya asked. "Now that is interesting. What did the others have to say?"

"Kitty giggled. She said that maybe Vivian had a crush on Josiah. Maybe she wanted the hair to do a spell that would make him attracted to her."

"Vivian Duckworth? I have a hard time believing that. She's not the type to be doing spells or fantasizing about men."

"Maggie laughed at the idea too and moved on to other gossip."

"You know," Jeenya said, "there is only one use I know of for hair clippings but it doesn't make sense. An Obeah Man uses them for his spells, sometimes to make a person love someone, or sometimes to cast an evil spell that might make someone sick or even kill him. But that makes no sense. Vivian is a Revivalist. She would never use Obeah spells."

After they finished their lemon pie, Zeke took the car to the garage and Jeenya visited the boutique. She thought about getting a haircut, but it really would be suspicious if she and Zeke got haircuts on the same day.

"I have a friend," Jeenya told Sarah. "Her daughter had a baby, and I thought I'd see if you have anything I could send as a baby gift."

Sarah directed her to the appropriate area and left her to look through outfits for little girls. They were so cute that Jeenya wished she really did have a friend with a baby girl. Maybe one of these days, Rick would get married and have a little girl. Jeenya finally gave up. She thanked Sarah, saying, "I can't decide. I'd better ask the mother what she still needs."

She went home and filled her purse with more samples of her newest tea mixture. As she worked, she thought about her efforts to help Rick.

The one time she really could have helped was at the beginning, the first time she talked to Rick and Hazel. She should have told them right away about Josiah and his women. She could even have told them about the two men who'd been threatening Josiah recently. She didn't remember their names, but it would have given Rick and Hazel something to work on. She still wasn't sure how they found out.

In the beginning, she really had believed that, because she knew these people so well, that she could be helpful, but now she had missed her chance. Now, what she and Zeke were doing was like playing games. It wasn't likely to be of any help at all.

Maybe her idea of helping Rick was just wishful thinking. She had always thought it would be exciting to be a detective. She remembered reading Nancy Drew books when she was a girl and thinking that if that girl could be a detective, then she could do it too.

Now seeing that Hazel was a woman and a detective, her childhood dreams had emerged again. She was certainly as smart as Hazel but she had no idea how to start. Maybe she was just a foolish old woman. Maybe she should leave the detecting to Rick and Hazel. It was nearly noon when she began to fix lunch.

23

Collette Cooper and her Father

Jeenya

Jeenya was running late and decided to fix sandwiches for lunch. She added tomatoes and onions to the left-over fish soup. Soup was always good with sandwiches.

"So how was your day?" Zeke asked Rick as they sat down for lunch. "Learn anything?"

"No. We made fools of ourselves, but the questions had to be asked. We went to see Sharona and probably should have talked to you first."

"About what?" Zeke asked.

"Our lieutenant suggested the murder might have been drug related. Sharona was clearly insulted when we raised the possibility. Is it really true that nobody uses or sells drugs around here?"

Jeenya laughed. "I can just picture Sharona's response. I don't imagine she was any too pleased."

"You got that right. Is this really a drug-free community as far as you know?"

Jeenya looked at Zeke. "I can't remember anybody here in Jamaica Lakes using drugs, can you?"

"Those Rastafarians out back," Zeke said. "They're probably smoking a little ganja now and then. But I've never actually seen them smoking. I've never even smelled it on them. It's possible a few of the teenagers are given a little something once in a while when they're with friends outside the neighborhood. That's all I can think of."

"Josiah gets the credit for keeping it this way," Jeenya said. "He refused to rent or sell a house to anyone likely to be into drugs."

"So Sharona was telling the truth," Hazel said. "I'm glad. I hate looking into drug-related murders. The only other thing we did this morning was visit Collette Cooper, the young lady who had Josiah's baby. She'd heard about Josiah's murder and was pretty upset."

"We saw the baby," Rick said. "I should say the young man. David is seven years old and adorable. He's in second grade but was home this morning with a cold.

"Collette has grown up too. With Josiah's money and her mother to help babysit, she finished high school on schedule with excellent grades. Now she's going to Indian River State College. She's set to graduate in May with a degree in education. She's going to be a teacher, an elementary school teacher."

"She told us where to find her father," Hazel added. "He's a manager at Taco Bell. He's immensely proud of his daughter for finishing school and he's delighted to have such a fine grandson. His face simply glowed with pride talking about the two of them. We certainly have no reason to suspect either of them."

Rick said, "Tell us about your morning of investigating."

Zeke began, "I learned one thing. Being a detective is boring when you do nothing but sit and wait for people to say something interesting. We had a morning snack in the café and they wanted to ask us what you found out."

Jeenya interrupted. "Loretta did tell us one thing. The word is getting around that people have far more to fear than Josiah's duppy because Sharona is an Obeah Woman, and far more powerful than Josiah because she isn't afraid of doing evil spells. They say she's doing spells every night, making Josiah's duppy more powerful, that it will even be able to kill people."

"We're not surprised," Hazel said. "She told us pretty much the same thing. What we didn't know was that she was making sure everyone knew what she was doing. I would guess that even more people are buying salt and that the killer, even if he doesn't believe in duppies or Obeah, will be getting worried.

'Let's get back to your reports," Rick said. "Zeke, tell us what else you learned."

"The men at the garage," Zeke said, "spent an hour working on the car while I sat and listened to them. They adjusted all sorts of things, but I still hear a rattle. The car's getting old and old cars rattle but I didn't learn anything helpful.

"The only strange bit of information I picked up was while getting my haircut." He retold the story of Vivian Duckworth dropping her keys and picking up a handful of Josiah's hair.

"My day," Jeenya said, "was even more boring. I took my new tea to three women, and I looked around in the boutique. The only interesting story was about all the women Josiah's duppy has been visiting since he died. I heard that one several times. Nobody knows who they are. If I had to guess, I'd say some idiot was kidding around and said he imagined Josiah's duppy was out visiting women in Jamaica Lakes. After a few retellings, it might have changed from a joke into a supposed fact with people adding details as they passed it along."

Jeenya frowned. "I keep thinking about Vivian Duckworth picking up Josiah's hair. That may be the only important information of the day."

"It is strange, I agree," Hazel said, "but what makes you think it might be important?"

"I could guess," Rick said. "I remember the name 'Duckworth'. Rev. Wolff mentioned them as part of his Revivalists. Then, I've either heard or read about human hair being used in rituals like Voodoo. I imagine it could be used with Obeah spells. Maybe they use it with a Revivalist ritual. What do you think, Jeenya? Am I getting close?"

"I'm shocked," she said. "First, you've never heard of Obeah. Now, you came to this conclusion faster than I did. I just thought it was weird."

"Then too," Zeke added, "one of the women suggested Vivian might have had a crush on Josiah. She suggested Vivian was planning to use the hair in a ritual to get Josiah to notice her. That threw me off track. If Vivian planned to put a spell on Josiah, Rev. Wolff wouldn't do it. I still can't imagine what is going on."

"My plan," Jeenya said, "is to visit Gladys Wolff after lunch. I'll give her a sample package of my new tea. Then I'll mention what Zeke overheard and see if she has any explanation.

"Next, I'll visit Miranda Pratt. If anyone in Jamaica Lakes hears all the gossip, it would be Miranda."

"That is for sure," Zeke said, rolling his eyes. "If I was

walking past her house and I was scratching my neck, the story would be around the whole neighborhood about my terrible rash or how the mosquitoes were biting."

"Miranda's a nice lady but, once you sit down with her, it's hard to get away. Enjoy your visit, my dear. I have a long shopping list. As I wander around the store, I'll see if I can catch any other interesting information."

"There's one person we haven't talked to," Rick said. "We haven't met Josiah's brother, Elijah. I don't know how much more he could tell us."

Zeke chuckled. "You haven't met Elijah? That's an experience you should not miss. Elijah is nothing like his brothers. I don't know how much help he'll be, but you will enjoy talking to him. After you ask your usual questions, you need to ask Elijah to tell you about his family."

Jeenya smiled. "Be sure to ask him about his family. Zeke is right. Elijah is a most interesting man; some might even say fascinating. Check with the ladies at the café. If he isn't there, they'll know where he is."

❖

24

Elijah's Story

Rick

Rick and Hazel found Elijah Overmon at the café and were welcomed warmly. "I've been wondering when the two of you would drop by," he said. "So now it's my turn to be interrogated? I have been looking forward to this experience. I can't recall ever being interrogated, certainly not pertaining to a murder.

"Before we start, however, you can use a cup of coffee, can't you? How about a slice of freshly baked carrot cake? Loretta makes the most delicious carrot cake imaginable."

As coffee and cake were served, Rick studied Elijah. He was even taller than Josiah, and very slender. The single word that described him best was "elegant." He wore a beautifully tailored grey suit that appeared to be silk with a pink shirt and pale green tie. His black shoes appeared freshly polished. His face was narrow with widely spaced eyes and he had a thin mustache.

"Now," Elijah said, "why don't we move to my office to talk? It is a little more private." His office was small but comfortable. Rick noticed that one wall had built-in bookshelves filled with books, and he wished he could see what sort of books were there.

"So, what can I do to help you?" Elijah asked cheerfully. "I'm at your service, ready to be questioned."

"As you know," Rick began, "we've talked to Dolly and Sharona. Sharona gave us helpful background about Jesus Juarez and Clancy Cottonwood, both of whom were upset at Josiah seeing their women. Unfortunately, it looks like both men might have good alibis. We're wondering if you know of any other women Josiah might have been seeing recently, or anyone else who might have had a reason to kill him."

"I am extremely impressed with your investigative skills," Elijah said. "I doubt that most policemen would have learned anything about my brother's personal life. I do wish I could tell you more, but you appear to know more than I do. I do my best to avoid discussing unpleasant situations like these. How else might I aid in your investigation?"

Rick wished he could think of something important. "Perhaps," he suggested, "you could tell us a little more about your family. We have absolutely no reason to suspect anyone in the family, but you might mention some little thing that could lead us to look in other directions."

Elijah Overmon appeared almost amused by this idea and then leaned forward. "I would very much enjoy telling you about my family. Has one of your friends informed you that this is a particular interest of mine?"

"Zeke suggested you might have helpful insights in this area," Hazel said.

"Zeke Birdsong is a good man. You are blessed to have Zeke and his charming wife as your friends. And he is certainly correct. The Overmon family is quite interesting. I've always thought a psychologist would enjoy studying us. While in college, I considered going into that field, myself, but I was far more interested in understanding our family than in spending hours listening to boring people describing their neuroses.

"Then too, Josiah didn't think I could make a living in Jamaica Lakes as a psychologist. So, I went from studying psychology with cooking as a hobby to the reverse. I studied culinary arts though I still read a little psychology from time to time.

"Let me assure you that observing the pleasure people get from my culinary creations is far more rewarding than dealing with unhappy people. Josiah insisted I also study business and bookkeeping. Absolutely boring at first, I must say, but Josiah was correct. They have become quite useful.

"Now, with the responsibility of managing the grocery as well as the café and the other shops here, I'm thinking of finding someone else to take over the bookkeeping. My daughters aren't interested. They run the beauty parlor and are quite satisfied. My son, Richard, runs a landscaping service, mainly cutting grass. He prefers working out-of-doors. I do have one son-in-law, Barry Goshen, who is studying business. I'm hoping he will soon be prepared to assist me.

"But here I am, talking about myself when I need to tell you about the rest of the family. To begin with, two people in the family were really quite brilliant. I'm sorry to say, I was not one of these. They were Josiah and Sharona. Either of them could have done or been whatever they chose.

"Sharona did not enjoy formal education and, after our father died, she quite willingly offered to work, along with our mother, to put Josiah through college but Josiah wasn't interested in college either. He just wanted to get away from our father, so he came here to Palm City to pick oranges. And what a success he was.

"And then, there's our other brother, Seth. Did you know he was our brother?"

"I wasn't sure," Rick said. "I thought he was, but sometimes people don't mention Seth when describing your family. What's the story?"

"Seth is our stepbrother. Our father was married to our mother but often visited other women. As I remember his story, Seth asked his mother who his father was and she told him he didn't have a father. But, since our father continued to visit her occasionally, Seth finally asked him outright, 'Are you my father?' Then, as I was told, Seth said, 'If you are my father, I want to live at your house and have people know I'm your son.' So, Father took him home, told Mother it was her responsibility to raise this son as well as Sharona, Josiah and me.

"And then there was another sort of sister we had. I don't imagine Jeenya ever told you this story. Jeenya and her mother had been living in Port Antonio. Her mother, Sally, had little or no education. She worked cleaning houses for other people. She had been working for an older woman in Port Antonio. When she died, leaving Sally without a job, someone told her about a job in Kingston.

"Our cleaning lady had just gotten married and moved away. Mother met Sally. liked her, and hired her. Jeenya was only five years old and Mother didn't want a child doing the cleaning and she didn't want her sitting alone in their small servant's room. She insisted that Jeenya should be like a part of our family, that she'd go to school with us and eat meals with the family. She only joined her mother at night to sleep.

"Actually, when we met her, she was named Virginia. I was only three years old and I couldn't say Virginia. I called her Jeenya, and soon everyone called her Jeenya. She'd been living with us for a couple years when Seth showed up.

"I'm not proud of this, but Sharona, Josiah, and I weren't very nice to Seth. He'd come from a terribly poor family. His grammar and manners weren't very good. He just didn't fit in very well so we tried to ignore him. The only person who was nice to him was Jeenya. She helped Seth with his schoolwork and helped him with his grammar and manners.

"Josiah and Sharona both said Seth would have been perfectly happy to hang around a garage the rest of his life. They said that being in charge of the garage here, was Seth's dream job, but I disagreed.

"Father trained Josiah and then Sharona in Obeah. Josiah wasn't interested. Sharona was more interested but chose to follow Josiah here to Jamaica Lakes. The person who was most interested was Seth, perhaps to please Father. After Father died, Seth couldn't picture starting out on his own as an Obeah Man. When Josiah suggested he join us here to run the garage, he came.

"Josiah suggested Seth go to a technical school and study automotive repair and he did quite well there. Since then, he has made a success of running his garage. But, somehow, and maybe I'm wrong, I suspect Seth might still feel the way he did as a child, that he isn't really a part of the family.

"Finally, we get to me. I'm the baby of the family. I always wanted to attend college. Josiah paid all my expenses but college wasn't easy for me. I've always seen myself as a highly educated person and it was easy to adopt the style of a college-educated man but my reading and math skills were never more than average. After two years in college, with Josiah's encouragement, I entered a culinary program and did well.

"But I have told you only about our varied intelligence and our educations. Our differences go far deeper.

"As you might have discovered by now, Josiah's real goal in life, what he truly hungered for, was power. Even as a child, he dreamed of dressing in royal robes and wearing a crown. He wanted to be king. He was delighted to discover that, in the Bible, there was an actual king named Josiah. He once told me he thought he might be the reincarnation of King Josiah.

"What a shame though, what a disappointment to discover there are no kings in America. Josiah noticed, however, that the people here with real power are not the politicians but the businessmen. He planned to become a millionaire and actually did quite well for himself. I assume you know about his real estate empire?"

Rick nodded. Zeke and Jeenya were right. Elijah was fascinating.

"And, seeing himself as a new sort of king, Josiah did and took what he wanted. As you know, this included women. He was never concerned with right and wrong. His only concerns were with getting what he wanted.

"Now, let us consider Sharona. Perhaps I should have begun with her. She is, you know, the oldest. She too, wanted power, but power of an entirely different kind. She spent far more time than Josiah learning all the secrets of Obeah from our father and grandfather. She was particularly fascinated with the darker side, what you might call Black Magic. Helping people was fine, as a means to get what she wanted, but Sharona's true desire was to control people's lives.

"If Josiah dreamed of being a king, Sharona dreamed of being a sorceress or, if you prefer, a witch. While Josiah ruled Jamaica Lakes and played the role of Obeah Man, Sharona had little to do but protect Josiah's reputation.

"Now that the king is dead, Sharona becomes both queen and sorceress. It will be interesting to see how many people are attracted by her power and how many of them turn away.

"Now, we must consider our other brother, Seth. He is shy and keeps to himself. He works hard and seems to do a good job, but I sometimes worry about him. I don't think he has any real friends.

"Now with Josiah dead, I imagine Seth was hoping that Sharona wouldn't take the role of the Obeah Man or Obeah Woman, so he might be able to do it. It would make people think he was someone important, that he was really part of the Overmon family. I'm not really sure. I could be imagining all this. He might be happy running the garage. If I had to come up with an image for Seth, it would have to be the Outsider.

"He'd tell you it was because we picked on him at first. Sometimes we were pretty mean to him, especially Josiah. But we were also mean to each other at times. It's just that Seth took it personally. Then, as we grew older and perhaps more civilized, we quit being mean to each other but Seth never stopped feeling like he didn't belong. Even now, even when we try to treat him like part of the family, you can tell he still sees himself as an outsider."

Elijah paused for a moment, and looked at the detectives. "I'm waiting," he said. "Aren't you going to ask how I'd describe myself?"

"I wasn't sure," Rick said, "that I should ask. But yes, of course, we are certainly interested in how you see yourself. The picture isn't complete without you."

Elijah nodded and smiled. "Elijah Overmon is a gourmet cook, an amateur psychologist, and an avid observer of human nature. If Josiah ruled in the political and economic realms and Sharona rules in the spiritual realm, I'd consider myself the philosopher, or the thinker, if you prefer. Mine is the realm of ideas and images. I study the people around me and try to discern the truth of who they are. I explore the human psyche."

Elijah paused for a moment as if waiting for the applause. "Questions?"

"I am delighted and honored," Rick said, "that you shared these descriptions and images with us. Every bit of it rings true as you describe the members of your family. I'd say you have a genuine gift. I can't say though, that I have any better idea about where to look for a killer. With the insight you have into what people seem to desire, do you have any idea at all who might have had a reason to kill Josiah?"

Elijah took a deep breath and let it out slowly. "I realize that I should have some idea. It pains me deeply that I cannot think of anyone with a serious motive. If it wasn't the husband or boyfriend of one of Josiah's women, I honestly cannot think where to look next.

"I can understand a motive of jealousy combined with anger or revenge but I can't see greed as a motive. No one would profit from his death. I can't think of anyone Josiah has really harmed. But let me assure you, I will focus my mind on this problem and, if I get any interesting ideas, I will certainly contact you. I do wish I could be of greater assistance.

"Now, before you leave, I would like to take my images one step further. And I must be honest at this point. While I take immense pride in my ability to observe and understand people, to see who they really are, I'm not the true expert in this field. You do know of whom I speak, don't you?" He looked straight at Rick.

"Someone I've met?"

"Yes, of course. A person you know quite well."

"Jeenya? You're talking about Jeenya, aren't you?"

"I glad you are aware of her skills. Your friend and mine, Virginia Birdsong, has more talent in this field than I could even dream of. Jeenya goes further than observing. She asks questions, apparently innocent questions and, before you know it, you're sharing with her, your most personal secrets.

"When I use images of king, sorceress and philosopher, I occasionally refer to Jeenya as the 'Earth Mother,' and at other times as 'The Woman Who Sees Through People.' But Jeenya Birdsong goes beyond seeing. She also speaks. She is the 'Wise Woman' who tells people what they need to hear.

"The best advice I can give you, detectives, is to listen to Jeenya. If the killer lives in Jamaica Lakes, Jeenya Birdsong is the one person most likely to know who it is and the only person likely to understand his motives. She can look into your eyes and know what you're thinking. She can ask you questions and you seem to have no choice. You will answer her questions and you'll tell her the truth.

Listen carefully when she speaks. Respect her intuition and insights."

Elijah paused now. "Wait," he said. "I just had a new insight. In this whole family, who do you think Mother loved the most?"

"Josiah?" Hazel guessed.

"Maybe Sharona," Rick guessed. "She was the only girl."

"I'd have guessed one of them when I was younger," Elijah said. But looking back now, I see things differently. The person Mother really loved was Jeenya, the cleaning lady's daughter. The rest of us received what she did for us or what she gave us and never thanked her. We just took it all for granted.

"Sweet little Jeenya was excited and grateful for everything she was given. Shopping together for new clothes was a delight for both of them. Each little dress seemed to be the prettiest one they'd ever seen.

"And then, I can remember when Mother read stories to us. Jeenya was a couple years older than me so she loved those stories. From what I've been told, I wasn't so attentive. I was a squirmy kid and tried to crawl away. Fairy tales never seemed interesting.

"Then, as Jeenya grew older, she sometimes read to Mother. Other times, the two of them simply talked. I can remember watching them and feeling jealous because Mother and I never talked together like that. Then I realized it was because I never wanted conversations like that.

"I remember Jeenya telling me about a conversation she had with Mother just before starting college. Mother had explained that she wasn't including Jeenya in her will, since she wasn't her own child, but that she wanted Jeenya to have enough money to last through college and maybe longer. They went together to the bank and opened up an account for Jeenya. I'm not sure how much money they put in it, but it was at least five thousand, maybe twice that. That day, you could look at them, Jeenya and Mother, and see how excited they were.

"At about the same time, Mother had a talk with Seth, explaining that he would not be in her will. After all, he wasn't her child but, she said, if he chose to go to college, she would pay for that.

"I still remember hearing her tell my father about the conversation. She said, 'Of all the children in our family, Jeenya is the one who is most grateful for what we've done and Seth is the least grateful. No matter how hard I try to treat him like the others, it is never enough. He never thanks me for including him in our family. He never thanks me for birthday gifts or Christmas gifts. I think I could give him every penny I have, and his response would be 'Is that all?'"

"But now," Elijah said, "here in Jamaica Lakes, Seth seems to have changed. He thanked Josiah for inviting him to join us here, He thanked Josiah for sending him to that automotive repair class, and several times I heard him thank Josiah for putting him in charge of the garage.

"I never thought about this before," he continued, "but I don't believe there is anyone in Jamaica Lakes, outside of our family, who knows that Jeenya grew up in our family and that, in some ways, Jeenya is actually more a part of the Overmon family than Seth."

As they headed back to Jeenya's house, Rick and Hazel looked at each other, hardly knowing what to say. Hazel broke the silence. "That man is someone I'll never be able to forget. He and Sharona both. His ability to define each member of his family with an image is uncanny. I wonder how he would describe you or me?"

"I might be Nosy White Boy," Rick suggested. "I certainly wouldn't qualify for a magnificent description like King or Philosopher."

"You," Hazel suggested, "could be Earth Mother's White Grandson."

Rick laughed. "And you? Perhaps Fire-haired Woman. What do you think?"

"We should probably have asked him," Hazel said. "Perhaps our personalities need to be more strongly defined to rate such an image. But Zeke was right. Even if he didn't help much in finding the killer, Elijah Overmon was absolutely fascinating."

"But he did help," Rick said. "He helped a great deal. You heard what he told us at the end. If the killer lives in Jamaica Lakes, if he is someone Jeenya knows, she will know who he is. She will understand his motives. And, if Jeenya talks to him and asks questions, he will eventually tell her everything."

"You actually believe that?" Hazel asked.

Rick knew Hazel wasn't sure if he was joking or serious. He wasn't sure, himself. But he *thought* he was serious. One statement Elijah made struck him as absolute truth. Jeenya could tell what a person was thinking. She could also ask questions that made people see themselves and their situation in a new light. It made sense but Rick wasn't quite sure that people would really tell her the truth.

"I'm not sure it would work," Rick said, "having Jeenya talk to a suspect, but it is worth thinking about."

25
Listening to the Gossip

Jeenya

Meanwhile, Jeenya called the parsonage. Twenty minutes later, she was sitting with Gladys in the parsonage kitchen.

"I heard from an old friend of my mother in Port Antonio," Jeenya said, "about a variation on my herbal mixture for tea. She said it's supposed to be mighty helpful for people with arthritis. I know you and Herman both have arthritis and thought you might like to give it a try. If it is helpful, I'll make up more for other people with arthritis."

Gladys asked the usual questions about what the Birdsongs knew about the investigation, and Jeenya gave the usual vague responses.

"The detectives talked to us," Gladys said. "Such nice young people, but I don't know if they can catch a killer in a community like this. They mainly asked questions about Revivalists. I guess that's puzzling to people who aren't Jamaican. They also asked for the names of people who regularly meet with us."

"Rick didn't tell us what you talked about," Jeenya said. "He keeps that kind of thing private. But he and Hazel did mention how much they liked you and Herman and that you had been very helpful.

"They asked us about Obeah and Revivalists first but Zeke and I don't know much about what you do. I know Obeah often involves spells. Although Josiah told me he'd never do an evil spell, he would do spells to help or protect people. What about your husband? Does he ever do spells?"

"Not really. Herman preaches against doing spells. He does the usual Christian rituals like baptism and weddings and funerals. At other times, he'll do special rituals designed to help someone, not hurt them. He tries to help someone stop smoking, stop drinking, things like that."

"That sounds good," Jeenya said cheerfully. "What does he use in these rituals?"

"It varies. Usually, there's something that belong to the person involved, maybe clothing they'd worn, maybe nail clippings or hair. Herman adds herbs, and a little pimento. He makes a small fire out in the woods, usually with cedar twigs. He reads a few Bible verses and prays while he burns these things."

"What I'm wondering…" Jeenya said.

"Yes? Go on, Jeenya. What are you wondering? You can ask anything you want. We don't have secrets."

"Zeke was getting a haircut this morning," Jeenya said. "He happened to overhear a strange story. Maggie was talking to Kitty Ferguson, talking about Vivian Duckworth."

"Kitty already called me," Gladys said. "We all knew

Vivian had gotten some of Josiah's hair. She was so sure nobody saw her do it. Apparently, Maggie saw her pick it up and stuff it in her pocket. She's been telling people about it, like it's something funny.

"I really would like to tell you what this is all about, Jeenya, but I need to talk to Herman first. You understand that. Herman will want to talk to the other people who were involved. Then, I promise, we'll give you a call. You and Zeke can call the detectives and have them join us if they'd like. It's much better if this is all out in the open. But I'll tell you right now. What we did wasn't anything to be ashamed of."

Jeenya nodded. She couldn't imagine what Gladys was talking about.

"I'd appreciate it," she said. "And, Gladys, if this new tea does you any good, please let me know."

Jeenya walked down the street looking forward to her last stop of the day. At ninety-four, Miranda Pratt was the oldest person in Jamaica Lakes. One daughter, Belinda, lived with her. Her other daughter, Miriam, was married to Elijah Overmon and lived next door. Jeenya hadn't been to visit Miranda for several weeks. She usually hated to waste so much time listening to gossip.

"Why Jeenya Birdsong, it has been ages and ages since I've seen you to talk to," Miranda said. "Please do come in and sit a while."

And sitting a while, listening to Miranda who always talked more than she listened, was exactly what Jeenya wanted to do. She gave Miranda a package of her new tea mixture.

"How kind of you to remember me," Miranda said as she poured them each a cup of tea. "I have so many health problems what with the arthritis and the diabetes, with my weak heart and my blood pressure, and swelling feet and knee problems and all, I'm sure your new tea will help something."

Jeenya nodded. She knew she wouldn't need to ask any questions. Miranda would ramble on and on without any urging.

"So much has been going on the last couple of weeks that I hardly know where to begin." Miranda described the angry man on the motorcycle and what she'd heard about the stranger who came to talk to Josiah that day. "From what I hear, that man told Josiah he was coming back to find him and he was planning to kill him. He was going to slit his throat. And that's what happened, isn't it? I assume the policeman knows about that man. They haven't arrested him yet, have they? If they did, I'd have heard about it for sure."

Jeenya was trying to keep up, nodding and shaking her head at appropriate times.

"I don't get out much nowadays, but I have a lot of friends who stop by to tell me what's going on. And then, I do spend most of my time sitting on the front steps or looking out my window. I'm sure I know things nobody else knows.

"I know when Elijah and Miriam are yelling at their children or grandchildren. I know when Frank and Eileen are having a fight. They've got to be close to seventy years old but, when Frank forgets and leaves the toilet seat up, Eileen's complaining is loud enough for me to hear everything.

"When poor old Frank visits a friend and he's fifteen minutes late coming home, Eileen simply throws a fit, claiming she was frantic, about to call the police, asking them to go look for her husband, which is ridiculous when she knew where he was all the time.

Then, one night last week, Eileen got a phone call when she was fixing dinner and she let the beans burn. Frank said he was almost mad enough to leave her. Can you believe that? That man's not in his right mind. He's over seventy years old and thinking about leaving his wife over burnt food. If he lived alone with nobody to cook and clean and wash his clothes, he'd change his mind fast enough, don't you think?"

Jeenya nodded, wondering if Frank was simply getting even with Eileen.

"I can also see all those men going to work in the garage and the people who bring in their cars to get fixed. Now that I think of it, I saw your husband taking in his car just this morning. Nothing serious, I hope?"

Jeenya shook her head. "Nothing but an annoying little rattle."

"Late in the afternoon, I sit out on the front steps and watch those men, the ones working in the garage, heading home. You can always tell who's in a hurry to get home, and who's taking his time standing around talking with the other guys.

"And then there's that poor Victor Hackett. I remember when his wife was alive. Elaenia was such a pretty little thing and so sweet. Back then, Victor was always in a hurry to get home. Now he hasn't any reason to hurry, going back to an empty house. But he doesn't spend much time talking to the other men. He goes over to the café, picks up his dinner, and carries it home to eat. And, once he gets home, Jeenya, you won't believe what he does next."

Jeenya shook her head. She couldn't imagine what Victor might do that seemed so interesting to Miranda.

"You know Zelda Dimmick. She lives across the street from Victor. According to Zelda, that poor man sits at his window like I do, only he seems to be looking down the street waiting for Elaenia to come home. Zelda says he's watching for her every single night. And it's been over ten years since that poor girl died. I've always wondered, you know, why a pretty girl like Elaenia with a husband who adored here, would go and kill herself like that. The only thing I can think of is, with her wanting a baby so much and then having a miscarriage, she could have been depressed. Or maybe she felt guilty, thinking it was her own fault she lost that baby.

"And then, Jeenya, I always enjoyed watching the people who stopped in to see Josiah in his Obeah shed. I knew why most of them were there, of course. There were times I could even hear if Josiah was able to help them. Like the night Josiah was murdered.

"Even though it was so black you couldn't see much, I was still watching out my window. What else is there to do, anyway? We don't have a television to look at. Elijah keeps offering to buy me one, but I don't want anything like that. I'd rather look out the window, watching real people.

"I was looking to see who went in and out of the Obeah shed that night. A little light came from his window so I could see people walking down the street, but the only time I could see who the people were, was when they stepped in the doorway and the light from inside lit up their faces. I'm getting older, but I've still got my eyesight, you know. I reckon I know just about every person who lives in Jamaica Lakes.

"The first ones to see Josiah that night were Seymour and Sarah Olsen. Seymour never lets Sarah come alone you know. I think he remembers the years when Josiah was having sex with a few of the women who came alone. Seymour knows Josiah hasn't done that for years, but he comes along anyway. Sarah has problems with digestion from what I've heard. She never stops to talk to me but I also hear she has terrible headaches.

"Next to come were Eula May Carter and that ugly little dog she calls Princess. Ugliest princess I ever did see but Eula May treats that little beast like it was her own child, taking it to see the Obeah Man for special doggie tea. That night, the stupid little mutt even got an herbal bath. Would you believe that? Eula May is claiming the herbs Josiah fixed up for Princess made her frisky as a puppy.

"While they were inside, I saw an old black pickup truck driving around, up and down every street like they were looking for something. After Eula May and Princess left, there was a break. Angela Armstrong was running late. I heard Angela is trying to get pregnant but not having any success.

"I wouldn't be surprised if that husband of hers was the one with the problem. They say George didn't want Angela going to see Josiah. Some say it's because George is part of that Revivalist nonsense and he didn't approve of Obeah magic, but it might just be that he doesn't want a baby.

"That night, the night Josiah was killed, I did see two things that were unusual. Just before the revivalists started up with their usual noise, I saw Victor go out. I couldn't tell for sure, but it looked like he was heading toward the garage. I guess he forgot something there.

Later, while Angela was in there with Josiah, I saw someone else. I don't know if it a man or a woman. It was terribly dark that night, but I believe this person went behind Josiah's shed. Then, just a few minutes after Angela left, Sharona left. She seemed to pause briefly. I wondered if she was talking to the person behind the shed. Of course, dark as it was, I might have imagined all of it.

"After Angela and Sharona left, Josiah was there alone. He often worked a bit longer before he left. The only other thing I saw after that was a very short flash of light. Then all was dark. I assumed that was Josiah heading home. By then, it was after eleven. I don't like staying up past eleven, so I went on to bed. I really wonder now, if I had stayed awake a little longer, what else I might have seen. It's scary to think I could have seen his killer go in. But, if anything else happened, I missed it. I was sound asleep."

"What about Belinda?" Jeenya asked. "Does she stay up later?"

"No. We had dinner together. Belinda fixed me a nice dish of red beans and rice and we had fried plantains for dessert. Then Belinda was in her room, reading a book, probably one of those scandalous romance stories. She doesn't spend much time watching out the window like I do. She came out at about ten to take her pills and said she was going to sleep."

26

George is Missing

Jeenya

It was nearly four when Jeenya got home. Zeke was already there.

"Jeenya," he said. "Gladys called less than five minutes ago. She wants you to return her call."

"I told Herman about our conversation," Gladys said, "and we have a few people who will be gathering here at the house at about five. Would you and the detectives be able to join us?"

Thirty minutes later, Rick and Hazel arrived. Along with Zeke and Jeenya, they walked back to the parsonage. As they walked, Jeenya tried to imagine what they were about to hear, but this time, her intuition failed her. She had no idea whatsoever.

Rev. Wolff began the conversation. "We understand," he said slowly in his rich baritone voice, "exactly why some of you were suspicious. You were correct to suspect something unusual was going on. We'd like to explain what we did." He nodded to Kitty Ferguson.

"It started with me," Kitty explained. "I was down at the

store about three weeks ago when that crazy man showed up on his big motorcycle, shouting all those obscene things at Josiah. Josiah wasn't even there to hear it.

"Zelda told me this man had done the same thing several times before. Obviously, Josiah had been having sex with this man's girlfriend. I said to Bunny, 'You'd think, wouldn't you, that if Josiah was determined to have affairs all the time, he could at least find a woman without a husband or boyfriend.' Anyway, Bunny and I told Vivian."

Now, Vivian picked up the story. "I decided we should do something about it. It wasn't good for the people here in Jamaica Lakes to have angry strangers coming through, shouting bad words and all. My husband, Eugene, came up with the plan."

Eugene nodded. "I agreed with the women that we should try to help Josiah. I remembered, back home, how the Revivalist preacher in our village sometimes did special rituals including a special cleansing ritual. We wanted to do something like that, a ritual to cleanse Josiah of his lust and his lack of self-control. We needed a little of his hair, something he had worn and other items from his home.

"The big problem was how to get Josiah's hair. Vivian is friendly with one of the younger girls who work at the beauty shop. The girl said Josiah was fairly regular with his haircuts. He came in every two weeks on a Monday morning, usually at about eleven.

"Meanwhile," Eugene continued, "we took turns walking past Josiah's house, looking for stuff. Dolly has a clothes dryer, so she wasn't going to make things easy, putting clothes out on a line. One day I noticed Josiah taking off a torn old T-shirt. He tossed it off to one side of the porch, saying it could go in Dolly's rag bag. That was perfect.

"Matt Venable and I went back that night, a little after midnight. We opened the porch door quietly, went in and took the shirt. On our way out, I stumbled over one of the children's plastic toys. The noise woke Dolly, who called the police. But Dolly and Josiah didn't notice anything missing."

Jeenya nodded. This helped explain the noises Dolly had been hearing in the night.

"Another time," he said, "we were there in the middle of the night getting part of the newspaper Josiah had been reading and a few dead flowers off that rosebush he was so proud of. Dolly heard us and called the police again. The other times she called the police, it wasn't us. I think she'd gotten nervous about little noises in the night." He turned and smiled at his wife.

"I was at the beauty shop," Vivian said, "that day when Josiah arrived. Maggie was done with me, but Josiah was still sitting there. I kept asking Maggie to cut it a little shorter.

"When Josiah left, I got up and dropped my house keys right in the middle of the pile of hair. As you heard, I reached down to get the keys and grabbed a handful of his hair. I was really pleased with myself and I was so certain no one noticed me taking the hair."

"Then," Kitty said, "we came to visit the pastor, and told him what we'd done. He'd never done a cleansing ritual, but he figured it should be similar to rituals to help people stop smoking. We didn't do it on a Friday night because we didn't want the word getting around town. People would have talked, I'm sure.

"So, all of us here got together on a Tuesday night, out in the woods. We had the Bible open on the table and a dozen candles burning like we always do and we were burning incense. Eugene built a small fire and each of us put something in the fire. While it burned, we sang a few hymns. The pastor read a little scripture and we all prayed for Josiah to be free from lust. Then we all went home, hoping it would work."

"When Josiah died…" Vivian Duckworth said with a worried expression. "When he was murdered, I heard the news and told the others. We all came to see the pastor. We were nervous, thinking somehow it could have been our fault. We were afraid that maybe, when the Lord cleansed Josiah, the cleansing could have killed him. We wondered, if maybe, the only way to get Josiah to stop doing those things was to kill him."

Rev. Wolff joined the conversation. "It is true that God's ways are mysterious and often difficult to understand. He answers prayers in ways we don't always expect. So, I led the group in prayer, a prayer for Josiah, that he be allowed to enter Heaven, prayers for his family, and prayers for forgiveness if we were in any way responsible.

"Later, when we learned someone had slit his throat, we relaxed. I can imagine God bringing a heart attack perhaps, but I can't picture our Lord cutting a person's throat. I agreed with most of the people in the neighborhood, that it was probably the man who went in Josiah's office that day, threatening to kill him just that way.

"We never mentioned our ritual again until today when Kitty called after the conversation in the beauty shop. As you probably know, she suggested Vivian could have taken the hair because she had a crush on Josiah and wanted his attention."

"I had to say something," Kitty said. "They saw Vivian take the hair, and that was the first thing that popped in my head."

"I laughed," Vivian said. "The last thing I would ever have wanted was to attract that man's attention. Besides, I'm not young and pretty like the women Josiah was attracted to."

"You understand," Gladys said to Jeenya, "why I needed to talk to Herman and why he wanted to talk to all these people. We wanted to tell you the truth. It's important, to us, to always be truthful."

Jeenya nodded. "I appreciate your sharing this. Your motives were good. You wanted to help Josiah, not hurt him."

"I'm glad we were included," Rick said. "It not only clears up the question of why Vivian took Josiah's hair, it also clears up the mysterious events that kept waking Dolly in the middle of the night. I'll tell her we found who was making the noises. I'll explain that there was no intention of hurting anyone and that it won't happen again."

Rev. Wolff frowned. "That's kind of you, Detective, but the truth is better. I shall visit Mrs. Overmon myself and tell her exactly what we told you. She'll understand that our intentions were only to help Josiah. I don't imagine, though, that she'll keep the story to herself. It will get around town. But we aren't ashamed of what we did. The people here don't understand why Vivian picked up the hair. It's best if they hear the whole story."

Rick and Hazel headed back to the police department to write their daily report and then headed home. It was almost six forty-five when Angela called Rick. He answered immediately.

"I'm really worried, Rick. George isn't home yet. It's almost seven, and he's always home by five-thirty unless he tells me he'll be late."

"Have you called any of the men that work with him at the Garage? They might know where he went. Call them, all of them. They might know if he planned to go somewhere after work. Call me on my cell phone and let me know what you find out."

"I'll be at the Birdsong's. If he's not back by seven-thirty, we'll go out looking for him."

Rick returned to the Birdsongs' house and, when he didn't hear from Angela, he called Hazel. She and Tim were finishing dinner. "It's probably nothing," he said. "But I wanted you to know. Sure, that's fine. We'll see you at seven thirty."

"Hazel is on her way," he explained to Jeenya and Zeke, "and her husband is coming with her. It should help having one more person looking, but don't go calling all your friends at this point. George could have stopped somewhere on his way home and forgotten to watch the time. But, if we can't find him and he hasn't shown up by morning, we might think about a major search.

"I'm heading to the grocery and the café," Rick said. "If there's any gossip about George, that's the place to hear it." He wasn't disappointed. The women near the café thought he and Angela had a fight and he was planning to spend the night with an old girlfriend."

One woman said, "I'm pretty sure I know where he is. I see him at least once a week visiting the house right across from me. I imagine they've been having an affair."

"That's too bad," another woman said. "I always thought George was a really nice man. I never pictured him doing something like that to Angela."

The men had gathered near the grocery. Rick recognized Chester who seemed to be listening but not talking. One man suggested, "When a man just disappears like that, he's probably done something wrong. I like George, you know, but he could have been the one to murder Josiah. George had his reasons to kill Josiah, what with Angela going to see him all the time, trying to get pregnant. I know Josiah said he would leave the women who live here alone, but Angela is a pretty lady. He might have changed his mind, you know."

Another man said, "What I've been thinking is that there's a killer here in Jamaica Lakes. He killed Josiah first. Maybe he's gone and killed George. I hope not, but murderers don't usually stop with one victim."

Back at Jeenya's house, Rick shared what he'd heard but said, "I don't believe any of that nonsense. I think they are all wrong."

As they waited, Jeenya described some of what Miranda had told her, starting with the black pickup wandering up and down the streets while Angela was with Josiah.

"That's helpful," Rick said. "Jesus Juarez drives an old black pickup. He told his wife he had gotten home at about nine or nine-thirty, then came here looking for her, that he went up and down every street. This confirms his story, at least to that point. I imagine other people saw his truck and didn't say anything. They assumed it wasn't important."

Hazel and Tim pulled up at seven-twenty. She introduced her husband to Zeke and Jeenya. "We drove around for a few minutes," Hazel said. "Tim wanted to see the neighborhood. I looked for George as Tim drove, but I didn't see him."

While they waited for Angela's call, Zeke and Jeenya shared other stories of her visit to Miranda. "The poor woman is so lonely. For a while, I was afraid she might never stop talking. One story that she heard from Zelda Dimmick was interesting. It's one of those stories where one person sees something perfectly ordinary and, by the time they pass it on, it's changed.

"Zelda lives across the street from Victor. She noticed that he looked out his window every night. The way Zelda explained it to Miranda is that Victor sits by his window every afternoon after coming home from work. According to Zelda, Victor is looking for Elaenia to come down the street."

"I love it," Hazel said. "I wonder if Victor expects to see his wife like she was when she was alive, or if he's looking for her duppy."

It was seven thirty-five when Angela called. Rick answered immediately.

"I'm really worried. I talked to every one of the men from the garage. George didn't say anything to them about going somewhere after work. George couldn't have gone far. His car's here in the driveway. He walks to work."

"First thing," Rick said, "you need to know that, unless there is evidence of foul play or the missing person has some kind of dementia, the police won't do a thing. You can't even file a missing person report for at least seventy-two hours. Even then, the police don't usually get involved. Adults have the right to disappear if they want.

"But, with everything else going on here, I'm concerned. Zeke, Jeenya, Hazel, and her husband and I are going to wander around the neighborhood looking for him. Angela, we want you to stay home so you can answer the phone. If George shows up or calls, let me know immediately.

"Now, one question. Where would George go if he stopped somewhere on his way home? Where would he go if he wanted to be alone for a while?"

"The only place I can think of," Angela said, "is Jamaica Lake. On nice days, George likes to walk around the lake or sit at a picnic table and look at the water."

Rick had flashlights in his car and Jeenya found a couple more on a closet shelf. It was starting to get dark. They began their search at the park. Zeke and Jeenya walked the path around Jamaica Lake. Rick, Hazel, and Tim divided the rest of the area.

It took them less than five minutes. Rick heard Zeke's voice. "We found him," he shouted. "George is in back here. He's hurt."

"I kept hoping you or someone would be out looking for me," George said. "I could shout all day and nobody would hear me back here. I knew it was late. I was hurrying along the path and tripped over that big root over there. Then, when I fell, I hit my head on this rock and it must have knocked me out. Now my head's okay but I'm pretty sure my leg is broken."

Tim went to get their car and Hazel called Angela while Rick and Zeke, with a little help from Jeenya, lifted George and helped him place his arms around the shoulders of the two men. They put George in Tim's car along with Angela.

The others went with Rick, all heading to the hospital.

As they passed the grocery, Rick stopped by the gossiping men. "You all guessed wrong," he said. "Nobody got killed. George is on his way to the hospital. He was just walking around the lake. He tripped on a root and fell and broke a leg."

Ida Lee was at her usual position, sitting next to the window.

"Hey, Miz Jeenya. Sounds to me like tings at your house be getting worse not better with all of you out looking for George. Some people I know were tinking he be dead too, that maybe the same person who killed Josiah killed George. Some tell me it was Josiah's duppy dat done killed poor George. What I want to know is how come you can go find George so fast when you can't find de person who killed poor Josiah. I'm afraid, if you don't hurry up and catch him, he's gonna go kill somebody else."

27
Meeting Vanessa

Rick

The next morning at the Birdsongs, Angela was there with a woman the detectives hadn't met.

"Rick, Hazel," Angela said. "I want you to meet Vanessa Augustine. She stopped by last night when she heard George was missing. She shared some interesting information; things I wish I had known a long time ago. I want her to tell you what she told me."

They settled around the table. Jeenya brought coffee and tea. "All right," Jeenya said, "We're ready to listen."

"I told Angela," Vanessa said, "that George and I dated a few times when I was just out of high school. Then he got married. I spent two years in college, worked in an office for a while and then got married. I moved to Jamaica Lakes less than a year ago, just after my divorce.

"I was in the grocery and saw George. What a surprise. I invited him to stop and talk, just to catch up on what we'd been doing. After that, he came by to talk from time to time. When I felt depressed about my failed marriage, he tried to comfort me. He knew how I felt since he'd gone through a divorce himself. Later, he came asking me for advice. He was terribly worried that he wasn't good enough for Angela, afraid she'd leave him."

"Tell them why," Angela urged.

"As I said, George was married back in Jamaica. He and his wife had four children. They got divorced when his wife found another man, one she liked better. He was an older man with more money and a fine new house.

"George decided the reason he and his wife had so many problems was the stress of having all those children around. So, he went and got himself a vasectomy.

"When he met Angela, she talked about wanting children. George was afraid to tell her about the vasectomy. I told him he should talk to her, that Angela would understand. But George couldn't build up enough courage.

"He was at my house most Friday nights while Angela went to see Josiah. He didn't want her to think he'd changed his mind and approved of Obeah methods, but he didn't want to stop her from going.

"The Revivalist meetings made a good story. He knew Angela wouldn't ask Rev. Wolff if he was there. He and I weren't having sex or anything, just talking. But nervous George wanted to keep it a secret. 'If Angela finds out I've been visiting another woman,' he kept saying, 'she'll leave me for sure.' I didn't argue. I agreed to keep it a secret."

"The terrible thing," Angela inserted, "is that I really didn't care whether we had children or not. When George and I talked about it, he seemed to think having children was important. I was going through all that, sneaking out to visit Josiah, thinking it would make George happy. I wish he'd had the courage to tell me. This is so crazy. He could have told me about Vanessa too. I trusted him. George had no need to lie. What a terrible mess we made of things."

"I have one question," Hazel said. "Last Friday night,

the night Josiah was killed, was George with you that night?"

"Yes," Vanessa said. "From about nine-thirty, until the Revivalists went home, he was there with me."

"Good," Hazel said. "That means George has an alibi. He didn't kill Josiah." She noticed Vanessa's startled look. "No, we really didn't think he did it, but he kept lying about where he was which seemed very suspicious."

"Rick," Angela said, "Vanessa told me something else, something that's really bothering me. She said George has been upset about something recently. I never sensed anything like this. Vanessa, please tell Rick and Hazel what you told me."

Vanessa began hesitantly. "It started about three weeks ago. George seemed to be nervous about something but he never told me what was bothering him. Each week, it seemed to get worse, especially when he was talking about Angela but I can't think of anything that might make him nervous."

"Interesting," Rick said. "Do you think he was upset about Angela seeing Josiah?"

"That doesn't make sense," Vanessa said. "He's known that for a long time and it never seemed to bother him before. He knew that Josiah mainly sold tea and that Sharona was always there.

Rick took a quick look at Jeenya. She seemed to be listening intently. He wondered if she knew something or if she was as lost as he was. He had a feeling that if he could just ask the right questions, if he listened very carefully, this might be something important.

"All right," Rick said. Did he do anything different? Did he talk about anything that might have upset him?"

Vanessa closed her eyes to think. "The only thing that comes to mind is that he spent more time talking to me about that friend he had at the garage."

"Victor? Was he talking about Victor?" Hazel asked.

"Yes, it was Victor. It could have been something Victor said."

Rick turned to Jeenya. "Can you help us? Do you know anything Victor might have said that would upset George?"

"Yes," Jeenya said, almost in a whisper. "Yes, I can. Most people around here know part of the story but not all of it. It was maybe ten years ago that Victor married the loveliest girl you can imagine. She was named for a little bird found in the forests in Jamaica, the Jamaican Elaenia."

"I've heard that name," Hazel said. "But I never tied her to Victor. Is she the girl who committed suicide?"

"Yes," Jeenya said, "but that's not the whole story. When she and Victor got married, they wanted children but, in that case, I think the problem was with Victor's sperm." Jeenya looked at Angela. "Like you, Angela, Elaenia went to Josiah. She tried the teas and the herbal baths.

"Then, when nothing worked, Josiah seemed to have suggested one other approach. I understand he told other women in her situation to first have sex with him, and then, that night, to sleep with their husbands. That way it would be hard to prove which man was the father.

"Elaenia told me later that she had thought it over for a week or maybe two. Finally, she decided to do it. Two months went by before I heard any more. Elaenia and Victor were going to have a baby. Victor was so excited, he bragged about it all over town.

"When she was about six months pregnant, Elaenia

came to see me. She was feeling guilty about not telling Victor the truth. I knew Victor pretty well, and I strongly advised her not to tell him, but Elaenia loved her husband and trusted him.

"That was the last time I talked to her. I would guess that she went home and told Victor the truth. What happened after that, I have no way of knowing. About two weeks later, she wasn't there when Victor woke up. Someone found her down by the lake. It was a place she loved to go. An autopsy showed that she had taken a large number of pills. They killed her and her unborn child.

"Since then, Victor has been miserable. Some people think it was his fault. They thought he must have done something terrible and, as a result, he lost the wife he loved so much and what could have been his son. Then the word got around that she'd lost the baby, that she'd had a miscarriage and was so upset she took those pills."

By the time Jeenya finished the story, both Vanessa and Angela were in tears along with Jeenya. Hazel was trying not to cry.

"Finally," Jeenya continued, "I imagine Victor knew you were visiting Josiah, Angela, trying to get pregnant. He might have worried that the same thing might happen to the two of you. George could have been torn between trusting that Josiah really had changed and worrying about having you pregnant with Josiah's child. Now, with Josiah dead, I expect George will be a little more relaxed."

"It would be interesting," Hazel said quietly, "to know why George was just nervous recently, rather than when Angela first started going to see Josiah. Maybe the question we should ask is if Victor talked to George about this from the beginning or if, for some reason, he just began discussing it recently. Then, of course, it could be something totally different."

When Vanessa and Angela left, Rick and Hazel went to see the bartender who had been up in the mountains. He looked at the picture and immediately recognized Jesus.

"Oh yes, I remember seeing him that night. It was the night before I left on vacation. Jesus came in, probably about nine, and was more upset than I'd ever seen him. He said he'd gone home but his wife wasn't there. He'd looked everywhere but couldn't find her.

"I did my best to help him cool down, telling him she probably went somewhere with a friend. That just made him angry. Jesus was there until closing time at two AM, just as he told you."

After they were done for the day, Rick went to visit his grandmother again. To his surprise, she remembered who he was. He suspected one of the nurses had been getting her prepared for the visit and he was grateful for her help.

Back in Jamaica Lakes, Ida Lee continued her evening rant.

"Hey dere Jeenya, you be a wonder woman I hear. But you don't know everyting do you? You didn't know George's girlfriend did you now? Plenty of other people here knew 'bout Vanessa but you didn't know. Not until she came to your house and told you all 'bout her and George. Plenty of us with nothing much to do all day, we watch out the windows and we know secrets you don't know. Someday when you get old like me, you'll know some of our secrets."

28
Seth's Story

Rick

The next morning, Rick and Hazel parked, as usual, in the Birdsong's driveway. As usual, Jeenya had coffee ready, this time with a plate of scrambled eggs, bacon and slices of fried breadfruit.

"We'd better have a talk with Seth today," Rick said. "He's the only member of the Overmon family we haven't talked to. I don't expect much, but talking to him could turn up something new."

He called Seth. "We were wondering if Hazel and I could stop by and have a long chat with you. We've talked to everyone else in your family and they've all been helpful. Now we'd like your perspective."

"Sure, I'm free all morning," Seth said. "We can use my office. It's comfortable enough and private. I'll get some doughnuts from the café and what would you and the lady detective like to drink?"

"That's great," Rick said. "I'll take black coffee. Hazel says she'd like a Diet Coke."

When they arrived, the black coffee was hot, one for Rick and one for Seth. The Diet Coke was cold, and there was a glass in case Hazel preferred her drink in a glass.

Even the doughnuts were hot and there was a neat stack of napkins next to them.

"We should visit you more often," Hazel said with a friendly smile. "This is really nice.

"Now," Rick said, "when we're investigating a murder, it often helps to know as much as possible about the victim and his family. We've heard part of the story of your early life, a little from Jeenya, but mostly from Elijah. I'm sure your memories are different."

Seth nodded his head.

"So," Rick said, "we'd like you tell us your story. Start wherever you like."

"My early years," Seth began, "were pretty miserable. The Overmons probably knew I wasn't happy, but I don't think they had any idea how terrible it was. My father, you know, was Adam Overmon, the father of all these other Overmons. He was an Obeah Man and needed to travel to make enough to live on.

"My mother, Betty Black, was very nice looking when she was young. There was a picture on the wall of her in a bright green bikini taken long before I was born. As the years went by, she got heavier and heavier; She didn't take care of herself. Still, my father stopped to see her two or three times a year. They had sex—I can't really call it love-making—then he left without ever saying a word to me.

"My stepfather, Billy Black, didn't want anything to do with me. I wasn't his kid. Both Billy and Betty had real dark skin. My father's skin wasn't real light, but a lot lighter than theirs. People just had to take one look at me and they'd know I wasn't theirs.

"Another thing was that they were named Billy and Betty and all their real children had names starting with a

B. There was Ben, Bobby, Bonnie, Belle, and Barbara.

"My father, since his name was Adam, asked Betty to name me Seth. In the Bible, you know, Adam and Eve had at least three children Cain, Abel, and Seth.

"But I didn't know all that until years later. All I knew back then was that my skin was too light, that my name didn't start with a B, and that I didn't have a father. They all called me 'Bastard.' I didn't know what that meant, but I decided, since it started with a B, that it must be good.

"That ended when I started school. I told the teacher my name was Bastard and she was terribly upset, saying she never wanted to hear me say that word again.

"When I was ten years old, I took a good look at Father one day when he came to see my mother. This man had light skin, and my mother seemed to like him all right. I put two and two together. This could be my real father. I stood by the gate where he'd left his car. I'd seen cars before but never touched one so I went over and touched it gently. I liked the feeling.

"When the light-colored man came out, I reached out and grabbed his hand. 'Please Mr., my name is Seth. They tell me here that I don't have a father, but I think you are my father. Are you?'

"He didn't say anything for a long time. He just looked at me. Then, slowly, he said, 'Yes, Seth, I am your father.'

"'Please Father,' I said, 'the people here all hate me. They call me names. They called me Bastard so much that I thought it was my name. I even told my teacher my name was Bastard. What I want more than anything is to go home with you. You are my father and I know you wouldn't let people be mean to me.'

"He just stood there not saying anything, not frowning

or smiling for a long time. Finally, he nodded. He sent me to pack up my belongings while he went to see my mother.

"When we left, my mother kissed me on the cheek, the first time she'd ever done that. 'Seth,' she said, 'Your father is giving you a chance to be part of his family. Don't you dare mess up and make him send you back here. You understand that?' I nodded. I wasn't sure what it meant to mess up, but I'd have done anything so they wouldn't send me back.

"Next thing, we stopped at a little cottage. I thought at first it was my father's house. He introduced me to Mr. and Mrs. Clarke. He never told me their first names. He gave them some money and asked them to clean me up, to wash me from head to foot, to throw away all my old clothes, and buy me all new clothes. Then he left, saying he'd be back in three days.

"I'll never forget the washing that I got. I was used to being the last kid in a lukewarm laundry tub. I'd never heard of soap. Here they soaked me in a hot tub of water, made me stand up while they scrubbed me with soap from head to foot, and then they turned on the shower and rinsed off all the soap. They told me to look at the water and see how dirty it was.

"They emptied the tub and did it all again. Then they cut my hair and gave me a comb and brush to keep it orderly. They gave me a toothbrush and some toothpaste. I'd never seen such things, so they had to teach me how to brush my teeth, how to use a proper toilet and how to wipe myself with paper.

"Then Mrs. Clarke measured me and went to a market where she bought me a pair of shorts, a shirt, and a pair of sandals. 'These will have to do,' she said, 'until we can buy you some proper clothes.'

"We rode in their car to a place with very tall buildings. I'd never seen the like. Finally, Mr. Clarke found a place to leave his car, and we walked down a sidewalk where you could see through glass windows and see fake people. That was amazing. About half way down the block, we went into one of these buildings.

"First thing Mrs. Clarke bought me was underwear. I'd never heard of underwear. Mr. Clark explained that I was to put on clean underwear every morning. Then we bought socks, shoes, three pairs of long pants, and five nice shirts, shirts with buttons. Then they found me a pair of pajamas. I thought it was funny to wear something to go to sleep.

"Finally, they bought me a fine suit, like the suits important men wear. They told me I was to wear this suit only on Sundays when Mrs. Overmon took me and the other children to go to church.

"As we headed home, I asked 'What is go to church?' As we drove, they explained. Then, that night at dinner, they showed me how to eat properly and how to be polite, like saying please and thank you."

"On the third day, they took me to a dentist who cleaned my teeth and fixed four cavities. Then we visited a doctor who checked me out. Finally, they took me to a barber shop where a nice man gave me a proper haircut. That afternoon, my father came back, told them they'd done a great job, and he took me home.

"The house where my father lived was like a mansion. Now, I'd say upper middle class. I quickly learned that it wasn't really my father's house; It was Ms. Overmon's house. My father also explained that he did a lot of traveling so I wouldn't see him very often. This was a shock. I was being left with a woman who wasn't my mother, and with some of her children. I hadn't gained much except that these people had more money. I hoped these children would be nicer to me than the children I used to live with.

"My father introduced me first to the mother who looked me over to see if she approved. Then my father took me to meet Sally. She was the cleaning lady. She took me to my room, showed me where the toilet was and the shower. She showed me where to put my clean clothes and where to put them when they were dirty, even if they still looked clean. I liked Sally. She was a good explainer, and she seemed to understand that I didn't know how to do things in a fine house like this one.

"The children were at school when I arrived. I heard them when they got home but, since no one took me to meet them, I waited until dinner. There, Mrs. Overmon introduced me to my new brothers and sisters. Sharona and Josiah were older than me. Jeenya and Elijah were younger.

"Mrs. Overmon explained that Jeenya wasn't actually her child, that Jeenya was the daughter of the cleaning lady but that it didn't matter because Jeenya was such a sweet girl, and they all loved Jeenya just as if she was a member of the family.

"This was a surprise, but it made me feel better. If Mrs. Overmon loved the daughter of the cleaning lady this much, perhaps she would love me too. I was wrong, of course. I was her wandering husband's bastard.

"Then she said one more thing, 'Seth, I've been thinking what you should call me. Mrs. Overmon is too formal. You shouldn't call me Mother. I'm not your mother. Perhaps you can call me Mum.' Then she told me where to sit.

"I started to reach for some food when Jeenya pulled my hand back and whispered, "Wait. Watch what I do." And that was just the beginning of what Jeenya taught me.

"But let me get to the point of the story, detectives, life was a whole lot better at the Overmon's house. I got a good education, I dressed like a gentleman, and I always had plenty to eat.

"Jeenya was nice to me. She was nice to everyone. But having the cleaning woman's daughter be nice to me wasn't what I wanted. Most of the others tried being polite for the first week or two. Then they ignored me, except for one person.

"That was Josiah. I don't know why. Maybe boys of that age are naturally mean. When the others were around, he ignored me, just like they did. But when no one was looking, he sometimes jabbed me in the stomach or the back and whispered things like, 'Don't you ever forget, you aren't really an Overmon,' or 'You understand, you are not my brother. You never will be.' He always finished with 'You aren't anything but a filthy bastard.'

"When Josiah invited me to live here, when he said I'd be the boss at the garage, I wondered if he'd still be calling me names. But he really had changed. He still didn't treat me like a brother, but he treated me decently enough.

"That's my history," Seth said. "What else do you have on your mind?"

"Seth, we want you to think again," Hazel said, "about who in Jamaica Lakes might have wanted Josiah dead, and why. The other Overmons don't seem to have any ideas."

"The only people I can think of," Seth said, "are the families where the wife was seeing Josiah but most of those, the people who were really upset, have all moved away. Of those who are still around, the only one that comes to mind is Victor. I don't know just what went on with Victor's wife and Josiah or if that had anything to do with her suicide, but I've heard Victor warning George to be careful about letting his wife see Josiah and it sure sounded like Victor blamed Josiah for his wife's death."

"Is there anything Victor has said or done recently?" Rick asked. "Anything we should know about?"

"Hard to say," Seth said. "Things he's done recently might not have anything to do with Josiah but, one day, Victor asked where he should go to buy a knife, a good sharp knife. He said he didn't want a kitchen knife; he wanted a knife to protect himself. He thought he'd sleep better with a good knife nearby. I suggested the sport store just across the bridge in Stuart. They sell hunting knives."

"Anything else?" Rick asked.

"Well, after that, Victor seems to have gotten interested in weapons. He asked me, maybe a week later, if I knew how to make a garrote. I think he watched something on TV about someone being killed with a garrote. He made one here in the Garage using an old broken broom handle and the wire from a phone that didn't work anymore.

"I asked if he was planning to add a gun to his collection but he said no, that he didn't like guns. That's all I remember. If I think of anything else, I will let you know."

29
Evidence

Jeenya

Having nothing else planned, Rick and Hazel headed back to Jeenya's house. Over lunch, they asked about her early memories of living with the Overmons and meeting Seth.

She found it surprising that any of them referred to her as the cleaning lady's daughter. "They just called me Jeenya," she said. "I knew I wasn't one of the Overmons. After all, I slept downstairs with my mother, telling her all the wonderful things I had learned or done that day. She was always so happy for me. But, with the Overmons, I really did feel like one of them.

"That changed when Seth came. At breakfast that day, Mrs. Overmon told us that we had another brother, a brother with a different mother, and that he'd be coming to live with us. 'Seth,' she said, 'grew up with a very poor family. I'm sure it won't be easy for him to get adjusted to living here. He probably never learned proper manners and I'm sure his English won't be very good.'

"She went on to say, 'I'm counting on all of you to treat the poor boy nicely. Be polite. Help him learn English and good manners. And Jeenya, sweetie, I'm counting on you the most. He will probably feel more comfortable being corrected by you than by the rest of us. Do what you can to help him.'

"When she said that, I had to think about why she thought I would be the best one to help him. I think that, just like Seth, I came from a poor family. I hadn't thought of myself that way before.

"After that, they all seemed to treat me differently. There were the Overmons and then there was me and Seth. The Overmons usually treated Seth politely, but not very nicely. They were still nice to me. They all liked me. What I never understood was why none of them ever liked Seth.

"The other thing I didn't understand was why Josiah was so mean to Seth. I never saw any of the others treat him that way. Josiah would poke Seth so hard that it hurt. I could tell it hurt. Then he'd call Seth names. Josiah called Seth a bastard, a word I'd never heard.

"I asked my mother what a bastard was. Then I asked her if I was a bastard. She said that since she wasn't married, I probably was, but since I was so nice to everyone, they probably would never think about it.

"I did my best to teach Seth English and good manners and he did get a little better, but his attitude never changed. I think that if Seth had been more friendly, they would all have liked him more but I don't think he knew how to make friends. I told Mrs. Overmon that and she said she thought I must be right.

"After we left Jamaica and after I got married, I was still treated as a friend but not as part of the Overmon family. And you might have noticed that when you talk about the Overmons, people mean Josiah, Sharona, and Elijah. They might add Seth as an afterthought. I know Seth talks about how happy he is working there in the garage and I know Josiah no longer hits him or calls him names. But I can tell that Seth still feels left out, and that he feels like nobody cares about him. As far as I know, Seth still has never had a real friend. At first, I tried to be his friend but, since he didn't like me back, you couldn't ever call that being friends."

We were still sitting at the table when Rick got a phone call. "Yes, I understand," he said. "I really appreciate your calling. You are right. This could be something very important. We'll be right over."

"That was Seth," he said. He's at the garage and was emptying a garbage can and noticed a bag with what seems to have bloody clothes in it. He seemed kind of shook up. about it. He's afraid he might even have found the knife used to kill Josiah and he's scared the killer might be one of the men working there in his garage.

"So, we'll pick it up, drop it off at the lab, talk to Nate, and be back as soon as we can."

"Rick, if you think one of those young men is guilty," Jeenya said, "don't take them to the police station. They'd be so scared that they wouldn't want to say a word. What you need to do is bring him here. They aren't scared of me. I could ask them what happened and you might be surprised how much they would tell me."

Rick nodded, wondering what Nate would say about that. In fact, he wasn't sure what he thought of the idea.

They arrived at the garage in three minutes or less.

Seth took them into his office and showed them the garbage can. Inside, there was a plastic bag with a torn corner where blood appeared to be seeping out. Something shiny that might be the tip of a knife was sticking out.

Seth brought a cardboard box. "Why don't you put it in the box?" he suggested. "I don't want the men to see you taking it out. I don't want whoever put it here to know it's gone. It will also be less messy. You don't want blood dripping on your clothes or on the seat of your car. If your people want to check the garbage can for prints or something, have them call me after five and I'll let them in."

Rick knew they shouldn't move evidence, but here, the evidence was in a bag. So, they put the bag in the box, thanked Seth for his help, and headed straight to the station. They dropped the box off at the lab, telling them about getting into the garage after five. They sat down and wrote up the report of the day's events. Then they went to talk to Nate.

Nate already had the first report from the lab. "The two of you really hit the jackpot," Nate said with a big grin. "In that bag you brought in, they found a bloody shirt, a bloody hunting knife, and a bloody garrote and they have someone's fingerprints on the bag, bloody fingerprints. So, what do you plan to do next?"

"The knife and the garotte," Rick said, "clearly points to Victor. According to Seth, Victor recently bought a hunting knife and made a garotte."

"What are you waiting for?" Nate asked. "Bring him in for questioning and let's see if we can bring this case to a very quick end."

"Not yet," Rick said.

He remembered what Elijah told them. He said that if the killer lived in Jamaica Lakes, Jeenya Birdsong would be the one person most likely to understand his motives and that she could ask questions and he would tell the truth. He imagined talking to those men again, day after day, and still not finding any hard evidence. Jeenya might be the one chance they had to learn the truth.

"We are working on a plan that might work better. Give us an hour or two and we'll be back with the plan."

Back in the car, Hazel asked Rick what he was planning. "Do you really think Victor is more likely to confess to Jeenya than he would at the station?"

"I don't know," he confessed. "I really don't know. That's what we're going to talk about when we get there."

Jeenya

Jeenya and Zeke still sat at the table. "All right," Zeke said. "We are waiting to hear what Seth found. Was it really some sort of evidence?"

Rick started by telling them what Seth had said earlier about Victor getting a hunting knife and making a garrote. "Those," he said, "were the weapons used by whoever killed Josiah. And what's in the bag? A bloody shirt, a bloody knife, and a bloody garrote that looks very much like the one Victor made."

"Looks mighty bad for Victor," Zeke said. "I'll bet the guys at the police station are ready to take all this evidence and lock Victor up immediately."

"The other possibility, of course," Jeenya said "is that someone else was the killer, and they planted that bag of evidence."

"The problem in that," Zeke said, is that the person who did kill Josiah would have needed to get a hold of Victor's knife and his garrote. That wouldn't be easy."

"That's true," she said. "At least, if we bring Victor

here, if you let him talk to me, he'll have a chance to tell us what really happened."

Zeke frowned but didn't say anything. Jeenya stared at her husband, knowing he was worried that it might not work.

"Zeke" she said softly, "I don't think Victor will confess to our detectives. But I'm just a friendly old lady and I can be very understanding.

She turned to Rick and Hazel. "If I work it right, Victor really might tell me exactly what he did and why."

"The problem," Zeke said, "is that as soon as Victor tells you what he did, he might feel like he has to kill you too."

"I am not stupid, Ezekiel Birdsong. I am not planning to talk to him by myself. We will all sit down together. I'll put Victor on one side of the table right across from me. You two detectives will sit one on either side of him. That's not only for my protection. Victor can't see you very well if you're on his side of the table. I want that man looking me straight in the eye. Zeke, you can sit off to one side but you let me do most of the talking. If I get stuck and one of you wants to join in, that's fine. But it's important that Victor talks to me."

Everyone was silent for a minute. Jeenya was starting to regret her suggestion. This was exactly what she'd been trying to avoid. She wanted to help Rick, but she hadn't wanted to take over. The problem was that she couldn't think of any other way to get the truth.

"You really think," Rick asked, "that Victor will talk to you?"

Jeenya nodded very slowly. "Yes, I think there's a good chance. He'd certainly tell me more than he'd tell you.

Rick looked at Hazel. "What do you think?"

Hazel frowned. "It's worth a try. I'd agree that he's likely to say more to Jeenya than to the police. I know I would say more to Jeenya than I would to the police."

"I don't like the idea of Jeenya talking to a killer," Zeke said. "It makes me nervous but, if my dear wife thinks she can get Victor to talk to her, I expect she really can."

Rick looked at Jeenya and then nodded slowly. "Jeenya, I wish there was some other way. But, if you think you can get Victor to talk, I think we should go for it."

Rick and Hazel returned to the station and went straight to Nate's office. "We decided to try our plan first," he said. He outlined the details.

Nate leaned back in his chair, his hands behind his head. "This Jeenya, she is someone you know well?" Rick nodded. "You trust what she says?"

"Yes sir," Rick said. "I think she's right, saying the man would be too scared to say anything here. But Jeenya has a way with people. People talk to her about all kinds of problems. She knows these people. She knew Victor's wife and talked to her just weeks before she committed suicide. If there's anyone who can get Victor to tell us what happened, it would be Jeenya."

"And the two of you will be there while she does this?" Nate asked.

"Yes sir. We'll be sitting on each side of Victor, listening to the whole thing.

"Well then, we will let your Jeenya use her magic. It is certainly worth a try. But I think we'll put a plain clothes man near the man's house until then just to be sure he doesn't try getting away."

Hazel went with Andy, the plain-clothes man who was assigned for the first shift, and found him a place to park near the garage where he could see both the garage and Victor's house.

That night, as if she knew what was going on, Ida Lee was laughing.

"Oh my, Miz Jeenya, I can't stop laughing. You don't do nothing to help those poor detectives, do you? I hear dey spent nearly all morning listening to Seth telling stories. And then what do they do?" She laughed some more.

"You make dem spend the afternoon listening to your stories. Just how are dey going to find dat killer when all dey do is listen to stories all day? I sure wouldn't trust any stories Seth is telling them and I have my doubts about your stories. So, what stunt you be planning next? I'll be sitting here waiting to see."

30

A Bowl of Goat Curry

Jeenya

The next morning, Rick and Hazel were there for breakfast. "So Jeenya," Rick said, "this is your show. What time do we start and how do we get Victor to come here? Would he come visit if you called him?"

"Give me a couple hours to plan," she said. "You and Hazel should get him here. You can tell him that I'm fixing something good to eat. "Men usually come running," Jeenya said, "when there's something good to eat."

"We can do that," Hazel said. "We'll check with Seth and tell Victor we'd rather he come here where it's more comfortable. What are planning to have for us to eat?"

"I like your thinking," Jeenya said. "I have some brownie mix. It won't take long. It will smell good when he comes in and he won't mind waiting until they're out of the oven. I never knew a man who didn't love brownies. I might even start with some left-over goat curry."

"This might work," Rick said. "First, we'll tell him about the brownies, and say we'd rather do the interview at your house so we can get some brownies when they're hot. We will say you suggested bringing him there to talk.

If Victor refuses to come here, we can suggest going to the police station. I think he'd rather come here."

Later as they drove to the garage. "Rick," Hazel said. "This just doesn't feel right to me."

"You mean about having Jeenya asking the questions?"

"Not that," she said. "It's like this is all too easy, with Seth just happening to find all the evidence." It seems to me like someone is trying to frame Victor."

"I've been thinking the same thing," Rick said, "but I keep telling myself that, if he didn't do it, we should find that out today but we cannot ignore all this evidence."

They parked and spoke briefly to Seth. Then Seth told Victor that Rick and Hazel needed to talk to them.

Victor frowned. "How come you need to talk to me? I ain't done nothing."

"If you haven't done anything wrong," Rick said, "There's nothing to worry about, is there? We decided to talk at Jeenya's house. She's even got brownies cooking in the oven."

"Guess I haven't much choice, do I?" Victor said, following them to the car.

As Jeenya waited, she tried to look cheerful, but she didn't feel that way.

Victor probably hadn't eaten homemade goat curry for years, and now, if they put him in prison, he might never have another opportunity to taste it.

As the car pulled up in front of the Birdsong home, Jeenya came out on the front steps to welcome Victor. She took one look at his hunched shoulders and the pain in his face and knew what she needed to do. She wrapped her arms around Victor and gave him a long, warm hug.

"Come on inside now, all of you. We're going to sit in the kitchen to talk."

The smell of chocolate filled the kitchen. "Those brownies smell awful good," Victor said. "It's been years since I've had fresh-baked brownies. I'd forgotten how great they smell."

"I feel the same way," Rick said. "This brings back memories of when Homer and I were young. You used to bake brownies for us, Jeenya. If my mother or grandmothers ever baked brownies, I don't remember it."

Jeenya busied herself pouring tall glasses of lemonade. Out of the corner of her eye, she saw Rick and Hazel take their seats, one on either side of Victor as planned. Zeke sat at one end of the table, leaving Jeenya the seat across from Victor. The table was already set with small dishes, forks, and white paper napkins.

"It will be awhile before those brownies are done," Jeenya told Victor. "If you're feeling hungry, I have some left-over goat curry. Maybe you'd like a bowl?"

Victor nodded. "Please. It's been years, Jeenya, since I ate homemade goat curry. I've heard people say your goat curry is delicious."

Jeenya took out the left-over curry and heated it in the microwave. Victor, she knew, wasn't just hungry for goat curry and warm brownies. The poor man was starved for love. When she hugged him, that was probably the first time Victor had been hugged in over ten years.

As Jeenya worked, Rick began the conversation as planned. "Tell me Victor," he said, "how you happened to come to Jamaica Lakes."

"Let me think," Victor mumbled. "First, my parents

lived here. I visited a couple times and then I just stayed. Later, my parents moved back to Jamaica because Grandpa was sick. I was washing dishes at a restaurant back then but looking for something better when Mr. Overmon decided to add a garage. I was friends with Abe Overmon and he said they were looking for men to work in the garage. I didn't know anything about working in a garage but Abe said they'd send me to a program where we'd learn how to fix cars."

"Thanks," Rick said, Now, why don't you tell us about your life since then?"

"Well, I met George and the others back in automotive school. That must have been fifteen or sixteen years ago. Later, Abe introduced me to Elaenia. She was my wife, you know. It was a couple years later when Abraham's wife, Ruth, introduced George and Angela. The four of us sometimes went to the movies together. Some days we had picnics at the beach. We had dinner together at their house one week, at our house the next. Back then we really were good friends."

Jeenya carried the bowl of hot curry to the table and placed it in front of Victor. "There you go. I had a feeling, Victor, that a bowl of goat curry might be just what you needed."

Jeenya watched as he held the bowl up to his nose and inhaled. She knew he was enjoying the smells and probably memories of happier times. He took a spoonful, chewed slowly and swallowed. He smiled at Jeenya. "This really is the best goat curry I ever tasted."

As Victor enjoyed his curry, Rick asked another question. "You said that back then you and George were good friends. Did it change?"

"It was different after my wife died. It didn't feel right having one happy couple and me without my wife. Awkward, you know. George and Angela would ask me to do things with them, but I'd say no. I really didn't feel like going out and having a good time. After a while they quit asking."

"You didn't socialize any more with George and Angela, but you and George were still good friends?"

"People thought we were. George was always going out of his way to talk to me, especially after work. He always had some stupid joke or a funny story to tell me like he thought it would cheer me up. But when you lose your wife, funny stories don't cheer you up at all. I thought they were annoying. I kept wishing he'd quit, but he didn't."

"I understand that," Rick said. "The friendship wasn't the same."

Victor scratched his head. "When I met George, we had a lot in common. We listened to the same music and both like pizza."

Jeenya watched Victor. She knew he watched her as she took the brownies from the oven and set them out to cool.

"Maybe being married wore George down," Victor said. "Angela wanted a baby but George didn't. When she didn't get pregnant, Angela might have blamed him. George wasn't as happy as he used to be."

Jeenya noticed that Victor's bowl was empty and went to pick it up. Victor smiled appreciatively and Jeenya had the feeling he had begun to relax. Rick was doing his job, continuing with questions that weren't terribly stressful.

"We learned something interesting about George," Rick said. "Apparently, after he and his first wife had several children, he went out and got a vasectomy so he couldn't have any more children. We understand he was afraid to tell Angela; afraid she'd leave him. Did he talk to you about that?"

Now Jeenya was cutting the brownies and putting them on a plate, but she turned to watch.

Victor scratched the back of his neck. "Yeah. George told me all that, but he told me not to say anything about it so I didn't. He knew Angela wasn't ever going to get pregnant, you know. He knew she'd blame him.

"Angela wanted to see Josiah to get herbal tea and all that. She thought it would help her get pregnant. George tried telling her not to go but Angela was really determined. It made George feel terrible, not being able to give her a baby. If it had been me, I'd have told her right off about the vasectomy. But George was afraid she'd leave him."

Jeenya paid close attention. The conversation had begun well. Now, if she could get Victor to trust her, if she could get him to open up and share his feelings, she might be able to do this. She'd need to take the conversation to a deeper level.

She liked Victor. She understood the pain he must be feeling, but her intuition told her something had happened, something that made him lose control. She needed to watch her step. She didn't want him to lose control again. But she did want to help Victor face what he had done.

31

Brownies Fresh from the Oven

Jeenya

Jeenya placed two plates of brownies on the table. As Victor and the others helped themselves, she sat down and quietly took over the conversation. "Victor, did you ever talk to George about how Josiah used to help women get pregnant?"

Victor stared at her. "I don't understand," he finally said. "Why are you asking me about that?"

Jeenya waited for him to answer the question. She took a drink of lemonade and looked at him.

"Sure. I told him. George needed to know about all that."

"Was he worried about Angela after you told him?"

"Maybe. Just a little. He'd heard about Sharona always being there with Josiah so he didn't worry too much."

"You had a good reason to talk to George, didn't you? Victor. You were remembering how Elaenia wanted to get pregnant, weren't you?"

He nodded his head.

"And, when she didn't get pregnant, Elaenia went to Josiah for help, didn't she?"

He nodded again.

"What happened, Victor? We know Elaenia stopped going to see Josiah. Why did she stop?"

Victor was silent.

"Did she stop seeing him because she was pregnant?"

"Yeah," he said. "She was so excited and so was I. We both thought having a kid would be wonderful."

"I remember, Victor, how you went bragging all over Jamaica Lakes telling people you and Elaenia were going to have a baby."

Victor smiled.

"But then, something happened, didn't it?" Jeenya gave him time to think about it. "Back in those days," Jeenya continued, "Sharona wasn't working with Josiah. Elaenia and Josiah had sex, didn't they, Victor? Did she tell you she was raped? Or did she tell you she'd agreed to it?"

"That's not true. It isn't. Elaenia would never have sex with anybody but me. You understand that? She was my wife."

"That's what you thought, wasn't it? It must have been a terrible shock when she told you. Then you both wanted to keep it a secret. You never told anyone, did you?"

"Stop. Please stop," Victor said. "You don't know what happened. You're imagining all this and I don't understand why, after all these years. Why are you asking me about Elaenia?"

It was almost as painful for Jeenya as it was for Victor, but she needed to get the truth out, the truth Victor had denied for so many years. "Your wife was pregnant with another man's child and you had to decide what to do about it."

Victor stared at her. His mouth hung open. The vein

in his forehead throbbed. "Okay," Victor said, sounding like the breath had been knocked out of him. "Elaenia was pregnant. She was going to have Josiah's baby."

He turned back to Jeenya. "I wanted her to have an abortion, but she refused. We fought about it. I said things I wish I'd never said. If only I had acted differently, if only I'd acted like I was happy about her being pregnant, if only I'd told her how much I loved her and that we'd both love the baby and it wouldn't matter who the real father was… If I'd done that, Elaenia would still be alive. None of this would have happened.

"But since you want to know the whole story, I'll tell you what happened. I lost my temper. I told Elaenia I wasn't going to raise some other man's bastard. I said that and worse. That night, when I was asleep, Elaenia got up. She went down by the lake. She went to the table where we used to go for picnics, and she took all those pills. She killed herself. She killed herself and she killed our baby.

"You want to know how I felt? I felt like I'd killed my wife. I murdered the only woman I'll ever love. It was my fault she did it. If only I had gone with her to see Josiah, it never would have happened.

"I couldn't see any reason to go telling people Josiah slept with my wife and that Elaenia was going to have his baby. Everyone just assumed she had a miscarriage and lost the baby. I let them think that. I told that story so many times I started believing it myself. Everyone thought she was depressed because she lost our baby.

"So now do you feel better, Jeenya, now that you know why Elaenia killed herself? Are you happy knowing that I killed the only person I ever loved? Is that what you wanted to hear?" Victor took the last brownie on the plate and took a huge bite.

Jeenya wondered if he thought having his mouth full would keep him from needing to answer questions. She felt a terrible sadness now, sympathy for Victor living all these years with so much guilt and pain.

"You must have felt terrible, Victor. You've been missing Elaenia and feeling guilty all these years."

Victor nodded. Tears were dripping down his cheeks. "I'll always feel terrible. There's no way I can forget."

"But it wasn't just your fault, was it?" Jeenya asked. "You also blamed Josiah, didn't you?"

"Of course, I blamed him. He got her pregnant. I can't believe she let him do that. Sometimes I think he used Obeah magic on her so she would let him do that. But, however he did it, I blame him, not just her."

"Now Victor," Jeenya said softly, "why don't you go ahead and tell us what happened Friday night? Victor took his time, chewing slowly, and then swallowing. He took a long drink of lemonade.

Jeenya glanced over at Rick. He was running a finger along his scar. She had a feeling he was thinking the same thing. She didn't feel victorious. She felt very sad.

"You know everything else, Jeenya. I don't know what sort of magic you use, but it seems like you know what happened better than I do."

"I know it's not easy, Victor, but you need to go ahead and tell us the rest. It will make you feel better to get it all out."

32
Victor's Story

Jeenya

Victor sighed. "After Elaenia killed herself, I spent a lot of time walking through the woods. One day, I found an old phone cord. I took it home and put it in a dresser drawer. Another day I found an old broom in the trash. I took that, cut two short pieces, and drilled holes in them. I used those as handles, one at each end of the phone cord. It's what they call a garrote. I saw something about that on television, maybe on one of the CSI shows.

"I hid the stupid thing in a dresser drawer under my sweaters. I never planned to use it. I just liked having a weapon. I showed it to Seth one day. He thought it was great. He even let me use some of the tools to make it smooth so it looked better.

"Seth said if I wanted a good weapon, I should get a knife, not a kitchen knife, but a hunting knife that's real sharp. He even told me where I could buy one.

"He didn't know it but, when I was a boy, I used to look at knives like that and asked my parents to buy me one. I asked for a knife for Christmas and for my birthday but I never got one. Now I had one. It made me feel good. I felt strong. I felt like I could protect myself.

"Seth was like my only real friend then. I never showed these things to George. He wouldn't understand. I even told Seth what I told you about why Elaenia died. He understood how much I hated Josiah. It really was Josiah's fault, you know, that Elaenia did it. Seth asked if I was angry enough to kill Josiah. I said I was, but I don't think he believed me. He said if I was serious, I'd go ahead and do it. I kept telling him, I wasn't ready, that it would take me a while to work up my courage. What I didn't say was that I didn't think I'd ever be brave enough to kill someone."

Victor stopped as if the story was over.

"All right, Victor," Jeenya said. "What happened after that?

"Victor took a deep breath. "What do you mean? I told you everything. What else do you want me to say?"

"What happened Friday night, Victor?"

"Friday night? Nothing happened Friday night," he said with his voice beginning to shake. "What are you talking about?"

"Victor," Jeenya said softly, "just look at me. I know this is hard to talk about. You're probably trying to convince yourself it never happened, aren't you?" Victor nodded. "Why don't you start by telling us what time it was when you went back to the Garage?"

"The garage?" Victor said. "How did you know?"

Jeenya sat quietly, waiting for Victor to continue

"All right," Victor said. "It was about nine that night, just as I was getting ready for bed, I got a phone call. Seth had never called me before. Anyway, he told me to bring my weapons, both of them, and come over to the garage. He had something he wanted to show me. So, I got dressed. But, when I put my weapons in my pocket, I had a strange feeling that something bad might happen. That seemed foolish. What would Seth say if I didn't bring my weapons? So, I left them in my pocket and went on over.

"Then, Jeenya, it was really weird. Seth had told me how he learned about Obeah from his father when he lived in Jamaica, but I thought that was all in the past. That night he had a small table set up with candles and other things. He had me sit there and place my weapons on the table. He lit the candles, speaking in what sounded like another language. My guess is that he was doing some sort of blessing. I didn't think that was going to help much, since I don't believe in Obeah, but I figured it couldn't hurt.

"Next, he took some sort of oil and mixed it with some dried herbs and then rubbed it on my face. He had me take off my shirt so he could rub in on my chest. He said he was rubbing it over my heart. And then, this was the strangest part. He had me unzip my pants and he rubbed the oil over," and here he hesitated. "Over my private parts, you know. That was sort of embarrassing.

"After he put away the oil, he took some feathers. They looked to me like chicken feathers, and he put them in a small bag, a black velvet bag. Then he took some dirt and put that in the bag. He added bones, hair, fingernail clippings, a small pink plastic heart, and even a small piece of cloth that he said was from Josiah's shirt, one he'd thrown away.

"He added a picture of a woman he called Nanny of the Maroons. She was supposed to have been some sort of powerful Obeah Woman in Jamaica who helped free a lot of slaves. Seth said her picture would free me from my fears. The last thing he added was a picture of Josiah. He put it on a dish, burned it, and put the ashes in the velvet bag. The bag had a long loop attached and Seth put it over my head like a necklace.

"Now he got out two glasses, ordinary glasses. He put a little ground up herbs into each of them and some sort of powder in my glass. He poured Coke into his glass and, since he knew I liked Dr. Pepper, he poured a can of that into my glass. He stirred both glasses while saying more in his strange language.

"Finally, he handed me my glass and said, 'Drink. Drink all of it. It will make you strong. It will give your courage.' So, what else could I do? I drank it. It tasted a little strange with the herbs in it, but mostly it just tasted like Dr. Pepper.

"After that, I'm not sure what happened. I remember feeling a little dizzy. Seth told me to lie down on the floor and it would go away.

"The next thing I remember was waking up. The lights were still on, but the table with the candles was gone, the little bag he put around my neck was gone. But right in front of me I could see my knife, but somehow it was all bloody. My garrote was all bloody and my shirt was there, all covered in blood. But that wasn't all. *I was bloody.* There was blood on my hands, blood on my chest and on my pants and my shoes.

"My first thought was that this was animal blood, and that it was all part of Seth's ritual. Then I started thinking what the other men would think if they came in and saw all this.

"I found a plastic bag, put all the bloody stuff in the bag and threw it in the garbage. I didn't want anyone to see it in the garbage so I found more trash and put that over the bag. Then I got paper towels from the bathroom and did my best to clean the blood off the floor. I didn't want to put those in the garbage with the other stuff so I flushed it all down the toilet, a little at a time. Then, since it was only about four in the morning, I went home, took a shower, and went to bed but I didn't sleep too well."

Victor paused. "I can't tell you any more, Jeenya. Really. Could I have another glass of lemonade?"

Jeenya nodded to Zeke and he refilled Victor's glass. "Take your time, Victor. I know this isn't easy but you are doing a really good job so far."

The room was quiet while Victor drank his lemonade, very slowly, one sip and then another, until, finally, his glass was empty.

"All right, Victor," Jeenya said softly. "We need to learn the end of the story. You might want to take a few deep breaths and try to relax. Then tell us what happened next. Did you begin to remember what happened?"

Victor took several deep breaths, letting the air out slowly. "That next morning," he said slowly, hesitantly, "everything was crazy. You remember. People were saying Josiah was dead, that he was murdered. People were putting salt around their houses.

"I went into work and Seth gave me a big smile and said something like, 'Good job, Victor.' At first, I didn't understand but gradually I figured it out. Victor thought I'd killed Mr. Overmon. But that didn't make sense. He knew I was sound asleep. I couldn't have done it.

"Then I started to wonder. I remembered all that Obeah stuff and I wondered if Seth had put a curse on me, a curse that made me kill Mr. Overmon. Even though I didn't remember doing it, I must have killed Josiah. That must have been where all the blood came from. I started to wonder if Seth had put a curse on me, did that make him guilty of murder or was I the one who was guilty?

"Next thing I did was run to the bathroom and vomit. I still couldn't believe it. How could I have killed Josiah and not remember anything? I might have done it, but whether I did or I didn't, I needed to act normal, like all that Obeah stuff never happened.

"After that, the detectives started asking questions. When they asked about the crazy man at the grocery, the one who threatened to slit Josiah's throat, I felt hopeful. I thought maybe he killed Josiah, not me. But then, I guess that man had an alibi. I didn't.

"I thought about running away, but I figured that they'd be sure to catch me and, even if they didn't, I'd never feel happy worrying about being caught. I tried to pretend it never happened. I hoped it really was a dream, a very bad dream, that I'd wake up and discover none of this happened.

"Now, I don't know what to think or what to do. I still don't remember doing any of this. I keep wondering if it is really possible to kill someone in your sleep. So, do you have any other questions? What happens to me now?"

"Now," Rick said, "we have to take you to the police station. Even if you don't remember what happened, we picked up that bag with the bloody knife, garrote, and shirt yesterday. With that kind of evidence, they will have to question you at the station."

"You know the whole story now. If I had a gun, I might just shoot myself. That would be easier than going to prison. But I don't have a gun. I guess it will be easier sitting in prison, knowing it's over. Otherwise, I'd be running scared the rest of my life.

"And Jeenya," Victor said. "I don't want you feeling bad about this, about getting me arrested. I'm glad it's over, just like you said I would be. And the brownies were awful good too."

Victor and the two detectives stood up. He was ready to go with them.

"Before you go, Victor," Jeenya said. "I have one important thing to tell you. You did NOT kill your wife. You have no need to go on feeling guilty about that. You and Elaenia were both young and impulsive. You didn't stop to think before you said those things, but Elaenia should have known that, if she'd just given you a few days to think about it, you would have apologized. You would have told her that, if she really wanted that baby, it would be fine with you.

"Like you, Elaenia was impulsive. If she had just thought things through for another few days, she'd have realized she had other choices too. She could have had the baby and given it up for adoption. She could have left you and raised that baby by herself. And probably, once that baby was born, you wouldn't have been able to help yourself. You would have loved that baby as much as she would have.

"You did NOT kill Elaenia. That was her decision and hers alone, a foolish, spur-of-the-moment decision, but it was hers. If you had suspected what she was planning to do, you would have stopped her, wouldn't you?"

Victor nodded.

"Don't feel guilty. It wasn't your fault." Jeenya reached out and gave him one last warm hug.

Rick took out his handcuffs. Victor nodded and held out his hands. Jeenya watched as the two detectives led Victor to the car. She was crying as Victor turned one last time and tried to smile at her. She waved. Victor, she knew, was not an evil man. A truly evil man would not have confessed.

In other circumstances, Victor and Elaenia would now be a happy couple, proud of their child, respected in the community. But Jeenya could not turn back time to give Victor or anyone else a second chance. If Victor did kill Josiah, he would be punished.

Zeke hugged his teary wife. "Jeenya, my love. You did what you had to do. And I want you to know what you were doing. You were loving Victor. You loved him with a hug. You loved him with food. You loved him by listening to him and showing that you really cared. For you, I think a spiritual advisor is someone who loves people who needs loving.

That night, Ida Lee sat at the window and cried.

"Miz Jeenya, at first it looked like you were having a party over dere. I could smell those brownies cooking. I wished you'd sent a few of them over to me. I do love brownies when dey are hot out the oven. Den I see Victor coming with the detectives. I smiled at first when you hugged him so warm and friendly like. I tink it must be his birthday.

"But then, at the end, poor Victor is wearing handcuffs and everyone be looking terrible sad and I know it wasn't no birthday. I 'spect maybe poor Victor went and killed the Obeah man. Victor probably tinking the Obeah man killed that sweet wife of his. I'm sure I'll learn the truth soon enough. What I really want to know, Miz Jeenya, is did you trick poor Victor into confessing?"

33

Perhaps Another Alternative

Rick

The next morning, Rick called Jeenya. "We've had breakfast, but we want to see you at about ten if that's all right. Yesterday, at the station, Victor told the same story, but he cut out some of the details. Even if he says he might have killed Josiah, that's not much of a confession when he doesn't remember doing it.

"They will have a psychologist talk to him this morning. He might have a case of repressed memory but Hazel and I agree that the problem could be something different."

"Ten or ten-thirty would be fine," Jeenya said. "Yesterday we got a list of herbs Sharona wants. Zeke is collecting some of the herbs. I'm getting ready to harvest the others."

Rick and Hazel arrived at the Birdsong's house just after ten. "Don't worry about us," Rick said. "We'll sit by the flower garden and relax a little." It was nearly eleven when Zeke and Jeenya were done and ready to talk.

"First," Rick said, "we talked to Seth the other day and there were some interesting differences between how he told the story and how Victor told it.

"According to Seth, Victor came to him asking for help to improve the garrote and Victor came to Seth asking where to buy a good knife.

"According to Victor, however, it was Seth who suggested he improve his garrote. It was Seth who suggested he buy the knife and told him where to buy it. That's not a big deal, but it is interesting. It was also Seth who asked if Victor was brave enough to kill someone."

"That's not all," Hazel said. "We didn't know about the garrote or knife until Seth told us about it. Then it was Seth who called us just a few hours later to tell us about the bag with the bloody shirt and weapons. You might wonder why he looked through the garbage."

"It wasn't Victor," Rick said, "asking for help to build up his courage. Seth planned the Obeah show to build up Victor's courage whether he wanted it or not. Then there was that drink to give Victor courage. We suspect the white powder was two, maybe three strong sleeping pills. Ground up like that, the pills would make Victor dizzy and, before long, he would be sound asleep. What do you think so far, Jeenya?" Rick asked.

"I'd say you're on to something," Zeke said. "It bothered me that Victor kept saying Seth did this, and Seth said that, and Seth told me. I wanted to tell Victor to stop doing what Seth said to do and think for himself."

"I felt the same way," Jeenya said, "but my mind was focused on what I needed to say next as well as listening carefully to every word he said. So, Rick, are you saying Victor killed Josiah in a trance like sleepwalking, or are you saying he just went to sleep and never killed anyone?"

"Well," Rick said. "That is the question, isn't it? Some

sleeping pills do occasionally cause sleepwalking. The problem is that most of the time, they just make people sleep. It seems unlikely that Victor was sleepwalking, that he picked up his garrote and the knife, that he walked down the dark road, and that he went inside and killed Josiah."

"The other alternative," Hazel said, "is that Victor just slept there on the floor until he woke up. Meanwhile, someone else took Victor's weapons, killed Josiah, came back to the garage and left the bloody shirt and weapons in front of Victor. There is only one person who could have done that."

"Seth," Jeenya said. "You are suggesting that the person who killed Josiah, who killed his own brother, was Seth."

"It looks that way to me," Zeke said, "unless Seth had an accomplice and I can't picture Seth having someone else do the killing. Jeenya, what do you think? You know Seth better than anyone else. Could Seth have done this?"

Jeenya nodded her head. "Yes," she whispered. "As much as I hate to believe Seth did it, I think he could have done it and that he was much more likely than Victor to kill Josiah."

Rick asked, "Did Seth hate his brother? Did he hate him enough to kill him?"

Again, Jeenya nodded her head and whispered, "Yes."

"What do we do now?" Hazel asked. "We have several choices. We could talk to him in his office. We could ask him to join us here. We could ask him to meet us at the police station, perhaps to talk about Victor."

Zeke spoke first, "I don't think he'd want to come here. He knows that Victor came here and left in handcuffs."

Jeenya agreed, "This isn't the right place, and neither

is his office. My choice would be the police station. I like your idea of starting by discussing Victor. That shouldn't be too intimidating."

"I have one suggestion," Rick said. "I'd like the two of you to be there, but I'd rather that Seth doesn't know you're there until we need you. We can put you in a room next to the room we're using. It has one of those windows where you can see and hear us but we can't see you. We will need to get you in place before Seth arrives.

"We'll start with the easy stuff, but as soon as he stops cooperating, then I want you, Jeenya, to join us. You said earlier that he had reasons to hate Josiah. I assume you are talking about when they lived in Jamaica. You're the only person here who really knew him then. You should be able to make it clear why he hated his brother, why he hated him so much that he could have killed him."

Hazel called Nate and made the arrangements. "We agreed to start at one-thirty," she said. "Everyone should have had lunch by then. Rick will ask most of the questions since Seth is fairly comfortable with him. Two other officers would be there ready to fill in if they are needed. Nate will probably join us from time to time. If Jeenya takes over, he wants to be there for that."

Then Hazel called Seth. "We're meeting at the station to talk about Victor. We need to have you join us to tell them what you told us. They have Victor's story, that he doesn't remember anything. Now, they want your story. Can we pick you up? Sure, we'll drive you home soon as it's over. Good. So, we'll pick you up at the garage at one-fifteen."

Hazel then took Zeke and Jeenya over to the station and showed them where to park in back out of sight. She introduced them to Nate and to the person at the front desk. Then she showed them the room where they'd be sitting.

Back in Jamaica Lakes, Jeenya and Zeke loaded wheelbarrow with bags of herbs and delivered them to Sharona.

For lunch, Jeenya just heated some canned tomato soup and made toasted cheese sandwiches. "Quick, easy, and good," Zeke said.

34

Rick Asks the Questions

Rick

Jeenya and Zeke left first. Jeenya brought some knitting to keep her hands busy. Zeke had a notepad. He could draw pictures or take notes. They were ready.

Rick and Hazel picked up Seth at one-fifteen. "After hearing Victor's story," Hazel said, "the detectives are eager to meet you. You were the person who discovered the only real evidence, evidence that might prove who killed Josiah."

They arrived and showed Seth the bathroom in case he needed it. Hazel asked if he'd like a Coke and brought him one. "Unlike in your office, there are no glasses here," she said with a smile.

Rick introduced Seth to Nate and the two detectives who would be sitting in part of the time. Andrew was young, good-looking and black. Aiden was older, taller, heavier, and had more experience.

When everyone was in place, Rick started the questioning. "First, I have to tell you that this session. as usual, is being recorded. Now, Seth, why don't you introduce yourself to Andrew and Aiden, the detectives working with Victor. Next to them is Lieutenant Holiday.

"Okay. My name is Seth Overmon. I'm the half-brother of Josiah, Sharona, and Elijah Overmon. We all live here in Palm City, in Jamaica Lakes. I run the garage."

"Now, Seth. Tell us how you know Victor Hackett."

"Sure. I met Victor when he moved to Jamaica Lakes to live with his parents. Josiah sent us and a couple other men to take the same automotive class so we'd be prepared to work together in the garage. That was about fifteen years ago.

"Both Victor and his friend, George, got married in the next couple years. Victor's wife died about ten years ago. Then recently, since I never married and Victor's wife had died, the two of us spent more time together. It wasn't like we were good friends or anything, but that we were both kind of lonely."

"Thank you," Rick continued. "Now, please describe what happened last Friday night, the night when Josiah was murdered?"

There was a minute or two of silence before Seth began speaking. It wasn't anything important. I was working late at the Garage. Victor came over and we had something to drink. He had a Dr Pepper like he always does, and I had a Coke. Victor was feeling dizzy, so he lay down on the floor and before long he was sound asleep. I hated to wake him up so, at about eleven, I finished my work and went home."

"Did you do anything that night involving Obeah?" Rick asked.

"Obeah?" Seth said, sounding very puzzled. "Of course not. Why do you ask that?"

"Did you put something in his drink?"

"Certainly," Seth said with a smile. "I always add a few dried herbs. I added some to both of our drinks. It's for good health and it even makes the drinks taste better."

"Did Victor have his weapons with him that night?"

"Yeah. He usually brought them along. He had a garrote and a knife. I don't know why he has them. He likes to talk about them but he's never used them as far as I know."

"Seth, do you think Victor Hackett killed your brother? Do you think he murdered Josiah?"

"Victor? That would be really hard to believe. He talked about wanting to kill Josiah but, as far as I could tell, my friend Victor was a coward. I know you have evidence that he did it but I wasn't there. I can't tell you if he did or didn't kill him. I guess, if Victor confessed, that he must have done it. "Now, if I've answered all your questions, I'd like to get back to work."

"Seth," Rick said in a serious tone of voice, "please stay seated. This was just the introduction. Now, we'd like to examine the reasons you had to kill your brother, the reasons why you hated him so much."

"Hate Josiah? That's crazy. He was my brother. He wrote me and asked me to come to Jamaica Lakes. He paid for me to learn about car repair. He gave me the job of being in charge of the garage. What reason would I have to hate him? That doesn't make any sense.

"Now, wait a minute. Is this the time when I should tell you I need a lawyer?"

"Sure," Rick said. "We would all be sitting here for hours while they find you one. It might even take a couple days. You'd be sitting in jail while we got a lawyer. But if you think you need a lawyer, we'd have to get you one.

What should we do?"

"Keep going," Seth said. "I don't really need a lawyer. I never did anything wrong and I sure don't want to sit in jail for a couple days."

"Seth," Rick said, "tell me this. If Jeenya Birdsong was sitting here in my chair, would you have said the same things to her?"

Seth didn't respond.

"What if Jeenya asked you the same questions about Friday night? Would you have lied to her too?"

Seth didn't respond.

"If Jeenya asked if you killed Josiah, would you have given her the same answer?"

Still, Seth didn't respond.

"Well, Seth, I'm happy to tell you that your childhood friend is here, and she's going to continue the questioning since we think you're more likely to tell her the truth. Maybe that's because she knows you better than anyone else. Isn't that right, Seth?"

Seth did not respond.

Within a few minutes, Nate had joined them, taking a seat to the side of the room and Jeenya had taken Rick's chair facing Seth.

35

Jeenya Continues the Questions

Jeenya

Jeenya smiled. "Hi Seth, before we get started, is there anything you'd like to eat or drink? We might be here a while."

Seth leaned forward. "Hi Jeenya. I'm glad you're here. You can tell them I'd never kill Josiah or anyone else." He paused for a long minute. "But, since you offered, you can tell the detectives I'd like a chocolate milkshake. A large chocolate milkshake. Tell them I'll talk to you if I get my milkshake."

Jeenya waved for Rick to come over. "Sure, I can get him a chocolate milkshake," he said.

"A LARGE chocolate shake," Jeenya said.

In just under five minutes, Rick reappeared with the large chocolate shake. He handed it to Seth. Now, after everyone had taken their places again, Rick introduced Jeenya and the next step began.

"Hello again, Seth," Jeenya began. "I'm here to help you and to help these detectives understand more about you. I want them to know that you had very good reasons to hate Josiah. I want them to know how he used to torment you. I will ask you some difficult questions Seth. If you choose not to answer them, that's okay. I will do my best to answer for you. To start with, could you tell us who your parents were?"

Seth took a deep breath. "My father was Adam Overmon. He was an Obeah Man in Jamaica. My mother was Mary Black. She was married to someone else."

"Thank you, Seth. Now, and I know it isn't easy, but would you describe what your life was like, living with Mary Black and her family?"

Seth frowned and rubbed his hands together. "They didn't like me. None of them did. They all knew I had a different father and they all called me 'Bastard.' For a long time, I didn't know what that meant. I thought it was my name. When I started first grade, the teacher asked me my name. I said, "My name is Bastard.' When I said that she got really mad. She said I should never say that word again. Then she told me what it meant.

"It's funny, that word. It means my father was not married to my mother, and that was true. It's also an insult, a real bad insult. I never knew that the children in that family were insulting me all the time. I never did anything to make them mad."

"Thank you, Seth. That was very helpful. Now, please tell us how all of this changed when you were ten."

Seth took a sip of his chocolate shake. "Since my mother didn't love me, I thought maybe my father would. I asked my mother who my father was, but she told me I didn't have a father. That didn't make any sense.

"I did have one clue. My skin wasn't nearly as dark as my mother, her husband, or any of their children. I decided that my father must be someone with skin more like mine. I kept watching people, mostly men who came to visit my mother. Months went by and I was feeling pretty discouraged.

"Finally, I saw him. This man with light skin like mine was visiting my mother. So, when he started to leave, I told him my name and asked if he was my father. When he said yes, I begged him to take me home with him. Finally, he agreed.

"He took me to some friends of his for a couple days. They threw all my clothes in the garbage. They cleaned me up and bought me some proper clothes.

"Then Father took me to meet his wife and children. In the beginning, they all treated me pretty well. But the only one who was really nice to me was you, Jeenya.

"In the beginning, I thought you were one of the Overmons, but then I learned you were only the cleaning lady's daughter. First, I was upset, thinking the only person who was nice to me was a 'nobody.' A few days later, I saw it differently. I saw how much the Overmons, especially their mother, loved you and I realized that if they loved you, the cleaning lady's daughter, how much more they should love me, their father's child.

"But it didn't work out that way, Jeenya. You were outgoing and friendly. You made friends easily. They all loved you. I wasn't outgoing. I wasn't friendly. In fact, I'd never had a friend. Before long, they all stopped trying to be nice. They weren't mean like in my first family. They just ignored me."

Seth stopped. He looked at Jeenya.

"Go ahead, Seth. You need to tell them about Josiah. Tell them what he did to you. They need to understand why you hated him."

Seth took another sip of his chocolate shake. "All of them ignored me except for Josiah. Josiah hated me. He ignored me like the others if they were around but, when the others weren't there, Josiah would poke me in the stomach or in the back. He hit me so hard it really hurt. He'd call me a fucking bastard, and much worse.

"Jeenya, you are the only other person to see how Josiah treated me. So, what was I supposed to do? If I told his mother, I don't think she'd have believed me. She'd have said I was lying. Even if she did believe me, I don't think she'd have done anything to stop him. The torture would just have gotten worse. And I couldn't hit him back."

"Go ahead, Seth," Jeenya said. "Tell them what you told me. Why couldn't you hit him back?"

"When I left my first family, the very last thing my mother said was, 'Whatever you do, Seth, don't mess up or they'll send you back here.' I never knew just what it would take to mess up, and I didn't want to find out. But that's why I couldn't hit Josiah when he hit me. They might say I'd messed up. They might send me back. At night I had bad dreams, terrible nightmares about me hitting Josiah and getting sent back where everyone hated me and where they all called me Bastard.

"Things were much better when Father took Josiah with him to learn the secrets of Obeah. Finally, I could relax. There was nobody torturing me. Then, when Josiah turned eighteen, he left his father and the rest of us and came here, to Palm City, to pick oranges. That was way back when most of Palm City was a huge orange grove.

"So, years later when Josiah wrote me, inviting me to come live in Jamaica Lakes, I was very suspicious. I was afraid this was some sort of trick, that Josiah was going to start torturing me again. But I was curious, so I came. He seemed to be a different person. Josiah apologized for his earlier behavior and said he wanted us to be friends.

"Josiah gave me a house to live in. He still owned the house but I could live there as long as I wanted, rent free. What a surprise! Then he asked if I'd like to run the garage. Right away, I said yes. So, he sent me to take a course at the community college, a course on automotive repair. That's where I met Victor, and the other men. Since then, things have been going pretty well. I can't say Josiah or any of the other Overmons have been really friendly. But they bring me their cars to fix, and they smile, and nobody is mean to me."

"Now, Seth, stay with me," Jeenya said. "You've been doing a great job so far. Now we need to talk about what's happened more recently. All right?"

Seth nodded slowly, perhaps suspiciously.

"Seth, you said everything was going pretty well. Nobody was being mean to you. Something must have happened to change that. Please tell us what happened."

Seth shrugged his shoulders. "I don't know what you mean. Nothing happened."

"You said Josiah wasn't treating you badly. Were you upset when you heard that he was treating other people badly?"

"Leave it to you, Jeenya, to understand me better than I understand myself. I think you're right. I think a lot of people got upset about Josiah having sex with other men's wives, I kept thinking what a jerk he was. When I heard about him getting a fourteen-year-old girl pregnant, I was furious. I couldn't talk about it, you know. Josiah was my brother."

Now, Seth began speaking louder. "I wanted to kill him every time he did things like that. And recently, with those crazy men coming around to complain, one about his wife, one about his girlfriend, it was really clear that Josiah had a terrible problem. For some reason, he just couldn't keep his pants on."

"That's helpful, Seth," Jeenya said. "I imagine you also talked to George and Victor about their experiences."

"Well, sort of. I was mostly listening. They did the talking. George's wife was trying to get pregnant but having no luck. She went to see Josiah once every week or two. He gave her teas to drink and sometimes his sister, Sharona, gave her an herbal bath. I can't see that either of those things were going to help her get pregnant. Then, finally, George told me and Victor that she never would get pregnant because he had a vasectomy years ago.

"Victor and George were friends and Victor kept warning George not to let his wife go alone to see Josiah. He talked about his own experience. He told us how his wife, Elaenia, was trying to have a baby and how she went to see Josiah regularly for teas and those herbal baths.

"Then Elaenia got pregnant. Victor was really excited about being a father. With him sharing the good news all over town, it didn't take long before everyone knew Elaenia was expecting. Then, one night when she was nearly six months pregnant, his wife went to the lake. She took a lot of pills and committed suicide. I can only guess what might have happened. Victor never told us why she did it."

"Seth," Jeenya said. "I can fill in that part of the story.

Josiah was trying to help a lot of women like Elaenia. If the herbs didn't help, he'd suggest having sex with the women and then told the women to have sex that night with their husbands. That way, it would seem like their husbands were the fathers."

Seth continued drinking his shake and nodding his head while he listened.

"Elaenia came to see me one day," Jeenya said. "She said Josiah was the father of the baby she was carrying. She wanted to know if she should tell Victor. She wanted to be honest but didn't want to upset him. I knew Victor fairly well so I recommended that she NOT tell him. I didn't think he'd take the news well.

"Elaenia went home and thought it over. She must have decided to trust Victor. She told him the truth. Victor just recently admitted that he'd been furious when she told him. He yelled at his wife. He said things like, 'I am not going to raise another man's bastard.'"

"If Elaenia had just waited a few days, Victor would have changed his mind. But that same night, Elaenia took those pills down by the lake. Now, Victor feels like it was his fault. He felt like he killed the wife he loved so much and their baby, a baby that would have been their son.

"Victor is still in mourning. He still feels guilty, but now he also blames Josiah. The more he thinks about it, the more he hates Josiah.

"So, Seth, tell me what happened in the past few months. What was Victor telling George?"

Seth began slowly. "Victor warned George not to let Angela to go see Josiah. He told George again and again what happened to Elaenia. All the time Victor was getting more and more angry."

"How did that make you feel?

"It made me mad. "Every time I heard about Josiah hurting people like that, I got more and more upset. When I was young and helpless, he hurt me terribly. Now, he was hurting other people."

Seth began shouting. "When Victor talked about Josiah killing his wife, killing his baby, and ruining Victor's life, I couldn't it stand anymore. Somebody had to kill this man before he hurt any more people."

Seth paused for a few minutes and was loudly slurping up the last of his chocolate shake. Finally, he placed the empty cup on the table.

"I really didn't want to kill Josiah. He hadn't hurt me for a long time. I was hoping Victor would do it. His whole life was so miserable already that even if you caught him and put him in jail, it couldn't get much worse. But Victor is a wimp.

"One day he showed me the garrote he made. I showed him how to make it better and I started to think he might actually do something about Josiah. I suggested he get a get knife and he went out the next day and bought one. He had some good weapons, but Victor is a coward. He didn't have the courage to use them.

"Finally, I decided I'd have to make Victor think he had killed Josiah, and, you have to admit, that almost worked, didn't it? I guess the detectives didn't quite believe him. That was my fault. I should never have given the detectives so much evidence at once. It probably made them suspicious.

"I really didn't want to be the one to kill him, you know. I didn't want Josiah to think it was because he picked on me and called me names when we were kids. I wanted him to know it was about all the women he had hurt, about how he hurt Victor and his wife and their baby. Just before I tightened the garrote, just before I killed him, I tried to tell him all that. I don't know what he thought. I only know it made me feel better."

There was a long silence. Seth had confessed. Finally, he continued, "The only thing I could hear that night was those damn drums out in the woods. I kept thinking of those people, people I knew, marching around, waiting to be possessed by a spirit. It seemed like they were in some other world.

"I had planned to kill Josiah when he left the shed, when I could surprise him with the garrote, but even after Sharona left, he kept on working. Finally, I couldn't wait any longer. I opened the door and walked inside.

"Josiah looked up and saw me. He even said hello. I told him he'd gone too far, that he was the one who killed Elaenia, and that I wasn't going to let him do that to anyone else.

"I'm not sure he knew what I was talking about. I don't think he ever realized I was serious. He was sitting at his desk trying to ignore me. He just kept putting his herbs in those little plastic bags, one bag after another.

"It wasn't hard, you know. I walked behind him and slipped Victor's garrote out of my pocket, flipped it over his head, and in less than a minute, less than thirty seconds I think, Josiah was dead. He didn't have a chance to scream. The only thing I heard was a grunt, and a sort of gurgle. Then it was over.

"That's when I got scared. I wasn't scared when I killed him. I was angry. I never believed I could kill anyone. But Josiah really was dead.

"The next part was harder. I pulled his body out onto the floor and rolled him over on his back. I took Victor's knife, and I cut his throat.

"I could never have cut Josiah's throat, you know, when he was alive. I took the knife in one fist, held my breath, and did the best I could to cut him from ear to ear. I figured, that way, everyone would think Jesus, that crazy truck driver, had killed him and he would get arrested. Even if that man didn't kill Josiah, I'm sure that man had plenty of other things he'd done wrong. I didn't feel bad about getting him blamed for what I did.

"I took a break then and looked around the room at all the neatly labeled teas and other herbs. I tried to imagine what it would be like if they let me take over as Obeah Man. I wasn't dumb enough to think they would, but it was fun to imagine.

"Finally, I did the hardest part. I didn't want people to think it was a robbery, so I didn't touch any of his money. I wanted everybody to know it was anger because of what he did to all those women. I kept waiting for it to be in the news, but they never did mention it."

Rick nodded. "Tell us what you're talking about, Seth. What was it you did last?"

"You know what else I did, don't you?" Seth asked.

Rick nodded again.

"It wasn't easy. I unzipped his fly, but I couldn't do it that way so I unbuckled his belt, pulled down his underwear. It was a mess down there. I'd heard about people messing their pants when they died, but I'd forgotten about it.

"I'd never handled another man's privates before. But it seemed like the right thing to do. Josiah's evil wasn't doing Obeah spells. His evil always involved sex. I unbuckled his belt, pulled down his pants and cut him there. The thought of cutting them off made me sick to my stomach, so I stopped halfway through. I just cut them enough so people would know that's why he was killed. But they didn't understand because you didn't tell people about that.

"After that, I smeared the garrote and the knife in the blood. I even stole one of Josiah's cups and scooped up as much blood as I could, and I walked back to the garage.

"Victor was still sound asleep. Yes, Rick, you were right. I did put up a couple sleeping pills in his drink. I put the weapons back in front of Victor where there were before. His shirt was there on the floor so I wiped my hands in it until it was bloody. Then I poured blood on his hands and his shoes and all over him.

"Next, I had to clean up all that Obeah stuff. It wasn't real Obeah stuff, but I figured it was enough to convince Victor it was real. Then I went home, showered, and had something to eat. After all that work, I was hungry. I took my bloody clothes and wrapped them in plastic bags and put them in a cardboard box. I put it in the garbage can of the old lady across the street. Nobody would look there. Then I went to sleep, and I slept well.

"I'm not sorry, you know. I'm actually PROUD of myself. Somebody had to do stop Josiah from hurting people. I had the courage to do it myself."

✦

36

The Questions are Finished

After a moment of silence, Zeke spoke up. "The whole story about that night, and about Victor killing Josiah but not remembering anything never made any sense before. Now it does."

"True," Nate said. "Sounds like Victor had been wishing for years that he could kill Josiah and had no idea that Seth or anyone else felt that way. Then, he sees that all the evidence pointed to him. The only thing that made any sense was that he was the killer."

Nate turned to Aiden and Andrew. "You two can take Seth, read him his rights, cuff him, book him, and drive him over to the jail."

Nate turned to Jeenya. "I want to thank you, Mrs. Birdsong for coming today. Rick was right. Having you know so much about this man made all the difference. And I must say that the way you handled the situation was amazing.

"We'll have to see if having a chocolate milkshake, a LARGE chocolate milkshake, makes any difference with the other men who don't feel like talking."

"It can be a lot of things," Jeenya said with a smile.

"With Victor, it was a bowl of hot goat curry and some brownies, straight out of the oven."

"I can see that brownies could be useful," Nate said, "but I don't think most of the men we have here would be too fond of goat curry.

Nate turned to Rick and Hazel. "You two can give Victor the good news. I'll see to it that he can be released as soon as possible."

"We'd be happy to give him a ride home," Jeenya said. "We'll be happy to wait until he's released."

When Nate left, Zeke poked his wife. "You did it again, my dear. You got that police lieutenant wrapped around your little finger."

Thirty minutes later, Rick arrived with Victor. This time Victor did the hugging. He hugged Zeke and then Jeenya.

"Rick told me, Jeenya, that you were the one who got Seth to talk. It's scary to think that I trusted Seth, and that he almost made me think I'd killed Josiah. With all that blood everywhere, it was hard not to believe."

On the ride back to Jamaica Lakes, Victor said, "Jeenya, I also need to thank you for what you told me before, when you kept saying I didn't kill Elaenia, that she killed herself. You were right. I was partly guilty but so was she."

It didn't take long for the news to spread. Hazel and Rick went to see Dolly, Sharona and Elijah and told them Seth had confessed.

Several people saw Victor coming home with the Birdsongs. Some hurried to find out what happened. Victor called George and it didn't take Angela long to pass the word. One of those people told Melissa who told her grandmother, Ida Lee, and Ida Lee told her other granddaughter about Jeenya making those brownies for Victor.

Melissa then walked across the street to talk to Jeenya. "My grandmother," she said, "sits by the window all day, watching everything you do. Then, for some reason, she leans out her window at night, screaming at you for what she imagines you did wrong. She was especially upset when you made brownies that time when Victor was visiting you, but you didn't think to take some over to her."

Jeenya laughed. "I can hear Ida Lee shouting at night but I never knew she was shouting at me. That poor lady must be lonely sitting there and looking out the window all day.

Now I know she likes brownies. I'll see what I can do. I have an extra box of brownie mix. I'll take some of them to Ida Lee. Thanks for telling me about your grandmother."

When the brownies were ready, Zeke took a dozen to Victor to celebrate. Jeenya took another dozen to Ida Lee.

"Oh, Miz Jeenya, I've been wanting some brownies and these are just the way I like them, fresh out of the oven. Now, you just sit awhile and tell me what happened today. I already heard that Seth was the one who killed Josiah but I want to know all the details, every little thing."

Jeenya, sat back and began the story. Ida Lee liked the part about Seth wanting a large chocolate shake.

"I reckon," Ida Lee said, "that if they arrested me for something, I'd like a large chocolate shake myself." After an hour with Ida Lee, Jeenya promised to come back to see her now and then, and hurried back to her house.

She joined Zeke who was sitting out in the garden and told him about her visit with Ida Lee. Above them, two mourning doves were cooing softly. "You hear those doves?" Jeenya asked her husband. "They call them

Mourning Doves because they sound so sad. Now I have the feeling they are performing a requiem, not just for the dead, but for all those in pain."

Zeke held her in his arms. "Go ahead and cry, Jeenya. Even if Seth is in jail for murder, I expect he was glad you were there to ask the questions. No one else could do what you did. That wasn't easy, I know, but you had to do it."

Now, as they went to bed, Jeenya went to the window and listened. "It's strangely quiet out there. I guess now, we won't be hearing Ida Lee shouting every night."

As she lay in bed, Jeenya wondered if what she'd done was being a detective. She decided it wasn't. Detectives never did what she'd done. It was different, something she knew how to do instinctively.

She remembered what Zeke told her. He said she was loving people, giving them the courage to tell the truth. Now that she thought about it, detectives generally use threats, trying to scare suspects into confessing while she tried to respect people, to treat them with kindness and to let them know she cared. She wasn't ever going to be a detective but, if anyone needed her to do this again, even knowing how painful it was, she would do her best.

"Zeke," she said, "I have something to confess. I've been thinking about what you said when we heard the old Patoo, when I thought it was a sign that someone was dying. My granny taught me to think that way.

"Now, I understand. You were right. It was just a plain old hunch. With the darkness that night and the drumming and shouting in the woods, it felt like something awful might happen. And I was right. Something awful did happen. But I was just imaging things when I thought the owl told me something."

Now, they heard the owl again and this time it was Zeke who did the interpretation. "It's your friend, Jeenya, the old Patoo. He's just telling you that there aren't any problems tonight, that all is well."